Dear Reader,

Home, family, community and love. These are the values we cherish most in our lives—the ideals that ground us, comfort us, move us. They certainly provide the perfect inspiration around which to build a romance collection that will touch the heart.

We are thrilled to have the opportunity to introduce you to the Harlequin Heartwarming collection. Each of these special stories is a wholesome, heartfelt romance imbued with the traditional values so important to you. They are books you can share proudly with friends and family. And the authors featured in this collection are some of the most talented storytellers writing today, including favorites such as Brenda Novak, Janice Kay Johnson, Jillian Hart and Patricia Davids. We've selected these stories especially for you based on their overriding qualities of emotion and tenderness, and they center around your favorite themes—children, weddings, second chances, the reunion of families, the quest to find a true home and, of course, sweet romance.

So curl up in your favorite chair, relax and prepare for a heartwarming reading experience!

Sincerely,

The Editors

CYNTHIA REESE

lives with her husband and their daughter in south Georgia, along with their two dogs, three cats and however many strays show up for morning muster. She has been scribbling since she was knee-high to a grasshopper and reading even before that. A former journalist, teacher and college English instructor, she also enjoys cooking, traveling and photography when she gets the chance.

HARLEQUIN HEARTWARMING

Cynthia Reese

Seeds of Trust

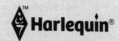

TORONTO NEW YORK LONDON
AMSTERDAM PARIS SYDNEY HAMBURG
STOCKHOLM ATHENS TOKYO MILAN MADRID
PRAGUE WARSAW BUDAPEST AUCKLAND

If you purchased this book without a cover you should be aware
that this book is stolen property. It was reported as "unsold and
destroyed" to the publisher, and neither the author nor the
publisher has received any payment for this "stripped book."

Recycling programs
for this product may
not exist in your area.

ISBN-13: 978-0-373-36560-9

SEEDS OF TRUST

Copyright © 2011 by Cynthia R. Reese

Originally published as WHERE LOVE GROWS
Copyright © 2007 by Cynthia R. Reese

All rights reserved. Except for use in any review, the reproduction or
utilization of this work in whole or in part in any form by any electronic,
mechanical or other means, now known or hereafter invented, including
xerography, photocopying and recording, or in any information storage
or retrieval system, is forbidden without the written permission of the
publisher, Harlequin Enterprises Limited, 225 Duncan Mill Road,
Don Mills, Ontario M3B 3K9, Canada.

This is a work of fiction. Names, characters, places and incidents are
either the product of the author's imagination or are used fictitiously,
and any resemblance to actual persons, living or dead, business
establishments, events or locales is entirely coincidental.

This edition published by arrangement with Harlequin Books S.A.

For questions and comments about the quality of this book
please contact us at Customer_eCare@Harlequin.ca

® and TM are trademarks of the publisher. Trademarks indicated with
® are registered in the United States Patent and Trademark Office, the
Canadian Trade Marks Office and in other countries.

www.Harlequin.com

Printed in U.S.A.

Seeds of Trust

To the women who have made me who I am.
I treasure you all. And in memory of
my Aunt Lou–the inspiration for Mee-Maw.

Acknowledgments

I couldn't have written this book
without help from a great many people–
too many local farmers in my area to name
individually here, but thank you all.

Thanks to Kenny Chesney for the music that
helped inspire this story and helped motivate me
when the going got tough. A big hug goes to my
better half and my daughter for putting up with
life on hold while I was writing.

Acknowledgments also go to
my critique partners Tawna Fenske,
Cindy Miles, Stephanie Bose and Nelsa Roberto,
and to Laura Shin, whose revision suggestions
really helped me turn the corner. Also, many,
many thanks go to Harlequin editors
Marsha Zinberg and Victoria Curran,
as well as Adrienne Macintosh, for
breathing new life into an old favorite of mine.

Rooster@yoohoomail.com: My favorite place on earth? Has to be my hammock by the pond. The hammock's rigged up under a willow tree my cousins and I bent double over the years when we pressed it into service as a catapult—bad for the tree, but it makes a nice, shady place to relax. What about your favorite place?

Sunny_76@yoohoomail.com: I'm restless, can't stay still, so I like to ride…just hop in my car and head down the interstate, no destination in mind.

Rooster@yoohoomail.com: You think one day you'll head to Georgia? After all these months, I feel like I know you, even though we haven't even told each other our real names.

Sunny_76@yoohoomail.com: Maybe…you never can tell.

CHAPTER ONE

CRAIG ANDREWS WAS moving in for the kill.

He'd trapped Becca Reynolds as neatly as any hound would trap a rabbit.

She swallowed hard, her mouth dry. To reach for the tumbler of water in front of her would be a sign of weakness, wouldn't it?

Yes. Better to have a mouth that felt as if a sandblaster had let loose in it than to have her actions prove it.

"Miss Reynolds…"

Andrews pivoted on his Testoni dress shoes and held up a single sheet of paper. The corners of his mouth lifted, but the expression bore about as much resemblance to a smile as a shark's chompers did.

"You based your conclusions on weather patterns and the very scientific NASA photographs."

"Yes. Yes, I did. It is my—"

But before Becca could explain how she knew the hailstorm had been nothing but cocktail ice and a few migrant workers beating plants down in the field, he held up one perfectly manicured hand.

Really. The fop spent more on his appearance than she and her father spent on their monthly office lease.

And now she was stuck on the stand, testifying in the first federal criminal-fraud case she'd investigated. The case was a slam dunk, or so she'd assured the feds and the insurance company who'd hired their firm.

It certainly didn't feel like that now.

"You even went so far as to say there were no tomatoes planted—"

She gritted her teeth. "No. I said there weren't as many tomatoes planted as Mr. Palmer said. His insurance claim forms indicated he had several hundred acres—"

"Yes, yes." He waved away her answer. "How much do you know of the weather in this part of the state?"

"I'm a private investigator, Mr. Andrews. I'm not a meteorologist."

"Ah, but you based your findings on meteorological evidence. So is it going to rain today, Miss Reynolds?"

With the prosecution's objection offered and sustained, and the laughter in the courtroom finished, Andrews came back. "Were you aware, Miss Reynolds, that this part of the county had heavy spring rains?"

Her stomach clenched. "No. My…recollection

of the rainfall levels indicated that they were a little above average but not inordinately heavy."

"But if your *recollection*—" Andrews's emphasis of the word dripped with sarcasm "—was faulty, would that impact your analysis?"

Becca swallowed hard again and this time succumbed to the call of the water on the witness stand. No way had she goofed those rainfall levels. She'd looked at them, standard procedure. She glanced at her father, the senior partner of Reynolds Agricultural Investigations. It was only after he glowered at her in a way that screamed "Don't screw this up!" that she answered Andrews's question.

"Possibly. It depends."

"You based your entire opinion on the analysis of photos. You said that you would be able to see evidence of tomato crops from satellite photos taken the week before, right? Isn't that correct?"

"Uh, yes. The red—"

"Would show up." Andrews spun again on his Testonis, this time to face the jury. "But if the fruit was unripened? If the tomatoes were still green on the vine…"

Becca wanted nothing more than to run from the courtroom and make it to the nearest bathroom stall. She didn't have the luxury of that option, so she stuck it out. "If the rains were heavy enough to delay planting, the ripening could be delayed, as well. But it would have to be extremely heavy rains—"

"Something like these?" Andrews turned back and dropped the printout into Becca's hands.

It was worse than she thought. She'd never seen this report—it totally contradicted her own research. If these figures were accurate, the farmers in the area would have needed an Evinrude on the back of their tractors to navigate these rains.

After he'd dragged the offensive numbers out of Becca and retrieved the printout, he said, "Your Honor, I would like to admit into evidence rain reports from the county extension agent in the early spring of that year."

Becca sat, numb, twisting her hands in her lap, her fingernails digging into her palms. Andrews smiled again.

"Did anyone from Reynolds Agricultural Investigations—um, how did you put it—go on-site?"

She closed her eyes.

When would I have had time? Would that have been between visiting my dad in ICU and keeping the firm open while he was out?

But she bit back the words, which she knew would open a whole other can of worms with Ag-Sure, their client. Opening her eyes, she forced out, "No. Because the satellite images showed clear evidence—"

"Of unripe tomatoes. Oh, yes. Right. Perfectly

understandable. I mean, you just get paid to rip apart farmers' lives. We wouldn't want you to get dirt under your pretty little fingernails. You should leave that to the farmers who are trying to scrape out a living."

Even before the prosecution could get out its objection, Andrews withdrew the question. "I'm done with this witness," he said.

"NOT GUILTY."

Becca's blood pressure spiked as she heard the bite in her father's voice.

"The jury's back already?"

"Yeah, while you *dashed* out for a bite to eat."

Her fingers tightened on the fast-food bag she had in her hand, supper for the both of them. "Dad, I wasn't gone—"

But her protest that she had truly been gone for only ten minutes got interrupted by another of his impatient growls. "The federal prosecutor isn't happy, and neither are the insurance-company suits. This verdict torpedoes their earlier turn-down. They aren't happy in the slightest, Becca. They're talking about using another firm."

"Because of one—"

"One verdict? No. It's not the verdict that they're mad about. It's you."

"Me?"

"Me?" he mimicked her. "Yes, you. You blew

that case. You should have been on that farm, interviewing the workers, interviewing the neighbors. You sure should have had the right rainfall figures. That lawyer sliced you up like a deli ham."

Becca gritted her teeth in an effort to hold her tongue. Not for the first time she asked herself why she wanted this job, why pleasing her dad was so important to her.

Uh, maybe because after the subject of a story you wrote sued you for libel, no other newspaper or magazine would hire you?

It hadn't been libel. Becca had written the truth in that article, and the target of her investigation just couldn't stomach it. She'd survived a humiliating lawsuit only to lose the fledging magazine she'd started up. In the countersuit she'd filed, the jury's decision to award her damages had come too late, and still, Becca had yet to see any money.

She tried to calm down by reminding herself who she was: An award-winning investigative reporter. Her dad had been the one, after his heart attack, to ask her to join his firm. It had seemed like a good idea at the time.

"Dad…you were sick, remember? You were in ICU with your heart attack. I couldn't be in two places—"

"What I needed you to be doing was looking

after the business. But I guess that's too much to expect from you."

"That's not fair! I worked hard, gave you my best effort—"

"If that case was your best effort, then I am expecting too much from you. Honestly, I thought you'd season up. I thought you'd have gotten smarter after—"

Her father stopped in midsentence. He shook his head and turned to head down the empty courthouse corridor.

Becca's anger bubbled up within her. She could not let her father's dropped conversation go. "Say it, Dad. You might as well say it. I'm a failure. I'm a disappointment. You took me on only out of pity. Say it. Because that's what you're thinking."

"Thinking? You really want to know?" He whirled around and stabbed a finger in her direction. "I'll tell you what I'm thinking. I'm thinking I'm a fool for ever thinking I could grow you into an investigator. I'm thinking I'm a fool for ever thinking you'd be grateful for me bailing you out."

"If you're referring to the libel suit…and the bankruptcy, why don't you just spit it out, Dad?"

Her father shot a look around. "If I want a prayer's chance of saving Ag-Sure as a client, they don't need to hear even a whisper about you getting sued for libel. But yes, that was what I was talking about. You go into business, start up that—that magazine against my best advice, you get mired in a counter-lawsuit you had no business even filing…"

Becca swallowed. The way he said those things, she might even believe she was a complete flake.

"I won that lawsuit, Dad. And that magazine had a name—Atlanta Insider. Couldn't you just once call it by its name and not hiss and spit? It was a going business until I had one bad break. It will be again. One day. Just because the judgment is being appealed doesn't mean I won't eventually get my money."

Her father blew out a long breath and looked off into the distance. "Let's focus on the problem, okay? Right now one of our biggest clients is going south. I just wanted you to do your job. You're here. You earn a paycheck. You know what to do. I've trained you." He ran a hand through his clipped cut. "You just…lose focus. Even with your own business, half the time you were cutting deals to nonprofits—"

"It was my business, Dad. I got to choose how I billed my time."

"Right. Well, this is my business, and I say you've screwed up for the last time."

Becca sucked in a breath. "Are you firing me?" The memory of her long series of fruitless job interviews with magazines and newspapers rushed back to her.

"It'd be the smart thing to do. I'd fire any other employee who screwed up like you did."

"I did not screw—"

"Take responsibility for this!"

Some men in suits filed out of the courtroom, and Becca saw her father's eyes track them. She lowered her voice and said, "Dad, you have to believe me…"

"Go home. I'm going to try to save this account. You just…" He gave her a withering look. "Just go home."

She watched him go after the suits, then she gripped the fast-food bag a little tighter in her hand and bolted for the stairs.

"Aw, honey, don't fret. You win some, you lose some."

Gert, the office manager who'd run her father's life for so many years that she was like part of the family, patted Becca's arm.

"But, Gert, Dad was right. I did screw up. Those farmers were guilty—all of them—and they got off. I should have seen that delayed-planting defense coming. I'll bet that county-extension agent was in on it from the get-go. Had to be. I checked as soon as I got loose from that courtroom, and the rest of the reported rainfall in that area was nowhere near as much."

"Which bothers you more? That they got off…
or that your dad was mad at you?"

"You have to ask?" Becca sighed and gazed off
into the distance.

"I thought so. Listen, I don't have to tell you
that your dad is a type A personality who doesn't
like to lose. He gets mad. He blows off steam. He
gets over it. By tomorrow, he'll be coming in here
like nothing's wrong."

"Yeah, right. You forget one little thing, Gert."

"Oh, yeah?"

"*You* get to go home. I happen to live with the
man."

Not for the first time did Becca grieve over the
loss of her own space. Just two years before she'd
had her little house, her business, a future separate from her father's. Then, bit by bit, she'd lost
it all.

First came the libel suit, stemming from a
puff-piece-turned exposé on a prominent Atlanta
businessman's not-so-squeaky-clean business
practices. Then, just to come on with a strong
offense, Becca had countersued with defamation
charges. Later, when she'd won the libel suit and
a half-million-dollar judgment from the countersuit, she'd counted on the money to help bail her
out of bankruptcy.

Only, it hadn't come. Neither had any job offers
from the multitude of weekly and daily papers and

magazines she'd applied to. Even if Becca had prevailed, just the fact that she'd been sued was enough to make an editor or publisher wary.

"Your father loves you."

"Yeah, but that box isn't on an employee performance review, and you know it."

Gert didn't contradict her, but then that was to be expected. They both knew Becca's father only too well.

Becca slid from the corner of Gert's desktop and made a beeline for her computer. The one thing that could make her feel better might await her in her in-box.

There it was: an e-mail from Rooster.

You nail that big presentation?

That was all, just that in the subject line. So like Rooster, straight to the point. She'd met him on an online farming community a few months before, and the two of them had hit it off.

"Uh-huh, I heard that sigh. It's that online fella again, isn't it?"

Gert's all-knowing smirk couldn't take away from Becca's pleasure.

"If you must know, yes."

"Sometimes I wonder. Why don't you go out with a real flesh-and-blood guy?"

"Like I have time."

"You would if you didn't stay on the Internet all the time, wasting your life away mooning over some guy who could be a psychopath, for all you know. He could be right here in Atlanta, right across the street with a telescope, casing the joint."

"Uh, Gert, I think you need to lay off the crime dramas. To put your overactive imagination at rest, Rooster and I agreed a long time ago not to mess things up by trading any identifying info. No real names, no locations, not even the names of pets. Simpler that way."

"If you say so. Me? I think you're just afraid of disappointing some other guy besides your dad."

Gert's comment hit close to home. Becca fretted at the pang she felt from it.

A part of Becca had been excited to work for her dad. Finally she'd had the chance to earn his approval and help him out with his investigative firm, to show him she could use her journalist skills on this job.

Today had left her feeling the eternal screwup, still haunted by her past bad decisions.

But before she could say anything, the office door opened, letting in a sweltering wave of Georgia heat—and her father.

Her dad's face was a perfect mirror of the weather.

He approached her desk and slapped down a file folder.

"Your last chance."

"What?"

"I'm a fair man. The suits at Ag-Sure have given us one more shot at getting things right, so I'm passing on the favor."

"They want us to reopen the case?"

"No. That ship has sailed. This is another one. It took me a lot of talking to convince them that we wouldn't make a hash out of this one, too. It's here in Georgia, about halfway between Macon and Savannah, so you get down I-75 and nail these guys. Fast."

Wow, Dad. Most fathers would have just said, "I'm sorry for losing my temper." In her heart, though, Becca knew how hard this was for her dad, how scary it was for him to let her take on a case that could well determine their future with Ag-Sure.

She met Gert's gaze across the room and took in the office manager's almost imperceptible nod. Yep, this was as good an apology as she was going to get.

She flipped open the file, scanned it. "Asian dodder vine? I've never heard of it."

"Never been east of the Mississippi, according to the insurance company. But there's a group of farmers claiming it's overtaking their cotton like kudzu."

"But, Dad, how can you fake kudzu?"

"That's your job to figure out. Get busy. You've

got a day to research, and then you'd better be packed and headed south. The insurance company wants to see results… If you don't get any, they'll have our heads on a platter."

Sunny_76@yoohoomail.com: I'm leaving on a business trip that I have to take, don't know if I'll have Internet access, so I may go radio silent for a few days.

Rooster@yoohoomail.com: I thought you just finished up that big project for work? Figured you could take a break.

Sunny_76@yoohoomail.com: I did finish it up, but it sort of imploded on me. I screwed up. So this trip is a penance of sorts.

Rooster@yoohoomail.com: Your job's not on the line, is it? Because if you're short on rent money there in the big city, you can always head down here, grab a hoe and remember what it's like down on the farm.

Sunny_76@yoohoomail.com: I miss being on a farm...well, my grandparents' farm, at least. Sometimes I wish I could go back.

CHAPTER TWO

"WHOA, LADIES! Easy! No call for fighting!"

But Ryan MacIntosh's exhortation fell on the deaf ears of a pair of six-year-olds bent on destruction. He pulled back just quick enough to escape a female fist flying for the other's face.

He made a grab for the fist, saw that the nails were done in a metallic purple nail polish with a constellation of stars. He closed his fingers around the wrist and shoved—as gently as he could—the two girls apart.

Stepping between them, his chest heaving, Ryan struggled for some earthly clue as to what to do next. "Enough!"

"But she started it!"

"She did! She was holding!"

Ryan squelched back his own temper, not an easy thing to do with the August sun beating down on his red hair. He set his jaw and gazed at the upturned faces of the two soccer players.

"Both of you. On the bench."

When they would have argued with him, he shook his head and pointed toward their respective benches. "Go on and you might get a shot at playing again before the game ends."

As the girls trudged off the field, Ryan could feel parental wrath lasering in his direction. A fight had to break out on the one game that the referee didn't show up for.

The other coach shrugged his shoulders and called for a time-out. Ryan indicated for his crew to get a drink. He didn't have to say it twice. They gathered around the Thermos like cows around a salt lick.

Cows would be easier, he thought. A chuckle brought him back from a momentary image of cows in shin guards, kicking a soccer ball up and down the field.

The chuckle came from Jack MacIntosh, his cousin—and the reason Ryan was here rather than on his John Deere, plowing his sadly neglected back forty.

"What?" he asked.

Jack laughed again. He adjusted the casted leg he had stretched out on a folding chaise lounge. "You nearly got clocked by a six-year-old. Doesn't say much for your reaction time."

"Hey. It was supposed to be you out there, re-member? I could have left your sorry—" Ryan did a quick edit, mindful of the small fry around him "—rump in a sling after you broke your leg."

"Begging your pardon, cuz, but you forget that I broke this leg hooking up your satellite antenna."

True enough. Despite Ryan's griping he enjoyed coaching soccer. This was Jack's cup of tea usually, what with Jack's daughter, Emily, involved in whatever the rec department offered. But since Jack was laid up with a bum leg, Ryan had discovered just what a great feeling it was to coach the kids.

He caught the glowering looks scorching between the two girls involved in the fight and sighed, amending his last thought. He liked coaching soccer—not preventing hand-to-hand combat.

He'd done enough of that earlier in the day dealing with Murphy.

Crooked jerk. Murphy's words came back to him.

"Some investigator type's supposed to be coming down here to sign off on these claims, Ryan. Now, don't muck it up. Just say what you gotta say, keep your mouth shut and we'll have a check cut before you know it."

Right. Slugging Murphy probably hadn't been the smartest thing to do, but the guy just would not take no for an answer. He wanted Ryan neck-deep in his scam, for insurance purposes if nothing else. It didn't matter that Ryan was as good as an accessory for knowing about the plan, even if he kept his mouth shut.

If I could only be sure Gramps hadn't been involved.

The Blue Devils coach hollered, "Hey, MacIntosh! You ready to finish up this game?"

Returning to the present, Ryan swigged down a healthy gulp of the orange atrocity he'd gotten from the Thermos. As he headed back for the game, he saw a woman pushing her way through the gate.

Even if she hadn't been a knockout, he would have noticed her. It was the way she dressed—a lightweight blazer paired with jeans that clung to well-proportioned legs. Who wore a blazer to a kids soccer game in south Georgia?

As he hollered for Emily to throw the ball in, Ryan stole another glance in the new arrival's direction. Honey-brown hair that would go golden in the summer sun, a little smile playing on her lips, more than a dab of confidence in her walk. This was a woman who knew what she wanted— and where to find it.

Ronnie Frasier's girl took off on a long drive the wrong way. Ryan hollered for her to stop, but his soccer player never heard him. Instead, the ball went into their own net with frustrating ease.

He stood, moved his cap from his head and used his forearm to wipe away the perspiration that had beaded there. Honestly, this was harder work than getting the harvest in.

If there is any harvest this year.

Ryan pushed the thought from his mind. He glanced over at Jack, saw his cousin talking to the new arrival.

Saw Jack pointing in his direction.

Ryan's stomach sank. Had to be that private investigator the insurance company had said they were sending.

Just his luck.

But then, he'd had a crop of bad luck for the past six months. If Ryan had believed in karma, he'd be convinced he'd been a scuzzball of the first order in a previous life.

All he'd wanted to do was save his grandfather's farm and look after Mee-Maw.

And avoid Murphy.

Somehow Ryan didn't think his goals would mesh with those of the pretty little thing waiting for him on the sidelines.

Just his luck.

BECCA SURVEYED the pack of girls running after the soccer ball. Some of them were pretty good for their age. Well, compared to her. But then Becca had entertained herself picking dandelions from a forsaken corner of whatever athletic field she'd graced.

Give her tai chi any day; it was more her style. No scoreboard to let her know how far along the game was. From the looks of the tall redheaded coach—Ryan MacIntosh, she knew from one of the parents—it had lasted too long already.

Still, MacIntosh seemed to remember why they were here. A few minutes after one girl scored on her own net, he stopped to give high fives for effort when his team managed to recover a turn-over.

He looked even better in real life than he had in the few photos she'd dug up on the Internet. He didn't look like the brain trust of a complicated farm scam.

At that thought, her father's words when she'd said as much came back to her:

"Becca, remember, he's a crook. A scammer. You're just buying into the stereotype that crooks look like crooks."

MacIntosh had that going for him. With his red-blond hair and his muscled legs that showed off a tan darker than usual for guys his coloring, he certainly didn't fall into the Wanted-poster cat-egory. He was good with the kids, patient. She'd seen him break up a fight earlier. He'd handled that well. Odd for a guy who didn't have kids of his own.

Becca had made it her business to find out all she could about Ryan MacIntosh before she'd arrived. Thirty-two. Never been married. No scrapes with the law. He'd graduated with an associate's from Abraham Baldwin Agricultural College and a bachelor's and a master's from University of Georgia. Then he'd taken a sales position with an agriculture chemical company. Moved to middle Georgia to run his grandfather's farm after his grandfather's death the year before.

The farm had been in his family for five generations. On it, Ryan MacIntosh had grown soybeans, corn and cotton. Lately, though, it seemed that MacIntosh's chief crop was desperation.

Right now, the farm was the smallest in acreage owned by any full-time farmer in the county—and in the past it had been in tax trouble. She'd turned up a few closed-out liens, as well.

Yup. Ryan MacIntosh was a desperate man.

And, according to her dad, probably a crook, even if he did give peewee-soccer players high fives.

The game played on with Ryan's Bulldogs taking a beating at the hands of the Blue Devils. Had he chosen that team moniker out of loyalty for his alma mater? What did a person do with a degree in agronomy, anyway?

"Hey, shove that Thermos over and have a seat. This thing could take awhile."

Becca glanced over at the dark-haired guy with the cast. "Really? I figured it was just about over."

"Nah. We got started late—the referee stood us up. I'm Jack MacIntosh."

She moved the Thermos and reached over to shake his hand. "Becca Reynolds. Any relation to Ryan?"

"Sure, first cousins, but we're more like brothers. Ryan hadn't mentioned meeting any ladies."

A smile tugged at her lips as she thought how Ryan was not going to like meeting her in the slightest. "We haven't actually met."

Jack raised an eyebrow. "Oh. One of those online deals?"

His words made her feel a little guilty as she thought about her own Rooster—whom she owed an e-mail and hadn't had a chance to pay that debt since she'd been researching MacIntosh and the other players in this scheme.

"No. This is business." Becca fished out a card and handed it to him.

"Reynolds Agricultural Investigations." Jack looked up from the card, a chill in his eyes. "You're what? A hired gun for a crop-insurance firm?"

Becca had seen that chill before. Farmer types didn't much care for her or her dad.

At least he didn't make a cutesy remark about me investigating how many peppers Peter Piper picked. "I'm a private investigator. I work as a consultant for the insurance company that covers several of the farmers in this area, yes. I wouldn't say a hired gun—"

"I know about people like you. I own an insurance agency."

Her alarm bells started jangling. "Crop insurance?"

He laughed, a derisive snort. "You kidding? You can't make any money selling crop insurance in south Georgia. No, strictly homeowners and auto, as well as life and a few health-insurance policies."

Becca nodded, staying quiet to see what else Ryan MacIntosh's cousin would volunteer. She didn't have to wait long.

"So why are you investigating Ryan?"

"Who says I'm investigating your cousin?"

A shadow fell across her, and Becca looked up to see the man in question standing over her.

"Hand me that stack of cups, if you don't mind."

Ryan's voice was clipped. She picked up the requested cups and extended them his way.

He knelt down beside her to get a refill. The hair on his muscled forearms glinted golden in the late-afternoon sun, and his T-shirt clung damply to a well-sculpted set of pecs that indicated he lifted something besides bales of hay.

He downed the sports drink and crumpled the cup in his hand. Rising to his feet on those marvelous legs of his, he stuck out a hand.

"I gather you're looking for me. I'm Ryan MacIntosh."

His clear blue gaze unsettled her. She felt heat rising in her face, struggled to remind herself that he was the one who should be on the defensive, not her.

"Becca Reynolds." She started to reach for another card, but Jack reached up and handed Ryan the one she'd just given to him.

It was telling that Ryan didn't even look at it. He never took his eyes off hers. Funny. She'd have sworn that a man with his coloring would have had green eyes.

"Richard Murphy told me somebody would be sniffing around. You already inspected his farm?"

"No. I thought I'd start with yours. I called ahead, and a lady gave me directions here, said I'd find you at the rec department."

"That'd be Mee-Maw." A small trace of pain flickered over his features. "She's my grandmother—our grandmother. She's nearly eighty-five."

"Really?" Becca chose to ignore his veiled hint to back off in deference to his grandmother. "On the phone, she sounded younger than that."

"Longevity runs in our family. Right, Jack?" But again, Ryan never took his eyes off Becca's.

"Yup. Gramps worked that farm till the day he died—and he was eighty-six when he passed on."

"I look forward to meeting her," Becca said.

Again pain crossed Ryan's features. Truth be

told, Becca did feel a stirring of remorse. She hated the way the firm's investigations caused so much collateral damage.

But as her dad so frequently reminded her, they simply exposed the ugly truth people tried to hide. They weren't the ones who'd created it. No, that lay at the feet of scammers.

Like this guy?

But he looks...honest. Direct. Straight.

"You want to see the farm now?"

"Why not?" she asked.

"Get it over and done with," Ryan agreed. "I hope you like chicken-fried steak. That's what Mee-Maw is cooking for supper."

Panic bubbled through Becca. Getting up close and personal with the family of her target wasn't in her plans. It was better to avoid all the messy touchy-feely stuff that could cloud an investigation. That was her father's mantra.

The beauty of analyzing satellite images was they couldn't charm the pants off you.

"Oh, I couldn't—"

But Becca's attempt to politely decline Ryan's invitation was met with a decisive shake of his head. "Mee-Maw would count it a personal insult if you came at suppertime and didn't stay to eat. Besides, if you're gunning for me, you'd best get a little nourishment before you get started, because it's going to be a long and thankless job."

Sunny_76@yoohoomail.com: No four-star lodging for me. The mattress is like concrete and the walls are so thin that I can hear people scurrying around in the next room.

Rooster@yoohoomail.com: Sure it's people? Could be a mouse, you know.

Sunny_76@yoohoomail.com: Well, you're comforting!

Rooster@yoohoomail.com: How come a farmer's daughter is afraid of a little ol' mouse?

Sunny_76@yoohoomail.com: If you could see the size of the cockroaches in this place, you'd be scared, too.

Rooster@yoohoomail.com: Where are you? Chernobyl?

Sunny_76@yoohoomail.com: Waaay in the backwoods, not a Starbucks in sight.

CHAPTER THREE

BECCA TRIED TO TAMP DOWN the adrenaline buzzing through her as she sat on the rough wooden bench. The second half of the soccer match was coming to a close now. She could tell by the way the parents were folding up their chairs and gathering up drink bottles.

If Ryan MacIntosh shared any of her nervous anticipation, he didn't let on. Instead, he kept his attention on his soccer team and didn't spare her a glance.

She discounted the flutter shimmering through her. Nerves. Way too much was riding on the outcome of this investigation.

My sweaty palms have nothing to do with that hunk on the field. He's a target, remember? At best, he's a material witness. At worst...

She'd know more once she had a look at his farm. Confident, wasn't he, to invite her out for a drop-in visit? But then, he had mentioned Murphy.

Richard Murphy had made a killing off of the weather the past few years. If he didn't suffer through a drought, then it was spring rains. If it wasn't the weather, then it was a bad lot of seed. Murphy was an inveterate frequent flyer of the crop-insurance programs. She knew that from the dossier the insurance fraud guys had put together for her dad.

Any friend of Murphy's should be suspect in Becca's book.

Beside her, Jack lumbered to a standing position, balancing on his crutches. When she would have helped, he forestalled her with one derisive look.

Right. She was the bad guy.

A blond-haired little girl dashed up. "Daddy! Daddy! Did you see the goal I made? I did it!"

Ryan came up behind the girl, ruffling her hair. "Next Mia Hamm, yes, sir. Jack, you and Marla may have that retirement problem solved after all."

"I won't stop the IRA contributions just yet," he told Ryan. A quick telltale glance toward Becca, and Jack added, "Uh, call me, okay? Let me know how things go."

Ryan didn't bother with circumspection. He eyed Becca openly. "How it's gonna go is she'll get the nickel tour, Mee-Maw's chicken-fried steak and then *adios, amiga.* Because there's nothing going on for her to find. Is there, Jack?"

Jack shifted. Becca couldn't decide whether the shift was to accommodate his leg or a sign of his discomfiture. "Right," was all he said.

Ryan grabbed the five-gallon beverage cooler. "Ready? Or do you know the way?"

"I have a map, but I'll follow you. Need a hand?" Becca reached for the cups.

One of his big hands scooped them up before she could retrieve them. "Not from you, I don't."

He marched off toward the gate. Becca looked over at Jack. "Is it just me or is he always like this?"

Jack shrugged. "The ladies around here tend to think he's hot stuff. So I'd figure...it was you."

She followed Ryan to the grass parking lot. He was busy loading the cooler and a couple of soccer balls into their mesh bag on the back of a dented pickup. The truck in all its rusty glory held her attention.

Becca had expected a big, shiny extended-cab model, fresh off the showroom floor. What she saw was a truck at least fifteen years old that bore the scars of work.

It didn't jibe with the typical scammer's profile.

Ryan shot her a smile that was short on any real welcome. "I'm about ready. Do you need a lift to your car?"

"It's right here. The red Mini Cooper."

He looked past her, toward the only Mini Cooper in the lot. Now his lips twisted a little. "That thing run on golf-cart batteries?"

She was accustomed to people teasing her

about her car; Becca didn't care. Buying that car was one of the truly profligate things she'd ever done—but her aunt would be smiling down on her for it.

Becca swallowed hard, wishing for just an instant that her aunt Mala were with her. Her father's younger sister had adored Mini Coopers when the imports had become popular, and she'd worn red until the day she'd died of breast cancer. She'd encouraged Becca early on to be a tad whimsical. Despite her father's pragmatic bent, Becca had to admit to succumbing to Aunt Mala's teachings with the car.

Besides, it reminded Becca of a time not so long ago when her own business was going great guns, she'd bought her own house and the future looked bright. The car was the one thing she'd kept from her old life.

Now Becca returned to the present. "Betcha my Mini would beat your old truck."

Ryan slid a hand over the dings and scratches. "This isn't any old truck. This belonged to Gramps. What's good enough for him is good enough for me. I wouldn't bet the farm on your little Matchbox toy, not until you've looked under the hood of my truck."

Maybe it was the way he'd touched the truck with such reverence. Maybe it was because he, too, let his choice of transportation be a way to connect with someone he'd loved. Whatever it was, Becca felt an immediate kinship spring up between them. For the first time, she allowed herself to hope that maybe things weren't as they seemed.

BECCA KEPT the Mini Cooper well back from the billows of dust Ryan's truck churned up on the dirt road. She couldn't decide whether it would be wiser to go slow over the washboard surface and save the car's alignment, or go fast—thereby missing most of the bumps and saving all the jostles to her neck and shoulders. They were stiff from the three-hour ride from Atlanta.

She'd stopped just long enough to get a room at the local motel, with its 1960s decor and its view of the pitted parking lot. Becca could have gotten a room at any of the el-cheapo but known motels in Dublin, but her dad had always advised to get a room close to the investigation. You picked up things that way, and you didn't waste time in transit.

Up ahead, she saw Ryan's brake lights pop on and the truck pull off on a narrow drive. It wound through two big pastures dotted with cows that seemed undisturbed by the truck.

Now she saw the tin roof of the farmhouse glinting in the setting sun. When she pulled to a stop, she gave the single-story house with its steeply pitched roof an appraising look.

The house was white-framed, with a deep wraparound porch graced by restrained ginger-bread trim, a swing and some rockers. The biggest chinaberry tree Becca had ever seen shaded the porch. A cracked and uneven walk curved between two beds full of red and yellow and orange roses.

This could be Nana and Papa's.

The homeplace wasn't just like Becca's grand-parents', of course, but the simple, unfussy style of the house was akin to many of the farmhouses in the south. Becca closed her eyes, sniffing in the late-evening air.

Yep. There it was. The redolent scent of honey-suckle.

"You gonna stand out here all night, or are you coming in?"

"Uh, sure." Becca was embarrassed that Ryan had caught her reminiscing. She closed the gap between them. "I was just admiring the house. It's beautiful."

"Tara, it's not, but I like it. Gramps built it him-self, just after he came home from the Pacific the-ater. He was in World War II."

"He seems to have been quite a guy."

"He was."

Again she heard that prickle in Ryan's voice,

that note of defensiveness. But before she could address it, the front door swung open.

"Ryan, that you? What you doing coming in the front door? Oh! You got company!"

The words, strong and vibrant and with a country twang, held a note of pleasure and came from the tall woman at the screen door. Her hair was thick and white and scooped up in a bun. Her tanned face seemed curiously smooth, except for a few deep crevices.

"Mee-Maw, this is Becca Reynolds. She's a crop-insurance investigator."

Amusement rippled over the old woman's features at the sour warning in Ryan's voice. "Well, Ryan, I guess everybody's gotta do something to keep body and soul together. Child, come on in. My grandson did invite you to supper, didn't he? Or did he completely forget his raisings? I sure hope you like chicken-fried steak."

"I do appreciate the offer, but I can get something in—"

"Hush, child. You won't get anything at all like my chicken-fried steak in town, so you might as well come on in and wash up. I was just getting ready to put it on the table, so you can get the ice in the glasses, how 'bout that?"

Ryan grinned at Becca. "Told you. When Mee-Maw gets her mind set on anything, you might as well just go along with it."

A hint of the supper wafted out, and suddenly Becca did want to sample Mee-Maw's cooking.

Or maybe you just miss your grandparents. Don't get too close, Becca.

Aunt Mala's whimsical nature—and the promise of a good homecooked meal—got the best of her. "Sure," she said, deliberately not looking at Ryan. "That sounds great. Just point me in the direction of the glasses and the ice."

"C'MON, CHILD, you know you can eat more—one little piece of steak is all you've eaten. There's plenty more."

Becca shook her head. The "little" piece of steak that she'd eaten was twice what she'd needed. To go with it, she'd tucked away a mountain of mashed potatoes floating with gravy, butter beans and thick slices of tomatoes.

"No, ma'am. I couldn't hold another bite. Besides, it's getting late, and I'd like to take a look around before dark."

"Pshaw, honey. It won't get dark until nearly nine. But you two young folks go ahead. I'll get the dishes."

That led to a tussle between Ryan and Becca to see who would take the kitchen cleanup task away from Mee-Maw. It at once felt odd and right to Becca to think of her target's grandmother as

Mee-Maw, but that was the name the woman had insisted she use.

"It's what everybody calls me," Mee-Maw had said. "The only Mrs. MacIntosh I ever knew was my mother-in-law—God rest her soul, 'cause I don't want that old battle-ax comin' back from the grave!"

Ryan ungraciously conceded that Becca could at least assist him with the dishes. They worked in silence. His familiarity around the kitchen told her that he'd done this before.

Maybe Dad was wrong. Maybe Ryan's not involved. I'm wasting my time here. It's Murphy I should be going after.

According to Ag-Sure's people, the insurance company was betting that the dodder vine had been planted intentionally. Since Ryan and Murphy had been the first in the area to submit a claim, Ag-Sure had tagged them as the most likely suspects.

Now Becca wasn't so sure. Maybe it wasn't a scam.

The last pot dried and put away, Ryan picked up a platter of table scraps. "Let me just feed Wilbur and I'll show you whatever you need to see."

"Wilbur?"

"That ol' dog!" Mee-Maw shook her head. "He's an old sooner that came wanderin' up last winter, nothin' but skin and bones. Ryan found him slippin' round the hog pen, survivin' off what food he could steal from my sows. I named the old mutt Wilbur after that pig in *Charlotte's Web*."

"So you have hogs *and* cows?" Becca's research hadn't turned up this.

Ryan shook his head. "After Gramps passed away, the guy who helped us took off. Guess he didn't think I could make a go of the farm. Anyway, it was too much work for one person, taking care of hogs, so we sold them. But we kept Wilbur. The name suits him—he sure thought he was a pig."

Hmm...a disappearing hired hand. That's a bit convenient. I wonder if this hand knew about the scam and was persuaded to get himself lost. She filed away the thought and commented, "I thought dogs weren't supposed to get table scraps."

Ryan chuckled. "Tell that to Wilbur—or whoever fed him scraps to begin with."

Becca followed Ryan out the kitchen door. A big brown dog loped up the back steps. He sat down on his haunches, pawed the rough floorboards of the porch and whined.

"Here you go, boy." Ryan dumped the scraps into a stainless steel bowl. Wilbur thumped his thick tail hopefully. "Okay, eat."

"Wow. You've got him trained. My old dog would be all over me."

"What sort of dog?"

"A collie. We lost her to cancer last year."

"We? You're married?"

Was that disappointment she detected in Ryan's tone? Becca shook her head. "No. I live with my dad. Kind of weird, I know. But it's just been me and him forever—my mom died when I was young. It's his firm that I work for—so we just, um, decided it was expedient to live together. Makes it simpler."

Becca hoped she hid her shame at having returned home.

"Hey, you're talking to a grown man who still lives with his grandmother." Ryan shrugged. "I did the single-bachelor deal and the roommate deal…and, you know, Mee-Maw beats 'em all when it comes to cooking and sharing a roof. Besides, this way, I get to keep an eye on her. It's been hard on her since she lost Gramps."

Again that feeling of kinship sprang up. They had so many things in common that, in other circumstances, they might well have hit it off from the start.

Becca covered her conflicted emotions by scratching Wilbur behind the ear.

"Ahem, well. Where's that nickel tour you promised?"

"Right. Let me put this up."

She stayed outside while he washed the final dish. Back outside, he rubbed his hands together—working man's hands, she noted, but with nails neatly trimmed and clean.

"So…where to?"

"Let me see this vine everybody's complaining about."

"Sure. But can we take a detour so I can feed the fish in the pond?"

"No problem. As long as I can get out of here by dark."

She fell in step beside him, crossing the back-yard to the pond that lay in a pool of golden sunset. "Oh, my. This is gorgeous."

"Yeah. It is. The rest of the world can keep its beachfront condos—this is my favorite place on earth. Me, my hammock and Wilbur at my feet."

Becca thought about Rooster and his hammock and his similar sentiments. Must be a man thing.

But the peaceful stillness of the pond stirred some understanding in even her restless soul. She finally got what Rooster had meant by needing a little solitude—and sitting still while you had it instead of racing down a highway.

"I don't see any hammock."

"It's over there. Underneath the willow tree near the dock. See the willow that's arched over? My cousins and I—"

Becca's breath caught. She didn't hear the rest of what he said. She couldn't, not over the thump of her heart. She stood stock-still and saw afresh the pond. The house. The dog who scarfed up table scraps.

She looked at Ryan, who stared back at her with a worried expression on his face. Ryan. The target of her investigation.

No.

Rooster.

CHAPTER FOUR

"ARE YOU—DO YOU NEED to sit down? You look like you're going to pass out. You're not a diabetic, are you?"

Ryan's words, as well as his hand on her shoulder, yanked her out of the swirling maelstrom of her thoughts.

Tell him. Tell him you know him.

No, you could be wrong. You'd sound like a nut, or a loser—a loser who has to go online to find someone to talk to and then doesn't even know his name. Wait. Be sure.

But Becca was sure, to-her-bones sure. She smiled at him in what she hoped was a reassuring way. "Uh, headache. I guess…the sunset?"

"Migraine?" Ryan made sympathetic noises that triggered a flood of guilt within Becca.

"My camera…I forgot it. I'll just…walk back and get it, okay? It's in my car."

He would have followed her, but she waved him off. "You feed the fish. I'll get my camera…and some medicine."

As if to make her words true, a headache blistered forth like a blacksmith's red-hot poker. Whether it was stress or punishment for the lie, Becca couldn't say, but she was grateful for the time alone.

At the car, she fumbled for her camera. The bag's heft felt dear and familiar in her hand. The camera had been one of the small things she'd managed to salvage after the debacle at the magazine. Becca pushed aside resentful thoughts of libel suits and searched for some quick-dissolve pain medicine.

She sat in the driver's seat and closed her eyes, hoping that the medicine would kick in before the pain settled for a long stay. The inner debate raged on. With some force, she managed to tick off the pros and cons of telling him the truth.

The biggest reason was her gut. It had never steered her wrong before—well, save one biggie in the form of her countersuit, but in the end, even a jury of her peers had said her gut had been right.

Maybe, though, her instinct to blurt out "Are you Rooster?" came from her distaste of lying, even by omission. Deceit never felt right to Becca.

But this situation was different.

You don't know if it's Rooster. You have no way to verify it, except for some story about a willow tree. He can't have been the only one who's ever put a hammock under a willow tree.

Yeah, right. And just what did her dad say about coincidence?

Her dad. Becca's stomach did a nauseating roll and twist the way it did whenever she'd topped a roller coaster and prepared for the final gut-wrenching loops. Her father would kill her. Becca could imagine the scathing words her dad would say to her if she trotted back to Atlanta to tell him some sorry tale about how she knew Ryan Mac-Intosh was innocent because he'd turned out to be her online buddy.

Knowing Dad, he'd say it was no coincidence at all. He'd think Ryan had targeted Becca.

The possibility niggled at her. It would explain how Becca, who never managed to win a door prize or a lottery ticket or even a bingo game, had hit the trifecta of coincidence.

But, no. She had six months of correspondence with Ryan, anonymous correspondence. She knew him—knew him how it counted. He couldn't be scamming her. He couldn't be mixed up in some complicated conspiracy to defraud the government and Ag-Sure.

Could he?

Okay, so she couldn't say anything to her dad. She had to go forward with the investigation if she wanted to keep her job.

So…

Maybe there was no fraud. Maybe it was some

wildly improbable, but still true, story about a vine that had somehow gotten transported from Texas to Georgia. Truth was stranger than fiction, right?

All she had to do was prove that the story *was* true. All she had to do was figure out how it got there. Then not even the insurance company could fault her.

If she did it quickly enough, Ryan wouldn't have to know now. Plenty of time to help him anonymously. Plenty of time to tell him later. He'd understand about conflicts of interest.

The tremulous panic within her subsided as she settled on a course of action. Becca drew in an easier breath. She could do this.

A tapping at the window made her jump. She opened her eyes to see a concerned Ryan crouched down, peering at her.

Right. Well, checking on her tallied with the considerate Rooster she knew.

She gripped her camera bag and opened the car door. Time to get the show on the road.

"I got worried," Ryan told her. "You looked so…"

"Thanks. I took some medicine. It happens, these headaches. I get stressed out and boom. A good night's sleep will put me to rights. Fish fed?"

"Yeah. Um…you have some different shoes? Those aren't exactly…"

She glanced down at her leather slip-ons. "Oh. Right. Let me change into the sneakers I brought."

Ryan dropped onto the grass while he waited for her to swap shoes. Wilbur nosed up to him and flopped down beside him. She watched the two of them roughhouse while she tied her last sneaker. It felt odd to see Rooster in the flesh, see him do the things he'd described in what he'd supposed was an anonymous way. They'd revealed more than they'd realized about each other.

The trick, of course, was not to inadvertently reveal that she was Sunny. That would be a devil of a dilemma. After all, hadn't she let Rooster—Ryan, she corrected herself—into her soul? Wouldn't it be as easy for him to spot her as it had been for her?

Becca gave an extra hard yank to her shoelaces and stood up. The quicker she could stamp *Closed* on this case, the better. "Let's take a gander at this vine, shall we?"

A FEW MINUTES LATER she was jouncing up and down behind Ryan on the back of a four-wheeler, with Wilbur running alongside them. Rows of cotton slid past them as they headed into the field.

She tightened her grip on Ryan to avoid being bounced off when they hit a rut—and was rewarded with the feel of rock-solid abs.

"Sorry!" he yelled over the roar of the two-cycle engine. "Didn't see that one."

His scent—a mix of soap and water, her favorite laundry detergent and the faintest trace of some sort of drive-a-woman-wild aftershave—tickled her senses. She inhaled again, this time deliberately. This was what she'd been missing all these months. Too bad e-mails didn't come with a scratch-n-sniff option; she would have discarded the blanket of anonymity months ago if she'd had a hit of this.

All too soon, Becca felt the four-wheeler slow and then stop. She climbed off the machine, tried to tell herself that the unrelenting vibrations were what had made her knees weak.

Becca couldn't convince herself of that one.

"Well. There it is. The giant Asian dodder vine. Ugly critter, isn't it?"

It *was* ugly. Thick vines with no leaves strangled the cotton. To Becca, the vines looked like nothing so much as some sort of monochromatic python.

She fumbled in her camera bag for her reporter's notebook and a pencil, old habits so ingrained that she never could get accustomed to using anything else. "Right. So how long has this been here? When did it first show up?"

Some of Ryan's earlier disgust came back. "Don't you guys even bother to read the insurance claim forms? Or are you hoping I'll trip myself up so you can stamp *Denied* on my claim and then go on your merry little way?"

Ouch. His tone had hurt. She was about to snap back with something like "Hey, easy, buddy, I'm on your side," but she stopped herself.

Don't assume that Ryan is going to treat you like he knows you. To him, you're the bad guy, remember?

Becca struggled for professionalism. "Yes, I have those forms—I've read them, I assure you. But I think it's best if you just think of me as a glorified insurance adjuster. I'm here to help, okay? The computer's flagged this and other similar claims for a variety of reasons. It's in your best interest to help me so that this case is resolved quickly. Then Ag-Sure's happy, you get your money and you're happy, too. After all, if everything's on the up-and-up, you've got nothing to hide, right?"

The color heightened in Ryan's face, and he glanced away. Oh, no. She wished he hadn't done that. It set all her alarm bells clanging.

Maybe he was still just mad.

"Right, Ryan?"

His nod lacked a certain ringing conviction of innocence. It troubled her that he didn't enthusiastically say "Of course I've got nothing to hide."

But she ignored her worries and focused on doing her job.

Because doing her job would be what saved both of them.

"So, then, how you can help is to tell me, to the best of your knowledge, the time line, how this vine came to be."

"I don't *know* how this 'came to be,'" Ryan growled at her. "All I know—all I can tell you— is that one morning, I got up to come plow my cotton and I saw this. Do you realize that I can't even plow it? Not this section, anyway. The vines are too thick. They wrap around the implements and the discs, and I spend half a day getting them unwrapped. Forget harvesting this in any sort of mechanized way—even the good plants that aren't affected—the vines are too close and mess up the harvester."

But Becca had already started counting off rows…and she realized something. The knots of snakelike vines were in a pattern. Several rows would be untouched, and then one lone row or two would be taken over by the dodder. Then it would repeat—within the distance of the common width of plows.

She looked from the field to Ryan. No. It couldn't be. But another count of the rows confirmed that the pattern was too consistent to be natural.

There's got to be an explanation for this.

But that desperate thought vied with another.

Face it. He's hiding something—and not very well.

Becca disguised her suspicion by taking pictures. She stepped back, steadied her pen on her pad and pressed on. "I have to admit, I know zip about this plant except what I could find online. And what the insurance company provided for me."

"Right, of course. I'm sure they were most helpful."

"It's your chance, Ryan. Tell me."

Becca willed him to come clean with whatever was so obviously on his mind. She could see something warring within him, knew instantly that he was experiencing the same inner debate she'd had earlier.

He'd tell Sunny.

For an instant, it was on the tip of her tongue to tell him the truth. Just blurt it out and see if he'd take her into his confidence. But then, maybe it was best that Ryan didn't know who she was. The insurance company would yank her and her dad off the case for sure, and then what sort of investigator would Ryan get?

No. Better to do it the way she'd planned.

He'd come to a decision, she could see that.

"From my research—and my experience, unfortunately—this stuff grows at, like, six inches a day. It has no roots, no leaves—doesn't need 'em. It just attaches itself to a handy plant and sucks it dry. Then it spreads to the next plant. And the next. I have no clue how it got here. A bit of a vine could have dropped here, could have been blown in by the wind from some of these other farms. It could have been trucked in. It just happened to drop in a spot, sniffed out a plant it liked and boom—suddenly I'm out of business. Bad luck. Bad timing."

"So herbicides won't work?"

"Sure. Kill the host plant and you kill the dodder vine. You don't make anything on cotton even when the rains come when they're supposed to and the weeds are the everyday garden variety. This is the scariest thing to hit cotton since the boll weevil."

Becca's headache came back full force. She realized that darkness had crept up on them when Wilbur came bursting out of a particularly thick patch of cotton.

"Um…look, I'll have loads more questions than I feel up to asking about tonight. Can I bug you tomorrow after I've had a chance to get some rest?"

"Do I have a choice?"

Again, her heart ached. She wanted to yell at him, "Don't hate me! It's me! It's Sunny! I'm here to help."

Until she knew what was going on, though, she didn't dare.

Ryan didn't wait for her answer. "C'mon. I'll take you back. We'll go a different way so you see how far down it goes.

"Listen…maybe I came across all wrong. I'm just really frustrated by all this. All I want to do is get this harvest in some way, somehow, or else call it a loss and take my lumps. Trust me. I'll make more money if I can get the harvest to market than I would with the insurance. All the insurance money will do is maybe pay off my seed money, my fertilizer and my pesticide bills. Diesel? Electricity? My labor? Forget that. But—"

She lay a hand on his arm. "I'm not the enemy, Ryan. I know how hard farming is, how dicey it can be. You have to trust me."

He nodded, an abrupt jerk of his head that told her he didn't, in fact, trust her.

Ryan seemed more rigid, less at ease, on the trip back. They left the field behind and came into the farmyard proper, whizzing past a big old barn, a grain silo, some outbuildings. Ahead, she could see the lights of the house, contrasting with the descending twilight.

They slowed as they passed a tiny but colorful vegetable garden.

"Wow! Look at the size of those tomatoes! You really know how to grow 'em!"

"That's Mee-Maw's. Want some? I need to pick the ripe ones for her anyway—"

He braked suddenly, the movement jerking her forward.

"What?"

Ryan switched off the four-wheeler's engine, stalked over to the vegetable garden and knelt down. With one hand, he began jerking up a perfectly healthy tomato vine by its roots, the careful framework of stakes tumbling to the ground.

Becca gasped. "What are you doing?"

He shoved it at her. "Pick off the tomatoes—ripe and green. Throw the vine down way over yonder—don't put it down near the garden. I need to check the rest of these plants."

Bemused, she did as he ordered, stacking the round red fruit on the seat of the four-wheeler. It was only as she turned the vine over in her hands that she saw what had made him yank up the bush.

Wrapped around the base of the tomato plant, as thin as a garden snake, was a young dodder vine.

CHAPTER FIVE

BECCA'S HAND INSTANTLY recoiled from the vine, though she told herself she was being silly. The plant, no matter how serpentine it looked, wasn't dangerous to anything but a hapless plant unlucky enough to be its target.

Behind her, Ryan half muttered under his breath. She turned from plucking the last of the green tomatoes off the bush to see him yanking up still more plants by their roots.

The investigator in her noted the placement of those plants. The vine had grown on host plants in a checkerboardlike pattern all over the garden. She'd been around farming all her life, and she knew that what she was seeing was not natural.

No, if this had been a natural invasion of a parasitic plant, the vine would have attacked one spot and spread outward in a radius.

How had it traveled all the way from the cotton field—far enough that it took a four-wheeler to get there—to the kitchen garden so close to the house?

Squash plants, pea plants, okra, cucumber—one

or two each joined the tomato plant Becca had discarded well away from the garden. Ryan crossed over to a shed, came back with a handful of kindling and a box of matches. He knelt, building a quick funeral pyre for the plants and tossed in a lit match.

"You're not playing around." Becca studied him for a long moment. Was his reaction normal frustration or a little too vehement?

For now, Becca was willing to give him the benefit of the doubt…but knowing her dad wouldn't do the same ate at her.

"If there's even a scrap of these left, the vine can spread. Mee-Maw's worked too hard on this garden for her to lose it now." His features were grim as he watched to be sure the plants caught.

The flames shot up higher and smoke billowed, hanging low in the twilight. Becca said nothing, still just observing, wanting to believe in Ryan. Abruptly, he turned and started back for the shed.

"Watch that for me," he said. "I need some old bricks to surround the fire. All I need is for this fire to get out of control. It's dry enough that it would spread. There's a water hose coiled up near the back porch if it spreads."

He was back again in a few moments, laden down with chipped and broken bricks. By the time Ryan had made a ring around the fire, the green plants had decided to succumb. Becca noted that the thicker dodder vines were more resistant to the flames than the tender green leaves of the vegetable plants.

Ryan seemed to read her thoughts. "First time I spotted this stuff in the cotton field, I thought that the best way to handle it was to burn it. So I doused a pile of cotton plants and vines with a little lighter fluid and tried to do just that. A day or so later I noticed that not all the vine had been destroyed and that it had latched on to whatever thick, bushy plant it found near enough to grab hold of. It's downright creepy, if you ask me."

The heat of the fire was suffocating in the muggy August evening, but Becca was still mesmerized. She pulled her eyes from the hypnotic flames. "So, you have to build this big a fire?"

Sweat had beaded up on Ryan's brow, and his T-shirt clung to him. "All I can figure is the vines have sucked so much water out of host plants that killing the vine itself is that much harder. You have to burn it a long time…kind of like getting seaweed started for an oyster bake. For a whole field of cotton, that's not so easy…but at least I know what to do to save Mee-Maw's tomatoes."

Mentioning Mee-Maw seemed to summon her. His grandmother swung open the back door and stepped out onto the porch. "Ryan? What are you up to? It's too dry and too late for a bonfire—not to mention it's got to be eighty degrees out here even at this time of night!"

Ryan sighed. "Help me carry these tomatoes to her, will you?"

Becca gathered up an armload of tomatoes and followed him to the back porch.

"Mee-Maw…I'm afraid that vine's spread to your garden. I had to destroy some of your plants, okay? I'm sorry, but if you want a chance at salvaging the rest of it, the host plants had to be burned."

Mee-Maw's face sagged, and suddenly Becca could see the woman's years. "Here, let me get a pan to put 'em in. We'll fry the green tomatoes, and the ripe ones needed picking anyway." She cast a nervous glance at Ryan. "You keep an eye on that fire. Should have got an old barrel out of the—"

"Yes, ma'am, Mee-Maw. I know. I should have."

The old lady hustled into the kitchen for a pan, shooing Ryan away as soon as he'd dumped his cargo. "You go on back to the fire."

Becca, though, followed her into the house, the dog at her heels. "Is it okay? The dog, I mean?" she asked. She piled the green tomatoes down atop the red ones. "They're beautiful tomatoes. It's a shame."

"Wilbur's fine. He likes to loaf, but he stays inside mostly. Thank you, ma'am, 'bout my tomatoes. Some of 'em are turning, looks like. You like fried green tomatoes?"

Becca nodded, gazing out the window over the sink at Ryan as he poked at the fire with an iron rake. When she turned her attention back toward Mee-Maw, she saw the woman was looking out the window, as well. "Yes, ma'am. My grandmother sure could make a mean fried green tomato."

Mee-Maw sank into her chair at the kitchen table and buried her head in her hands. "First I lose Mac, and then J.T. has to leave the day after Mac's funeral…then that blamed vine starts springing up. Bad enough it got into the cotton, but now the vegetables? And with money so tight!"

"Mac?"

"My husband. Ryan's grandfather. Mac's daddy gave us this little corner of land to build the house on. He was in the Pacific, Mac was, during World War II. Spent the whole entire war surrounded by water. Swore if he could ever make it back on dry land, he'd nail his feet to the ground, and he just about did. Don't get me wrong—we battled hail and sleet and drought and floods and just about everything, but I never thought I'd see anything like this…this awful vine."

"Is J.T. one of your sons?"

"J.T.?" For a moment, Mee-Maw looked a little

startled. Her face resembled Ryan's as it closed down, defensive and wary. "No. J.T. helped us out around the farm. Me and Mac, we were no spring chickens, you know, and we needed someone with a strong back. Ryan was on the road with that chemical company back then, and Jack's always so busy with his insurance agency."

"So your children…"

"Jack's dad got killed in a wreck, oh, ten years ago. And Marshall, Ryan's dad—he's my youngest—he's teaching at the agricultural college. That's a good three hours away."

Mee-Maw sighed again. "I didn't know what I'd do when J.T. had to leave. I thought for sure I'd have to give up this place. But then Ryan came back and helped me keep the farm going. He'd been itching to for years, but he kept putting it off. Besides, he didn't want to seem like he was pushing his gramps out of the tractor seat." She snorted. "As if anyone could have, even if he'd wanted to."

"Why did J.T.—"

But before Becca could get the question out, Mee-Maw had pushed up from the table and crossed to stand beside Becca at the white enamel sink and drainboard, muttering something about Ryan and the fire.

"Ma'am?"

"Fire. Hate the stuff. Lost everything we had to

a fire when I was a kid. An old cookstove messed up—ain't nothing sadder than to stand outside in the middle of the night and see every stick of furniture, every scrap you own, everything you worked for…gone. Makes me the pack rat I am, I guess.

"Go on out there, will you? Make sure he banks that fire. I know he will, mind you, but just humor a silly old woman."

Becca crossed the backyard to the bonfire—and stopped in her tracks.

Ryan had stripped off his T-shirt and laid it aside. The fire lit the planes of his chest, highlighting well-developed pecs and a firm, flat abdomen.

His skin was damp from his exertion and the heat of the flames licking over the dodder vine at his feet. Ryan seemed intense, focused, apparently unfazed by the smoke and the crackle of sparks that shot up from the wood into the dark night sky.

The sight made Becca's belly flutter. She tried to quench the butterflies with a good dose of common sense.

First she'd mooned over his scent and now she was ogling him? Her dad would yank her off this case so fast… She knew better than to get involved with the target of an investigation.

But you're already involved.

"Mee-Maw said to be sure to bank the fire."

Ryan jumped. "You scared me. I figured you'd gone by now."

"No. You know, I should have gotten pictures of the vine before you burned the plants."

"Yeah, well, chalk that up to my thinking it was more important to get a harvest than an insurance settlement."

Or was it to cover something up? She silenced her dad's whisper in her head, but it was there for a reason. While she'd always prided herself on being objective and open-minded, she had enough of her father in her to avoid being led down many a primrose path.

"Ryan…" Becca fought the urge to touch him. It was so hard to act as though she'd only just met him. "Before I close out this investigation, I'm going to need detailed time lines, to establish where this vine first popped up, how it spread. Your claim forms are pretty scant on details like that."

"You see how it spreads!" He scowled and gave the fire a jab with his rake, sending off an explosion of sparks. "It's like toadstools—one day it's not there, the next, it's strangling half a garden. Fill out all the blanks and check all the boxes you want to on your forms, but it all comes down to the same thing—I don't know how it got here. I can speculate, but it doesn't change the fact that I'm fighting something here—we're all fighting something—that could wreck agriculture in this part of the state."

"Whoa. A bit of hyperbole, isn't it?"

"No. Another farmer who has this stuff in his fields says it's resistant to the one herbicide that ought to kill it."

"I thought you said if you kill the host plant—"

"If you starve it out, sure. But in his case, the vine just found something else to latch on to. Look—I know insurance companies don't want to pay out claims. They've got shareholders, and I know whose tune those insurance execs are marching to. But rather than send us someone to *investigate* us—" this he made sound like the basest of insults "—why not send us someone to *solve* the problem?"

"And who might that be? What experts have you called in?"

Again, Ryan gave her a look that screamed his discomfiture.

"Well? Surely you—"

"I've put in calls to every expert that might have the faintest clue of how to get rid of this vine. They all say the same thing—drag a firebreak around the affected acreage, throw in a match and watch what little profit you have left go up in smoke. Believe me, I've been tempted. And to-night…tonight I'm past temptation."

"No! You can't do that. It could be evidence—"

"See? You do think I'm running a scam."

"Evidence can prove you either guilty or innocent, Ryan. But if you destroy it, you destroy any chance of me helping you."

"You? Helping me? Why would a hired gun from Ag-Sure want to help me?"

Frustrated, she ground her teeth. "I am not a hired gun. The outcome of this case—at least from my point of view—is not a foregone conclusion, okay? But you're being so paranoid that you're sure acting guilty."

"Sorry," he mumbled. "I'm just frustrated, okay?"

"Okay. But believe me. I'm here to help. Surely you can't have tapped out all the experts on this sort of problem."

The flicker of hope in his face died, and the corners of his mouth twisted. "You might as well know since you'll find out sooner or later—if you don't already know."

"What?"

The bonfire crackled as the flames fed on the pine resin. Bits of ash rained down on Becca and Ryan, but she waited. She tried to read anything but misery in Ryan's expression.

She couldn't.

"One of my last projects with the ag chemical company I worked for was on a farm in Texas with this same dodder vine. I didn't have a clue what to do to help them, and neither did anybody else. And I sure," he bit out, "don't know how to get rid of it here. I was there, on-site, equipped with means and opportunity to bring the vine east. So, you still think this case has no foregone conclusion?"

Sunny_76@yoohoomail.com: Have you ever wondered about me? I mean, what I look like, who I am? If you've ever passed me on the street?

Rooster@yoohoomail.com: I know pretty much everybody on the streets I've been on, but I've wondered, yeah.

Sunny_76@yoohoomail.com: What would you say if you met me, but you weren't *sure* it was me? If we did meet up?

Rooster@yoohoomail.com: I probably wouldn't say anything—what if it wasn't you? She'd think I was nuts.

Sunny_76@yoohoomail.com: So do you think one day we ever will meet?

Rooster@yoohoomail.com: Maybe…but part of me doesn't want to spoil the way things are.

CHAPTER SIX

RYAN'S PATH WAS BLOCKED by a four-foot-ten-inch pixie with the saddest eyes he'd ever seen.

"Charlotte, I promise. I don't know where J.T. is," Ryan told the diner waitress. "I haven't heard from him in months—since Gramps's funeral. You just need to…"

Ryan tried to swallow the anger he felt whenever he thought of the disappearing J. T. Griggs. The man had taken advantage of at least two women—Charlotte and Mee-Maw—left them high and dry, and still they defended him.

"You just need to forget J.T."

Charlotte Hooks shifted her weight from one rubber-soled foot to the other, the carafe of hot coffee sloshing dangerously in her hand. "I can't. He was a good man. I—I just don't understand it, Ryan. J.T. just wouldn't vanish this long without telling me where he was going. He wouldn't leave Mee-Maw in a crunch, leaving right after Mr. Mac's funeral. He had respect for Mr. Mac, and you know that. He flat worshipped the ground that man walked on."

"Maybe he went back to Texas?"

Her brows drew together in an even darker frown. "They have phones in Texas, last I heard. If he's that tight for money, he could at least send me a postcard. Besides, J.T. said he wasn't ever going back there. Wasn't anything there for him, he said."

Ryan eyed the glass door leading to the private dining room, the one where Murphy was holding court—and waiting for him.

He didn't need to be here. He needed to be out plowing—and making sure that vine hadn't taken any more potential harvest.

Ryan had been on a tractor, in fact, when Murphy had called this impromptu meeting this morning. Some people didn't apparently have to work for a living.

But calls from Murphy—what with his web of connections to local politics and his big fat checkbook—were the equivalent of a command performance. Mee-Maw—and what she might have done to protect Gramps's memory—was part of this equation, as well. Ryan hated the doubt and suspicion that had clouded his thoughts about her lately.

Besides, Ryan had a few things to unload on Murphy.

Not that it would do any good.

First, though, he had to get past Charlotte.

"Scout's honor, I have no clue where J.T. is. He hasn't called me, hasn't written, hasn't left a crop circle or a message in skywriting. But if he should, you'll be the first to know, okay? I know…I know you miss him, Charlotte."

Her mouth twisted, and tears gathered in her eyes. "I'm worried. That's what I am. He had so much going for him. He was finally getting his life together. He wouldn't throw it all away. He wouldn't."

Maybe he didn't have a choice.

Ryan shook off the dark thought. "That's right. I'm sure he'll let you know where he is and what he's doing. How about getting me a cup of that coffee and bringing it to me in the back dining room?"

"That's another reason why I thought… You never come here anymore. I thought maybe you knew something and weren't telling me."

I never come here anymore because I'm flat broke and even a dollar for a cup of joe is hard to come by.

"If I find out anything about J.T., I'll tell you. Now, how about that coffee?"

After Charlotte trudged off for a cup, he proceeded back to the dining room.

Murphy looked up from his plate of grits, eggs and bacon. "'Bout time you got here. We've been waiting on you."

The *we* included a motley crew of area farmers, some clearly straight from the fields as Ryan was, others in pristine golf shirts free from any signs of true labor. Murphy was part of the latter, his white knit cotton stretched taut over a big belly. Five minutes in a tractor and that shirt would have been history.

It also, Ryan realized with a sick twist of his stomach, included Jack.

Ryan pulled out a chair and sat down. He gave Jack a penetrating look, but his cousin merely shrugged in reply. The other men stared at Ryan, waiting for him to speak. When he didn't, Murphy forked in another bite of fried egg, chewed, cleared his throat and spoke.

"The fellows here are hoping you can tell them what to expect from that lady investigator. Understand she started with you last night. And stayed pretty late."

"Now you've got me under surveillance?" Ryan glanced Jack's way. Had his cousin told Murphy?

"Small town, Ryan. You know that. A gnat can't fart in this town without someone knowing about it."

The crude comment evoked a titter of uneasy laughter from the men at the table, but it did nothing to ease the tension.

"Well? Tell us about her. What's she like?

What's she askin'?" a farmer named Steven Tate finally blurted out.

The whole scene did not sit well with Ryan. He hated feeling as if he was a spy.

"Ryan, your grandfather knew how important it was for all of us farmers to stick together. You could learn a thing or two from Mac."

That not-so-subtle warning from Murphy served to goose Ryan into reluctant action. "She's nice enough. She asked the obvious questions— when did it start? How did it start? What had I done about it?"

Nobody spoke, not until Murphy had sopped up his grits and cheese with a bit of biscuit. "She seem satisfied with your answers?"

Translation: was Becca Reynolds going away anytime soon?

"For now…but she wants to nail down a detailed time line of the spread of the vine. She really wants to know how it got from Texas to here."

That last bit was inspiration on Ryan's part. Maybe he could force Murphy into revealing just how he'd pulled that trick. Murphy had been hinting for weeks that Gramps had had a hand in it… and the threat had a way of keeping Ryan in line.

But Murphy simply spat out a foul curse. "Detailed time line? What's the point? It's here. She could see it. You showed her, right?"

"You have to admit, Murphy, it looks suspicious. No reports of infestation between here and Texas? Of course the first question the insurance company is going to ask is what train it rode in on."

"Maybe we could buy her off," offered Doug Oliver, who fidgeted with his cap. "She look like the type who could come to some sort of understanding?"

Murphy shot a quelling look at Oliver. "It's too soon for that. But it raises a good question. She the type, you think, Ryan? If push comes to shove?"

"No. And I won't be a part of it." Ryan's blood hissed in his ears.

Murphy's answering chuckle was a short, sharp bark. "You're already a part of it. You're here, aren't you? This dodder vine was your idea, wasn't it?"

Ryan made to push his chair back. "I'm here out of respect for Gramps's memory and his long association with most of you. You keep saying this whole thing was my idea, but I don't have a clue why you think that. I had nothing to do with any of this."

"Nope. Not a clue. Didn't tell Mac anything about a slam-dunk way to get crop insurance to pay off, did you?"

Ryan seethed at the way Murphy was twisting

the truth. He would have shot back a reply, but Murphy had moved on.

"What'd you tell her? What's she got planned?"

Believe me. I'm here to help. That's what Becca had said to him last night, and he believed her. But why? Why would she go out on a limb for the likes of him? What made her think he could be saved—was even worth saving?

"Ryan?"

Ryan dragged his thoughts back from Becca's motivations. "She seems pretty bent on doing a thorough investigation…but on the flip side, she's ready to give us the benefit of the doubt."

"Maybe she's angling for a little grease on the wheels, eh?" Oliver said.

Everybody ignored him. They waited for Murphy's answer.

"She's here for the long haul? Say anything about inspecting the other farms?"

"No, but I expect she will. She seems to know her stuff."

"I don't like it," another farmer spoke up. "I thought this was supposed to be a slam dunk like Murphy said. After that insurance adjuster came, they were supposed to cut a check, and then we could start burning off our fields. As it is, I'm spending out the wazoo to tend a crop I for one didn't think I'd have to be fooling with at this point. Pretty soon, I'll be in the hole, even with the insurance money."

"You'll get your money," Murphy told him. "Everybody just stick together, stick with the story, and you'll get your money."

"Maybe you guys should just cut your losses," Ryan said. "I'm telling you, you let this stuff go unchecked for much longer while you wait on an insurance company to decide, and it'll gain a foothold. Then next year you won't even be able to put in a crop. You just don't understand how bad this particular vine can be. It's already jumped the cotton fields and got into Mee-Maw's garden."

To his satisfaction, Ryan heard a collective gasp. That's right, scare 'em into doing the right thing.

But Murphy seemed unperturbed. "Well, now, Ryan. Guess that shows you how important it is that we get this woman in and out on the double-q. Before anything happens to y'all's precious Mee-Maw. Glad to hear you're grasping the situation."

It took a moment for Ryan to catch Murphy's drift. "You—" Now he was on his feet, with Jack struggling to get up, too, but hampered by his leg. "You were the one who planted that stuff in—"

"That's no way to talk to your gramps's friends, is it? Mac never talked to us like that. All I was saying is that we need to answer this woman's questions and send her on her merry way before that stuff spreads any more. After all, you know what it can do. So it's in everybody's best interest to persuade her to get this investigation over and done with."

Tate leaned forward. "Murphy, if we can't persuade her, then we might have to—" the farmer scratched his chin "—consider other options."

The double meaning in Tate's brief statement was enough to sink a flotilla. Ryan could barely hold on to his temper. The thought that Murphy had deliberately put that vine in Mee-Maw's garden was enough to leave him speechless with rage.

But Tate practically threatening violence?

Murphy gave his head an abrupt shake. "You leave the Reynolds girl to me. Last thing we need to do is get her more suspicious. I know how to handle her kind. They come on strong, but when they see how things work in the real world…"

Behind Ryan, the glass door swung open. He turned to see Becca, clad in blue jeans and a V-necked T-shirt, taking in the gathering. Her eyes went from one farmer to the other, finally landing on Ryan.

Was it disappointment he saw in them?

BECCA KNEW A WAR ROOM when she saw one, and despite its Rotary banners spouting "Is it the truth?" this was most definitely a war room.

She looked past Ryan, his face taut with emotion—rage? Worry? She couldn't be sure—and met the cool, implacable gaze of Richard Murphy.

At least that's who she thought the man sitting at the head of the long table, radiating authority like a lord over his fiefdom, must be.

"Good morning, gentlemen," she said. "I was looking for a Mr. Richard Murphy."

She hadn't been wrong. The man pushed back his chair and rose to his feet. "That'd be me."

"I'm—"

"Becca Reynolds. Ryan here was telling us all about you."

Becca took in the way Ryan's mouth turned down even more at the corners.

He's not happy about whatever is going on.

"Well, good. That saves me the trouble of explaining things. I was wondering if you'd be available to show me your…infestation later today."

"We all will. Right, boys? We certainly want to cooperate with Miss Reynolds so she can get her job done."

"That's—that's great." This was creepy, the way the men around the table—including Jack MacIntosh—all nodded enthusiastically at Murphy's directive, though their expressions looked anything but.

"Uh…Becca. You said you had some more questions for me. We can handle them now, if you want to follow me back out to the farm. Or are you here for breakfast?"

Ryan's voice seemed strange, forced. Was he following orders or just using her as a handy excuse to ditch the meeting?

It didn't matter. She knew him in a way she didn't know the other men in the room. If she was going to get to the bottom of this, she'd get the full story out of Ryan quicker than she would anyone else. She was convinced he wanted to tell her the deal.

Or maybe you're just fooling yourself.

"Sure, I'll follow you. I've already eaten."

Ryan threw down a couple of bills onto the Formica table. He exchanged a long look with Jack, but he didn't, she noticed, say goodbye to anyone. Everyone else seemed to be waiting for her to get out the door so they could resume the meeting.

"Looking forward to seeing you later today, Miss Reynolds. Just come on when you will."

Murphy's invitation reeked of phony goodwill as his words didn't match the hard, speculative light in his eyes.

"I'll do that, Mr. Murphy. Ryan? If you're ready?"

They headed outside into the early-morning sunlight. She took a stab at loosening some details from Ryan.

"I didn't mean to drag you away from your breakfast buddies."

"They're not my buddies," he growled.

Well. That was a reaction. It cheered her immeasurably, save for a niggling doubt about what Ryan's cousin had been doing there. She tackled Ryan about it. "Not your buddies? What about Jack?"

Ryan's dark glower morphed into worry. That was then smoothed into something more inscrutable. "He was probably there for the same reason as me—waiting to see what Murphy had to say."

Maybe. But Jack did sell insurance—though not for crops—and he wasn't happy to have someone poking around. She'd need to keep an eye on Jack.

The thought that someone other than Ryan could be the focus of the scam eased some of the anxiety eating at Becca. She'd spent an insomnia-plagued night second-guessing herself, and then had been awoken at 6:00 a.m. by her dad's phone call.

Becca hadn't exactly lied to him, she just hadn't spilled the whole truth. It was too complicated, and she wanted to figure out a few things first. He'd been satisfied to hear that she thought something hinky was going on.

"Thought so," her father had said. "Mighty funny that a guy with MacIntosh's know-how is at the epicenter of a bunch of claims on some parasitic plant. Mark my words, he's in it up to his neck."

Becca looked at Ryan now. She hoped that he'd talk to her, come clean about whatever had been said in that room. If it were a conspiracy, he would be considered just as guilty as the rest of them if he knew what was going on and said nothing.

"Mee-Maw wanted me to invite you to lunch today. It's leftovers, mind you, but Mee-Maw's leftovers are better than a lot of people's fresh-cooked."

"I'll definitely take her up on it."

"She likes you."

What about you, Ryan? Do you like me? Don't you see any of Sunny in me? Won't you trust me?

"Ryan!" a woman called from the diner's door. She hurried over to where Becca and Ryan stood.

"Charlotte, I told you—"

"I know, I know. I'm a worrywart, and you want me to quit nagging you about J.T."

J.T. again. Becca tried to fade into the background to hear anything that might prove enlightening.

Ryan shot a sideways glance toward Becca. Was he in a hurry to cut the waitress' conversation short?

"I promise, when I find out anything, you'll be the first to know," he answered the woman cryptically. "Becca? Are you ready? I'm already so far behind I'll never get caught up."

With that, he strode off toward his pickup.

CHAPTER SEVEN

RYAN PUT THE TRUCK in gear but held the clutch for a moment longer as he stared in the rearview mirror. Becca was in a deep conversation with Charlotte.

His stomach flipped. Just what he didn't want—both Becca and Charlotte asking questions and comparing notes about J.T.

Real smooth, MacIntosh. You couldn't have been more obvious if you'd circled Charlotte *with a pen and scribbled* Clue!

Becca handed Charlotte something, a card probably, and headed for that oversized-lawn-mower car of hers.

Ryan gnawed at his lip, considering. What could he safely tell her? He'd be dumb as a load of bricks to fall for her "I'm here to help" routine. She probably did that to all her targets.

Highly effective on a sap like you, too, isn't it?

He groaned. *Gramps, I wish you were here.* This was the kind of deal Ryan always went to him about. If Gramps were still around, they'd pop open a couple of colas and a pack or two of peanuts, and Ryan would tell him the whole sorry tale. By the time the peanuts were gone, Gramps would have kicked his behind and put him on the road to right.

He ran his fingers over the dash of the truck, closed his eyes. With a sigh, he shook off the grief and the longing to dump this whole mess onto the capable shoulders of someone wiser, more experienced.

No point in it. He had to get back to the farm, answer what questions he could, avoid the ones he couldn't and do it as quickly as possible.

His cell phone buzzed. Ryan fished it out of his pocket, keeping one hand on the wheel.

"Hey, Ryan, I wanted to explain—"

Ryan cut off Jack in midsentence. "Yeah, I'm waiting. What were you doing there this morning?"

"Same as you. Murphy called me first thing. I aim to keep him happy—and you should, too. You know what he's got over us—over Mee-Maw."

"You don't have to remind me."

"I think I do sometimes. Look…we've talked about this before. Let's just keep our heads down, get through this season as best we can, start fresh next year. For Mee-Maw's sake."

"He planted—"

"Because he thinks you're not playing ball,

Ryan. I don't like it any better than you, but…
we've got no choice. You know that. Right?"

Ryan expelled a long breath. "Right."

"What's the deal with you and the Reynolds
woman, anyway?"

"What do you mean?"

"You know what I mean. I saw the way you
were looking at her. Don't fall for it, cuz. Don't
let a pretty smile take us all down."

"What is it—" Ryan bit back the protest he'd
been about to utter. "Look, I'm just cooperating
with her. You heard Murphy. We're all supposed
to make nice. I'll talk to you later, okay?" He hung
up and glanced in the rearview mirror to see Becca's Mini behind him. If only he and Becca hadn't
met like this.

Maybe Jack was right. If Ryan was going to
dig his way out of this mess, he couldn't afford to
waste time stewing over regrets or missed good-
byes to Gramps. He had to think of Mee-Maw.

MAYBE IT WAS SILLY, but to channel Gramps's
wisdom, Ryan pulled out two bottles of Coke
and the peanuts and laid them out for Becca. She
sat across from him on the front porch, in the
chair he'd always sat in for long confessionals
with Gramps. As he sat in Gramps's high-backed
rocker, he didn't feel worthy of the seat. He'd

screwed up and he didn't know quite how to fix things. Had Gramps ever felt that way?

Ryan worried that maybe, in those last days, Gramps had.

Don't even think that, MacIntosh. Gramps was as straight as an arrow, despite what Murphy says.

He waited for whatever Becca would unload on him. My, she was pretty. He could almost fool himself that this was a Sunday-come-a-courtin' conversation and that the biggest thing at stake was whether he'd get a goodbye kiss.

Be nice if it were that simple.

"So...you farmers frequently have meetings first thing in the morning?"

Ryan harrumphed. "That wasn't first thing in the morning for any self-respecting farmer. And no, we don't. At least I don't. Who has time to fool with breakfast out when you've got a to-do list that stretches to the moon and back?"

"It felt like a board meeting."

"Murphy'd like that analogy. He's a little full of himself, you ask me."

"You mean, you're not best buds with him?"

"'Fraid not. First of all, Murphy doesn't have time for a Podunk farmer like me. He's not the, um, mentor I'd choose for a fount of wisdom. He got where he is by a few lucky breaks and the money that came from them."

Becca lifted a honey-colored brow. "Funny. I'd say, looking back at all of Murphy's crop-insurance claims with Ag-Sure, that he was one of those guys you don't stand near in a lightning storm for fear that when he'd get struck, you'd get hit, too."

"You ask Murphy, he'll tell you a sad story, all right."

"I will ask him. I'll ask everybody. But I'm starting with you. So, do you have anything you might want to share?"

He couldn't meet her eyes. The way she made him feel was the way Gramps had over the years. Whether he found a garden snake in the house, an unexplained dent in the bumper of the truck, an angry girlfriend, Gramps had always used a soul-searching stare and unrelenting silence to get the truth out of Ryan. Becca was no different.

"I've pretty much said it all, I think."

She looked disappointed. But she didn't waste time dog-gnawing him or haranguing him. "I got the distinct impression this morning that I was about as welcome as the tax man. I assume that meeting was called to discuss how to handle me?"

Direct. He liked that, even if he squirmed a bit under the question. "I don't know if Murphy got everybody together just to talk about you, but he called me in, I think, because I was the first one you'd talked to. Why was that, anyway? Why start with me?"

"MacIntosh comes before Murphy."

This time she gave him a small, even smile and waited in silence. So the insurance company had a special interest in him...or Gramps.

Ryan didn't want to meet her assessing gaze. He cleared his throat and plowed on with the conversation. "Well, you certainly take the bull by the horns, don't you?" he asked. "Charging in like you owned the place. How'd you find out about the meeting?" For the first time, he wondered if maybe she had met Charlotte previously and that Charlotte had given her a heads-up.

"Would you believe luck? I'd gone out to Murphy's place this morning to find he'd run into town for breakfast, so I figured I'd find him at the diner. I didn't bet on walking in on all of you."

Ryan gave her a long look and took a swig of his Coke. Her words worried him. He'd assumed she'd gone in there with a plan. It had looked for all the world as if she was taking on the whole lot of them, calling their bluff.

But if she'd just stumbled into it... What if Murphy thought she knew more than she did?

Ryan recalled Tate's willingness to "consider other options" when it came to handling Becca. A little chill speared through Ryan despite the already oppressive morning heat.

Ryan's own costs for this past season were upwards of a half-million dollars. Murphy's farming operation was three times the size of his, and he easily had a million plus tied up, at least on paper. Tate's stake was similar in size. The crop insurance alone would be worth that. What lengths would Murphy and Tate go to for that much money?

"What?" Becca asked him. "You're looking at me like—"

"You just need to be careful with Murphy, okay?"

"Did he threaten me?" Becca's spine stiffened. "Because if he did, I'll have a warrant sworn out on him so fast—"

Ryan groaned. So much for a word to the wise.

"No, he didn't threaten you. Not in so many words. He just wants you out of here."

"Then he must have something to hide."

We all *have something to hide.* "Look, just because he doesn't want this dragged out doesn't have to mean he's up to no good, okay? I mean, look at me. I'm here, talking with you, after I wasted a good hour with Murphy this morning. Think how much disruption an investigation like this creates."

Ryan opted for a soft-pedal approach to pull her back from her inclination to play chicken with Murphy. "Murphy just thought it would be boom, bang, boom, and he'd get his check. Stands to reason. Like you said, this ain't the first time he's been at the crop-insurance rodeo. But this is the first time it's been drawn out."

"So he's not going to have his henchmen waiting at the end of some dark, deserted alley to rough me up?" A smile touched Becca's lips. She leaned back easily in her chair, crossing those long legs of hers as she settled in her seat. He yanked his thoughts away from what her legs would look like in shorts.

The way she'd reacted to his warning did, indeed, make Ryan's fears seem a little over the top. He felt foolish, as if maybe he'd painted Murphy as something other than the crooked farmer he was. He wasn't the Godfather, after all.

Still, a little caution would do Miss Hothead good. "No alleys—you won't find any of the alleys around here long enough or dark enough for mischief like that. He just…er, is pretty well connected. He's hardwired into the political scene, not just local and state, but federal, too, and he, well, let's just say he uses it to his advantage."

"I'll keep that in mind."

A moment of silence stretched between them. Just as Ryan was about to push up from his rocker and beg off to head for the fields, Becca stopped him cold with her next words.

"I take it that the waitress at the diner knew

your hired hand pretty well. J. T. Griggs, wasn't it? She's worried about him. From the way you mentioned that he left, I assumed he'd headed for another farming operation here. But he's...what? Disappeared in the night after your grandfather's funeral? Just dropped off the radar?"

Ryan's stomach knotted. He knew Charlotte and Becca talking to each other spelled trouble.

"I didn't really know J.T. all that well. He was a drifter of sorts, bounced all over the place. He was never one to settle down. I think maybe Charlotte read more into the relationship than J.T. might have intended."

"So his disappearance isn't tied up in all this?"

The screen door pushed open and Mee-Maw came out brandishing a broom. "Lawk's a-mercy," she said, scrutinizing the Cokes and the peanuts. "I sure hope that's not your breakfast, Becca. Back in my day, we didn't have junk food before noon. Of course, you young people live off that high-octane fancy coffee, so maybe a soft drink in the morning ain't so bad, considering."

"I had breakfast, thank you," Becca said. "I got a bite to eat at the diner this morning."

Mee-Maw made a derisive noise in the back of her throat. "They can't keep good help at that diner. Why, last I heard, they had somebody there who didn't even know which end of a can of pork 'n' beans to open. I expect you'll be staying for dinner, as late in the day as it is?"

Becca glanced at her watch, frowning. "It's just ten. I thought I'd—"

"I get my dinner started 'bout half past ten. That way, the kitchen don't heat up. Besides, usually Ryan's been out in the fields for a long spell by then and he's ready for a break."

Ryan wondered at Mee-Maw's intentions. Had she been eavesdropping? He knew well enough the broom was just a ruse because Mee-Maw swept that porch every day right after she put on the morning coffee.

But if she'd been trying to save him from some hole he was about to step in, why invite Becca to lunch?

The questions gnawed at him, started afresh his worries about the extent of Gramps's involvement with Murphy.

"My grandmother did that, too, at least in the summer," Becca was saying. "I've just lived too long in the city, that's all."

Becca's words stirred a memory of another city girl he knew—Sunny. She'd be somebody to bounce this whole mess off of. Ryan could count on her to give him good common-sense advice on a whole host of topics.

But could he bear to risk losing the friendship he had with her by confessing the workings of this scam? He had not mentioned a whisper of any of Murphy's scheme because he didn't want her thinking he was...well, a criminal.

Considering how telling e-mail could be, was it a good idea to spill his guts online? If the government decided Ag-Sure's investigation had merit, they'd follow suit and open up a federal investigation. In recent years, what with the budget being as tight as it was, they'd taken to making an example out of cases like this. That's what, he figured, had created Becca's firm's bread and butter.

"You young people just about through here? I don't want you spoiling your appetites with all that junk food." Mee-Maw gave the two of them a fierce look she'd most likely perfected when Ryan's dad was a kid.

"Mee-Maw, are you telling me in your not-so-subtle way that I should be off my backside and on a tractor?"

"Well, now—" she began a brisk attack on non-existent cobwebs in the far corner of the porch "—I wouldn't want to interrupt your visiting and all, and I know Miss Becca's got official business to do, but now that you mention it, that tractor ain't gonna run itself."

Mee-Maw was trying to give him an out, after all. "Okay, okay, you win. Gramps always did say you were a champion nagger."

"A woman like me has made many a good man

better than he ought to have been," Mee-Maw observed with a wink. "If you menfolk didn't drag around so, eatin' peanuts and drinkin' colas all morning long, we wouldn't have to nag, now, would we?"

Ryan made a show of giving Becca a "what can I do?" shrug and rose to his feet. Becca did the same.

"Mee-Maw, what time will you have dinner on the table? I can go over to Richard Murphy's and talk with him this morning if I have time before lunch. I have to admit, I'd love to avail myself of more of your cooking," Becca confessed.

Mee-Maw made a face at the mention of Murphy. "Better you talking to that man than me. I don't hate him, mind you, but that don't mean I have to like his ways. He's hard on his help. He's greedy, too. Plus, he's lazy. One thing I can't abide is a lazy farmer." She finished sweeping the steps. "I'll have dinner done about half past eleven. That's plenty of time for you to get your fill of Richard Murphy."

CHAPTER EIGHT

FROM THE COPPER-TRIMMED sign with its professional graphics to the brand-spanking-new metal barns, Richard Murphy's operation reeked of money. Becca pointed her Mini Cooper through pastureland and fields of cotton, noting the young pines that served as a backdrop.

The paved drive, a far cry from Ryan's rutted dirt road, led up to one of the barns, which had a brick-faced office attached. Becca parked the car and took a moment to flip through the dossier Ag-Sure had provided.

Ten claims in the past eleven years. They'd started small—Becca wasn't sure if that was a sign they had been legitimate or whether he was testing the system. Regardless, Murphy had been after a bigger piece of the pie in the past couple of years. This time, he was claiming that his entire cotton crop was a disaster—to the tune of eight hundred thousand dollars. And his entire farming operation was leveraged out the wazoo.

She sighed and closed the file folder. This morning's meeting made the sudden appearance of the vine in Georgia seem to be the product of a well-oiled conspiracy. Had the farmers taken advantage of a natural event and made it worse? Or had they dreamed it all up and actually imported the vine?

And what about J. T. Griggs, the farmhand who'd disappeared? Charlotte, the waitress at the diner, had told her that the man had been an ex-con from Texas. Before his sudden departure, he'd convinced Charlotte he was intent on going straight for her.

J.T. had hailed from an area of Texas plagued by the vine, again according to Charlotte. Was it just a weird twist of fate? Becca didn't believe in coincidences.

She found herself hoping that Ryan wasn't a part of it.

But he'd been there. He'd obeyed Murphy's summons. So what did that mean?

Rooster is not that kind of person. I'd know it.

Becca retrieved her camera bag and her reporter's notebook. Might as well get this over and done with. No point in dragging it out. Besides— and this thought cheered her—the sooner she was done, the sooner she could head back to Ryan's.

Inside the office, a fluffy-haired girl in her very early twenties regarded Becca for a long moment. The girl punctuated her scrutiny with a few pops of bubble gum. "Mr. Murphy is on the phone," she said finally. "*Long distance.* I'll just tell him you're here. I don't have you on his appointment calendar."

Becca managed to swallow her laughter at a farmer who required appointments. Good thing she'd asked one of the hired hands about his boss's whereabouts when she'd come earlier this morning—left to this bubble-gum bubble brain, Becca would have gotten no information.

While the girl nipped down a hallway, Becca helped herself to one of the pristine white brocade chairs in the reception area. Obviously, the hired help knew better than to soil the cushions.

The moment stretched into two, then three. Interrupting that all-important *long-distance* phone call must take time, Becca decided. Then the girl returned, gave her an inscrutable smile and took her seat behind the desk.

"He knows." That was all the receptionist said. She turned back to her computer without enlightening Becca as to whether she would get an audience.

Ten minutes later, Murphy bustled down the hall. "Miss Reynolds! I do apologize. You must wonder where my manners are, keeping you waiting. Come on back, come on back."

Becca preceded him, coming to stand just inside what was apparently his office. No beat-up metal desks or rough-and-ready furnishings greeted her. This office was done in Early Banker or Newly Arrived Big Shot, complete with the requisite prints of fox hunts on the walls. The only thing that spoke of who Murphy might really be was a huge mounted moose head with an impressive rack. It stared down at Becca from its place of honor just behind Murphy's desk.

"Nice moose," she offered.

He beamed. "Bagged that one in Canada a couple of years ago. Don't suppose you're a hunter? Well, even so, you should come up to the house sometime, see my trophy room—I have a collection from all over the world. The only reason the moose is in here is that I ran out of room in the trophy room, and Eileen wouldn't let me put it anywhere else in the house."

A farmer who could take extended vacations out of the country? Amazing. That was a luxury most farmers didn't have, which was why Ryan had sought the online community; it was hard to have much of a social life when you were tied to a farm seven days a week. YooHoo was supposed to be for farmers and their families only, but Becca had found she had more in common with the people she "met" on it than in other online communities.

So she'd fibbed a bit. She was the granddaughter of a farmer, and she worked with agriculture. The other members—including Ryan—wouldn't have welcomed her if she'd admitted she was a private investigator who hired out to crop-insurance firms.

Murphy made a show of stacking up the few papers on his desk and setting them to one side. "There. Now I can give you my full attention. I am anxious to get this done and over with so that Ag-Sure can finalize the claim. All of the farmers in this area who've been hit with the vine are just as eager to help as I am. To tell the truth, Miss Reynolds, we're getting pretty desperate."

Desperate? This office didn't shout desperation. It shouted pretension, certainly. Desperation? No.

She flipped open the reporter's notebook. "Well, then, let's dive in, shall we. I have inspected Ryan MacIntosh's fields, and the vine does look fairly pervasive."

Murphy made a clucking sound of regret. "Poor boy. His first year running his grandfather's farm has turned into a nightmare—I'll be surprised if he can hold out. You're right about the vine—he's got about the worst case of it. It showed up first there, you know."

A sick feeling pooled in her gut. "No. I wasn't aware of that. Of course, I've not finished speaking with him."

The farmer's face registered fake guilt. "Oh, dear. I just assumed…"

When he broke off, Becca didn't push it. "Tell me about your infestation."

"I believe ours spread from Ryan's front field. Our parcels of land border each other. One of the hands found it at first by sheer accident. The vine is tough and stringy, and when it wraps around the plows, it has to be removed by hand. I didn't even know Ryan was having any problems until I mentioned this strange weed to him—he's got the background, you know. Worked all over the country researching noxious weeds. I'd called in our county agent, and the whole mess just left him scratching his head. He'd not seen anything like it."

Hmm. A lot of information for Murphy to volunteer in one gulp—especially about Ryan. Her gut told her Murphy was too eager to paint Ryan as the one with the means and the opportunity.

Or is that your infernally optimistic heart?

Becca covered up her inner debate by giving a slight nod. That was all the encouragement Murphy seemed to require.

"It's bad stuff. The plowing, well, we can get by without. Lot of us had gone to the no-till method—" He paused to be sure she understood what he meant and continued after seeing her nod again. "So that's not too bad. The harvesting's the thing that's going to be tough. My foreman assures me there's no way, even after we defoliate, that we can run the harvester through the portions affected by that vine."

She asked a few more questions before jumping to the big one: "Mind if I see how it's affecting your crop?"

"Not at all, not at all. Just let me get my keys and we'll drive around."

Soon after, she was ensconced in Murphy's extended-cab pickup, the hot leather seats biting through her cotton shirt and her jeans.

When she remarked on the heat, he nodded enthusiastically.

"I tell you, we can't catch a break. It's so dry that the governor's about to declare these counties a disaster anyway—I talked with the ag commissioner earlier this week. Irrigation is killing us. 'Bout the only thing that'll grow is that vine. Wish we could come up with some sort of commercial use for it."

"Actually, in Asia it's grown for medicinal purposes. So who knows? Maybe it'll turn into a big bumper crop for you." Becca shot a sideways glance at him and was rewarded by a downward turn of his mouth.

She let that go, adding, "So, will you apply for disaster relief based on the drought conditions?"

"Of course. Why not?"

"Well, honestly, I'm not seeing heat stress on the cotton that we've passed."

Murphy's frown deepened. "You would if you were around to see the stunted size of the bolls when they form. Plus, the dry weather makes the plants more vulnerable to insects."

Something about his stubbornness, coupled with his earlier urbaneness and the slick pretentiousness of his office, aggravated her. At least, that's what she told herself later when she said what she did. "You should know. You've certainly submitted enough claims over the years."

If she'd sought to rile him, she didn't get much for her effort. His frown pulled down an eighth of an inch more and his fat, sausagelike fingers gripped the steering wheel.

"Sounds like you came down here with your mind made up about me, Miss Reynolds. I'm just an ordinary farmer with a real bad run of luck— or maybe not luck. Some people say that farming is so bad these days, you come out ahead if you don't try to plant anything.

"We'll have to walk from here. The vines you'll want to see—the ones closest to the MacIntosh spread—are right up ahead."

BECCA GOT FINISHED with Murphy by eleven-thirty, then raced her way back to Ryan's for the promised lunch. On her way, she reported in to her father about the mysterious J. T. Griggs.

"I'll start doing a search for him. See if you

can't get me a full name and a social-security number," her dad told her. He tagged on, "Good work, Becca."

The unexpected praise warmed her. When she got to the MacIntosh farm, however, her good mood soured. Though Mee-Maw had waited on her, Ryan had not.

"He just grabbed a bite and headed back to the field. Said he'd lost too much time this morning. I expect he has. We got an ailing cow he needs to run over to the vet's office later this afternoon, so he needs to get as much done as he can. I tell you, a farmer can stay busier 'n a one-legged man in a butt-kickin' contest."

"Was it like this for your husband when he was alive?" Becca tucked into batter-fried pork chops, green beans and last night's creamed potatoes that had been reheated—and of course, tomatoes.

"Yes, gracious. Well, not after J.T. came along, and we always did manage to keep at least one person working with us through the years. Back in the sixties, Mac had two or three full-time people helping out. That was when a person could make a living farming. Before those big corporations took over."

The mention of J.T. gave Becca the opening she'd been hoping for. "Charlotte's plenty worried about J.T.," she said, couching the words in what she hoped was a confidential tone.

"That girl… She's goodhearted. J.T. liked her well enough, but maybe she cottoned on to him more than he did to her, and he didn't quite know how to let her down easy."

"So he just left? On account of Charlotte?" *Talk about commitment phobia, if that's the case.*

"Some men are like that. Don't you agree? I mean, after all, you're—I don't mean to insult you—but by the time I was your age, I was married with a baby and another on the way." Mee-Maw pushed up her last bite of green beans with a corner of crisp corn bread. "And I married late 'cause of the war."

Becca squirmed now that the hot light of interrogation was shining on her. "I, uh, just haven't found the right guy."

Mee-Maw grinned. "There's plenty of Mr. Rights around here. You stay down here and you'll find a fellow who knows how to treat a lady."

Becca couldn't help but think of Ryan. In their months of corresponding, she'd found him to be kind and considerate, ready to listen when she needed to vent. Ryan, in all honesty, was exactly the kind of Mr. Right she wanted.

If he doesn't end up in a federal prison, that is.

"I'm curious. What did J.T.'s initials stand for?" Becca asked as she forced her mind back on her job.

"I don't rightly recall. You know men when they

don't like their names—they don't like sharing. So what's your plan for the rest of the afternoon? Ryan asked me to see if you needed to talk to him some more today."

Becca registered Mee-Maw's evasiveness and made a mental note to contact Charlotte to see if she knew J.T.'s full name. If Mee-Maw was hiding something—and her cagey answers certainly made it appear that way—Becca didn't want to tip her hand now.

"No, I won't bother Ryan, not today at any rate. I think I'll make a quick tour of the various farms that are affected by this vine."

"Won't get that done today. Most every farmer in this area has got it, to hear Ryan talk. Not just in this county, but the next one, too."

"Well, I can start on it. I need to see them, you know? With my own eyes."

Mee-Maw nodded. "Yup. I'm like that, too. But—maybe I'm out of line—I just want you to know, Ryan's sure counting on that insurance settlement. He really doesn't think we're going to be able to harvest the cotton this year. At least not the cotton in the front field."

Becca covered Mee-Maw's veined hand with her own. "I'll do my best, but I won't lie. I've got a lot of questions that need answers."

"Well, then. Leave the dishes and you get on to answerin' them questions of yours."

TWILIGHT DEEPENED as Becca pulled out of the drive-through of the local burger joint, her cholesterol-laden supper in a sack.

The hamburger would be a far cry from Mee-Maw's cooking. Becca was alarmed to find she missed the company that both Mee-Maw and Ryan offered.

Enough. You need to stay objective. You're already coming up with major conspiracy theories to figure out a way Ryan could be uninvolved.

Everything she'd seen today on the two farms she'd gotten to fed those conspiracy theories.

For instance, the stories were just too similar, too pat. How could farmers just walk out one bright morning and suddenly find a weird, exotic vine choking the life out of their cotton? Hadn't they been looking for signs of infestation once the news of its appearance had spread?

Also, the spread pattern just didn't make sense. True, life was stranger than fiction, but she needed to check with some experts to see if there was any way the dodder could have disseminated in the way she'd seen.

Becca yawned as she parked her car and retrieved file folders, her camera bag and her hamburger. She'd eat her dinner, take a shower to rinse off the dust she was covered in and then try to get some work—

She stopped abruptly as she rounded the front of the car.

There, hanging from the doorknob to her motel room, like a vile do-not-disturb placard, was a length of dodder vine.

Fashioned in a hangman's noose.

CHAPTER NINE

BECCA FROZE AND stared at the hangman's noose for a long moment. It swayed slightly, though Becca couldn't detect much of a breeze.

The observation kick-started her into action. She backpedaled her way to the car quickly. Inside, she hit the door's auto-lock button. With fingers that trembled more than she liked, she fumbled for her cell phone.

Did this county have 9-1-1 service from cell phones? A lot of rural counties didn't, and she couldn't remember Rooster/Ryan ever remarking on it. Her brain frothed until she allowed it a moment to digest on what it wanted to.

Who put that thing there? Who did she rile so much that they'd want to warn her off? When did they put it there? Just now? How'd they know which room was hers? She needed to get a photo of it, needed to get a police incident report done.

Her cell phone buzzed in her hand. She looked down at it, a shiver of paranoia running through her. The number was a local one. Could the call be related to the threat?

Becca answered it with a hesitant "Hello?"

"Becca? I'm sorry to call you so late, but—"

At the sound of his voice, she relaxed. "Ryan!"

"Wow. You sound glad to hear from me. Lonely?"

"No. Uh…a bit, um…" She gazed at the noose, just making out a hint of the vine in the dimness. "Someone graced my motel-room door with a dodder vine—in the shape of a hangman's noose."

"Where are you?"

"In my car. About to call 9-1-1 to get a patrol car here. I just found it."

"You're staying at the motel here in town, right? I'll be right there. Sit tight."

He hung up before pride made her protest that she didn't need rescuing. She could sure use the company, though.

She dialed 9-1-1 and got the wireless provider to patch her through to the local sheriff's department. Becca was requesting a patrol car when she saw headlights pull up behind her.

Squinting, she made out Ryan's old truck. He was tapping on her passenger-door window a minute or so later.

She hit the unlock button. Ryan swung open the door and proceeded to try to fold himself into the little car.

"This thing's a torture device for guys my

height," he said, bumping his head. "Sure you don't want to wait in my truck?"

"You're almost in now. It would be a lot of agony to get yourself out. Don't you need a break first?" she teased.

He managed to slide the seat all the way back and arrange himself. Becca hit the lock button again. For a moment, they sat in silence.

"Someone put a dodder vine on your door?"

She flicked the headlights to augment the dim, flickering fluorescent lighting that ran along the front of the motel-room doors.

Ryan shouted when he saw the hangman's noose.

Darkness settled after Becca switched off the headlights. "Was this what the farmers were planning at that meeting this morning?"

"No! Well…"

Becca glanced at him sharply. "Well, what?"

Ryan scowled, his mouth tight. "Murphy—and everybody else—wanted you out of here as quick as possible. They know they won't get any settlement until your investigation is through."

"This is the way to make me think the dodder vine is some freak accident of nature and tell Ag-Sure to start cutting the checks?" Becca didn't bother to hide her sarcasm. "Sorry. Threats usually tell me the opposite."

"They— Murphy's too smart for this. He would have never done it. Who else did you see today?"

"A guy named Tate. And another farmer called Oliver."

"Either Doug Oliver or Stephen Tate would have been hotheaded enough to do something like this. Or…"

"Yes?"

"It could have been any of those guys there this morning. Except me and Jack, of course."

She gave him a wry smile while she decided whether Jack should be excluded from the list. He'd been at the meeting, and he appeared more comfortable with those men than Ryan had. But to Ryan, she said only, "Of course. Guess it comes down to means. Who knew which room was mine?" she mused.

Ryan's chuckle was a grim one. "In this town? That wouldn't have been hard to find out at all."

"Well, it doesn't matter, does it? It just tells me that I've probed a tender spot."

He sighed at her words. "Maybe…maybe they were just trying to say… Oh, I don't know, that the dodder vine was strangling all of us."

"What?" She stared at him in amazement. "You don't really believe that, do you?"

"No, but what guy wants to believe that the people he knows are willing to scare a woman?"

"I'm beginning to think the people you know—

at least some of them—are crooks. Just how long does it take for the sheriff's department to respond, anyway? I called them right after I got off the phone with you, and you had to drive all the way into town."

"They have only one car on patrol at night and it sticks to the interstate. If you called them after I called you, it shouldn't be too much longer. What do you think they can do about this anyway?"

"Make a report, at the very least. Don't get me wrong. I'm not expecting a CSI-type response, but it's standard operating procedure. When you get a threat in the field, you report it. The report then becomes part of the evidence." Becca rummaged in the fast-food sack and hauled out the now-cold hamburger. She took a bite of it, frowning.

"This tastes like a brick. Are they any better when they're hot?"

"Not much. Only a desperate person would eat that. Why didn't you come back out for supper? Mee-Maw had plenty. I was…a little disappointed that you didn't show up."

Her heart warmed at his words. Disappointed? Did that mean he'd missed her? Becca hid her smile. "You must be the only farmer in this county who actually wants to see me, then."

"We, uh, we just got off to a bad start, you and me. Call me crazy, but…it's like I know you. It's like, I don't know, maybe we've met before. But

I know we haven't because I sure wouldn't forget a woman like you."

You do know me. "Ryan, I, uh, I think you—" She started to spill the fact that she was Sunny and she had a feeling he was Rooster, but more headlights flashed in her rearview mirror and lit the bank of motel-room doors.

"That'll be the sheriff's deputy. Let me go talk to him." Ryan bailed out of the car as if it was on fire. Was he running from the intimacy of the previous moment, or did he want to say something in private to the deputy?

She joined him on the pitted pavement in time for her to hear his greeting to the deputy. Ryan grinned in her direction and when she came to stand beside Ryan, his arm went around her in a comforting way.

"This is Becca Reynolds. She's down here to see about that dodder vine we have in our cotton. She, um, got a nasty welcome tonight."

The deputy, about Ryan's age and just as tall, turned to Becca. He held out his hand. "Deputy Brandon Wilkes, ma'am. What seems to be the problem?"

She showed him the vine and was glad to see the deputy look taken aback at the hangman's noose. He asked her to open the door with her key.

Inside, nothing looked disturbed. The bedside lamp cast a pool of yellow light over the room.

Housekeeping had made the bed. Becca's suit-case sat at the end of the spare double bed, and the room appeared its depressing, dank self.

They stood just inside the door, taking it all in.

"Uh, what exactly are you doing around here? Whatever it is, somebody doesn't think much of it."

"I'm an agricultural investigator. I'm consulting for a crop-insurance company, Ag-Sure, trying to determine just how the dodder vine came to be in this area."

"I know about the dodder vine. My uncle's a farmer, and he's got that mess. Says you can't do anything with it." The deputy frowned. "This doesn't make us look too good, does it?"

"Who's your uncle?" Becca asked.

"Jake Wilkes. He's got a small farm on the southern side of the county. Ryan knows him."

She turned to Ryan. "Was he at that meeting this morning?"

"No. The only farmers there were the big dogs in the county."

"So you're a big dog?" she teased.

"Not me. I was only there because Murphy—" Ryan hesitated "—suggested I be there. I didn't stay long."

"What's this about a meeting?" Brandon asked.

Becca filled him in on the specifics of the meeting. He asked Ryan a few more questions, looking even more disturbed.

"Just between us, Ryan, I don't like it that Murphy called that meeting, and then that hangman's noose shows up on Miss Becca's door. Ma'am, I don't know who you've managed to tick off, but I…I would proceed with caution from here on out."

"So you think Murphy is capable of this? And dumb enough to think it would work?"

The deputy and Ryan exchanged long looks. "Murphy's pretty much capable of anything when money's involved, but you're right. He's too smart for an overt threat that would make you take a closer look at him. Personally, I wouldn't put much past Murphy, but I think he'd draw the line at something like this," Wilkes told her. "Farmers like Ryan and my uncle, well, they don't have too high an opinion of guys like Murphy. Right, Ryan?"

Ryan nodded. "Can't say that I disagree with you. I tried to give Murphy the benefit of the doubt when I first moved back here, but maybe it's just because I respect the old-timers like Jake more than I do guys like Murphy."

Wilkes turned his attention back to the doorknob. "I'll write this up in a report. I can't do much more about it than that, though, I'm afraid.

Wish I could, especially since I know Murphy might be involved."

"Not a little bitter, are you there, Brandon?" Ryan asked.

"Yeah, I'm bitter. Just wait till Murphy takes half of your farm out of some rigged tax deal, then you'll see how Uncle Jake feels."

"I know. I know. It was a raw deal."

"Well, water under the bridge now. Let me grab my digital camera out of the car, and I'll snap a picture or two for the report."

Becca went back to her car and grabbed her own camera. As she snapped her photos, Wilkes looked at the camera in open admiration.

"That an SLR?"

"Yeah. It's a couple of years old now, and doesn't have anywhere near all the bells and whistles that have come out in the past few months. But—" she smoothed her fingers over the camera's housing "—I like it. It has interchangeable lenses, which is great."

"Sounds like you're a real serious photographer."

Becca thought about the magazine she'd birthed—and watched die a premature death. She thought about the years she'd spent behind a camera at various daily newspapers. "I was," she said, her voice hollow, "in a previous life."

Wilkes nodded in comprehension. "I used to

work on my uncle's farm—was a full partner— but then we lost half the farm and he couldn't really justify having me on, you know? I like this job well enough. I've been with the sheriff's department part-time for a long time anyway, just to make ends meet. I was lucky the sheriff could put me to work full-time, but I miss being on a tractor. A patrol car gets kind of cramped when you're used to the wind on your face."

Becca looked from Wilkes's pensive expression to Ryan, seeing a kinship there. She realized how big a part of life farming was for these men. She knew, from her own experience, how it felt to be ripped from doing what you loved and put instead to doing what you were merely good at.

"Well." With a shake of his head, the deputy brought the conversation back to why she'd called him here. "I've got what I need. I'm going to talk to the desk clerk—they usually have someone there until midnight. Maybe they saw something," Wilkes said. "Want to come with me?"

Becca nodded. "Yes, I do. I'd like to hear it for myself."

"She needs another room, closer to the motel office. This here—" Ryan looked up in disgust at the fluorescent light that had halfheartedly flickered on "—this is just asking for trouble."

"I agree," Becca told him. "Surely they've got a room that's better lit."

The desk clerk could give them no assistance. He swore that he'd seen no headlights until Becca's—he'd recognized the Mini Cooper. But as he produced another key for a room near the office, he said it was possible someone had been by, as he'd taken an extralong supper break.

Outside, Wilkes shook Becca's hand. "You can pick up a copy of the report tomorrow. I'll be on in the evening, so I'll be sure to swing by here on my way out to the interstate. That might convince that clerk to do a better job. Ryan, good seeing you again. I'll tell my uncle you said hello."

"Good seeing you, too."

Becca and Ryan headed for the new room. It was a carbon copy of the old one, albeit a little more stale and airless.

"Here. We'll leave the door open while we move your stuff," Ryan told her.

All that was left for her to do was sweep her toothpaste and other toiletry items into her bag. Ryan insisted on carrying it to her room for her. Inside the new room, he pushed the door closed.

"Brandon is right, Becca. You've sure angered somebody. I know you have your job to do, but as much as I'd like you to stay around longer, I don't want to see—" he looked off in the distance "—anything happen to you. Maybe whoever did this just wanted to make some juvenile warning, but if they were dumb enough to do that, they might be dumb enough to try something else."

Her mind remembered his earlier words. "You want me to stay around longer?"

The color in his face heightened. "Yeah. I do. But not if some dumb yahoo is going to try to scare you—or worse. I want you in one piece."

"Then tell me what was going on at that meeting."

His face closed down. "I did. I can't help it if *you* don't believe *me*."

"I want to believe you. I want you to believe that I'm here to help. But I guess I can't help it if you don't believe me."

He regarded her for a long moment, ready it seemed to say something. "It might be helpful for you to go see Jake Wilkes tomorrow. Give you another small-farmer view of this thing."

Becca accepted his suggestion for what it was—a reach across a divide he didn't seem to be able to bridge. "I will."

"Jake's an old bachelor, can't cook worth anything. So why don't you come out to the house for dinner tomorrow when you get through with him? Mee-Maw will be glad to see you."

"Just Mee-Maw?"

He reached over and traced the curve of her face. For a moment, she held her breath, waited for the kiss she was sure would come. Her pulse accelerated.

Ryan let his fingers graze against her cheek for a moment longer. He took a step back, his eyes registering the same deep conflict she felt.

"No," he said finally. "I have to be honest. I'll be glad to see you, too."

With that, he was out the door like a man on fire.

Sunny_76@yoohoomail.com: Haven't heard from you… What's up?

Rooster@yoohoomail.com: Things are crazier than ever. Look, it's pretty confusing for me right now. Maybe it's not fair to you… No, I know it's not fair to you. But you need to know that I've met a woman. I haven't got an earthly clue how long it will last, and I'm not fool enough to ask you to wait until I find out.

Sunny_76@yoohoomail.com: This is your goodbye, then?

Rooster@yoohoomail.com: Don't make me feel any more awful than I already do, okay? It's safe with you…and scary with her. And there are other things—things about me that you might not like if you knew them. So, yeah, I guess this had better be goodbye.

CHAPTER TEN

RYAN ARGUED WITH HIMSELF all the way out to the farm, up the back steps, down the hall past Mee-Maw's room. By the time he'd stripped off his clothes and got in the shower, the argument in his head was as loud, at least to him, as any barroom brawl.

It came down to one question, really: should he have come clean with Becca? Told her not only everything he knew, but what he feared and suspected, as well?

He'd told only one other person even part of the truth, and that was Jack. Jack had held fast to the idea that the best thing they could do was keep their heads down, muddle through, hope for the best.

Up until now—up until Becca—Ryan had thought Jack was right.

The hot water pulsating on Ryan's back eased some of the soreness from the day's labor. He still wasn't used to it, not even after nearly nine months on the farm. How Gramps had done it day after day, and in his eighties to boot, was amazing.

But then Gramps had an amazing partner in Mee-Maw. Woman could probably still outplow Ryan in a competition with a mule and a set of plows. She was tough but still so vulnerable.

Thinking of Mee-Maw brought his thoughts back to Becca. And thoughts of her and the kiss he'd just passed up—and the promise of maybe something more in the future—left his hands shaking so that the shampoo bottle slipped through his fingers.

Ryan smothered a curse and retrieved the shampoo from the bottom of the old cast-iron tub that was too small for a man his size.

As he did a quick lather on his hair, he tried to separate the hormones-gone-wild from the more dangerous attraction he had for Becca. In so many ways, she reminded him of his grandmother—sounded freaky when he thought about it that way, but it was true.

Mee-Maw was the one woman he'd admired above all other women. She had a good, compassionate heart, but she was willing to roll up her sleeves and get dirty if that's what it took to take care of her family. She was smart and funny and she knew people.

All things that Becca was.

So how did he know all this? He hadn't met Becca but a couple of days ago, but what he'd bumbled out to her earlier—right before he high-

133

tailed it out of there before he could make a complete idiot of himself—was true. Ryan did feel as if he knew her.

It wasn't just the instant kinship he felt, it wasn't that he truly sensed that she wanted to help. It was the way she said things, the words she used. Sometimes he could almost predict how she was going to react to situations.

It was her appreciation of rural life. Now that was different from the last woman in Ryan's life. Lily had sure cut and run when she found out he planned to give up the high-paying job with the ag-chemical firm and instead move here and run the farm for Mee-Maw.

But Becca…he knew she wouldn't have done that.

He would have kissed her tonight. Wanted to. But then he'd thought about Sunny and Jack's warning to keep his head down for Mee-Maw's sake. Kissing Becca just hadn't felt right.

But, man, he'd wanted to. Which was why he knew, no matter how it hurt, he owed it to Sunny to end things with her. They'd had a deal—if either one of them met someone in the real world, they needed to pull the plug on their cyber-relationship.

Give up that easy friendship with Sunny? The very idea ripped something inside him. But he might as well get it over and done with. A man was only as good as his word, after all. Better to e-mail her after he got out of the shower.

Ryan groaned in frustration and splayed a palm on the cool tile surround of the tub. Why was he always getting himself in these impossible situations? Either Becca was buttering him up to get him to confess all—in which case she was a complete phony—or else she was the real deal. Truth be told, that was almost scarier.

Because no relationship could ever be built on deceit. Or even half-hidden truths. Until he came clean, Becca wouldn't really know who she was getting involved with.

But these secrets weren't his own; they could hurt Mee-Maw. Maybe even result in her losing the farm she'd lived on all these years.

Ryan cursed again. No. If it were meant to be with Becca, it would be. It just wasn't the right time for them to start anything. He wouldn't force it and risk Mee-Maw's homeplace.

Because he owed Gramps that much. No matter what.

WHEN BECCA WOKE the next morning, the sun was bleeding around the edges of the motel room's heavy drapes. She'd not had a restful night—not only had she still felt unsettled over the hangman's noose, but she'd also had to deal with her dad.

He'd chastised her for not being more aware of

her surroundings. "Should have scoped out that door before you got out of the car. Could have been worse. You were lucky."

He had given her grudging praise for not over-reacting, but it was so much easier for the bad things, the negative things, to stick in her head.

Becca yawned, threw back the covers and headed for the shower. First thing she was going to do was get something to eat, then head out to Jake Wilkes's place. She wondered why his name hadn't been on the list of claimants Ag-Sure had provided.

He must be key to all this—or was that just hope that Ryan had finally decided to trust her enough to leave some breadcrumbs as a trail?

Out of the shower and dressed, Becca spotted the vine still on the dresser. She let her fingers trail along the thick vine. Ugly. But then most parasites were.

The morning was bright and hot already. Char-lotte at the diner hadn't known J.T.'s full given name, but she'd been able to provide detailed di-rections to the Wilkes farm, and Becca easily found the place.

What she saw when she pulled up at the gate was a far cry from Murphy's slick operation. Here, the fence was constructed from rusty wire and creosote posts, sporadically reinforced with bits and pieces of scrap lumber. The barns and outbuildings looked just as dismal, and the house was a tiny ranch-style that had seen better days.

Becca pulled to a stop in the space between the house and the large barn. She opened the car door and stood, peering around for signs of activity.

In the distance, she heard the squealing of pigs and hogs—and the sound of hammering.

Becca followed the noise and the scent to find a gray-haired man bent over a section of fence. Hogs snuffled excitedly around him. He kept butting them back with an elbow or a foot.

"Cornelia, I swear, you get out of this pen again, you'll find yourself on my plate, you got it? Pork chops, that's gonna be your future. Now least you could do is just get out the way and let me—Baby, you, too. I know you was in on it. Cornelia never does anything without you helping her."

Becca grinned at what she heard, amused by a pig farmer on first-name basis with his charges. From the affection in his voice, even if it was tinged with frustration, the pigs were in no danger.

"Mr. Wilkes?" She cupped her hands around her mouth and tried again when he didn't seem to hear her. "Mr. Wilkes!"

He looked up, frowned and hollered, "Just a minute. Let me get this finished up, else they'll be out again, quick as a flash."

Wilkes banged away on the patch some more until he had it to his satisfaction, then tucked the hammer into a loop on his belt. With a casual scratch behind the ear of the nearest hog, he made his way through the pack. A big black-and-white sow rubbed up against him.

"Oh, all right, Geraldine. You get a pet, too. I'm not mad at you—you always do stay in the pen. Now, go on with the lot of you. Y'all got mud to play in and slop to eat. Go on, git!"

With that, he clambered over the fence, grabbed a hose and squirted a jet of water over his waders. He stepped out of them, revealing worn brogans that, like his farm, had seen better days.

"Yes, ma'am? I wouldn't get too close to me if you can't abide the smell of hogs. I sure am sorry. If I'd known I'd have company—well, no, guess not. Got to fix the hole or else those hogs'll get out all over again."

"It's okay, sir. I know a thing or two about hogs. My name is Becca—"

"Reynolds? That crop investigator? Should have guessed. Brandon called me last night after he talked to you. Said you might be around. Nasty, the way they put that noose on your door. But then what can you expect from people like that? Ain't got quality, I say. Quality always shows, so if it don't show, well, 'tain't there."

"Yes, sir. Your nephew was telling me that you had some dodder vine—"

"Some? Some! One whole field of cotton just

about gone. I'm 'bout ready to burn the lot of it. Who knows if I don't, it's just gonna get worse."

"Yes, sir." She waited to see if that response would trigger another flood of rants. When it didn't, she ventured, "I was wondering why you weren't on the list of claimants. From Ag-Sure, I mean."

"Simple. Can't afford crop insurance."

"Kind of risky, isn't it?"

"Don't know about that. After all, what good has it done these fellas who have it? Don't see Ag-Sure cutting any checks, or did I miss something? In any case, if you can't afford it, you can't afford it. And me, I can't afford it. I can barely afford my mortgage as it is. I'm in the hock for fertilizer and pesticides and seed—and don't even get me started on what diesel costs these days."

"So, when did you discover dodder vine in your crop?"

He took off his cap and rubbed his forehead with the back of his arm. "Lemme see…this is August, I'd say, hmm…June."

"June?" This was earlier than any of the others had claimed they'd found dodder vine.

"Yes, ma'am. One day, I'm seeing some of Murphy's day workers skulking around in my field—his land borders mine, you know—and so I run 'em off. I figure they're after, I dunno, whatever ain't nailed down in my barns and they're sneaking in the back way. Few days later, I find these little ol' vines that look like snakes every few rows. Well, now—" he replaced his cap "—it don't take no rocket scientist to put two and two together.

"Murphy's been after that plot of land for a while—ticked him off good-fashion when I managed to scrape up the money to save this half of the farm. So I yank up the vines and I burn 'em. When they're young, they burn pretty easy."

"Then…"

"How come I got dodder vine in my cotton? There's only me. I can't watch the field day and night—I gotta get work done, gotta get some sleep—and these pigs of mine'll worry a man loose from his soul if he lets 'em. I snatched up what I could when I found it, but some of it I must have missed. It took root and spread like wildfire. But I dragged a big firebreak between it and the rest of my crop and I burned enough off so that it didn't have any way to spread. I keep thinking Ryan'll come up with some way to kill the mess and I can save my crop, you know?"

A pang went through her at the mention of Ryan's name. Becca pulled her attention from that and focused on the topic at hand. "Could you identify the men who had been in the field?"

"Naw, don't say that I could. Not a positive ID." He shook his head sorrowfully. "Besides, Murphy

hires so many illegals, his farm looks like a re-
volving door. Hardly ever see the same folks for
more than a month or so at a time."

"Illegals? Undocumented workers?"

"Yeah, poor men. Murphy makes 'em kick back
part of their wages for their rent—and in cash,
to boot. They live off down behind me along the
creek. That's why Murphy wanted my property,
I figure, 'cause it's got easy access to water. Ain't
none of 'em got any wells down there."

Things began to click into place for Becca.
Murphy was paying his workers with checks to
document losses for insurance purposes—but he
was getting a chunk of that money back in cash.
It was a fiddle, a common enough one.

The men would be in the fields, but Becca
wanted to see for herself this settlement of migrant workers. Perhaps she could find someone
there to question.

"I'd like to talk to them. Is it far?"

Wilkes shrugged his bony shoulders. "Nope,
not to me. I can drive you to the back fence—you
can take a gander at the dodder vine on the way if
you'd like—and you can walk from there."

A few minutes later, Becca was standing at an
overgrown fencerow, looking over the crest of the
field behind Wilkes' property.

"See the tops of them trees? That's the creek
right there. 'Tain't more than a fifteen-minute

walk back on in there. I should know—I take the rascals some food and other stuff on occasion."

"You do?"

"Yeah. Murphy makes sure they stay pretty desperate, but I wouldn't treat my hogs thataway." He shook his head in disgust. "Want me to walk back there with you?"

"Not if you don't think there's any danger. They might talk more without anyone else around."

"Suit yourself. But if you ain't back in…say an hour and a half, I'll come lookin' for you."

"I have a cell phone."

"Mightn't get reception that close to the creek. But then again, the way these dang cellular towers are popping up, it might. Brandon got me one of them contraptions to carry with me—" he patted his pocket "—in case I fall or something. Bunch of bother, you ask me, but he pays for it. Give me a call when you get back to the fence and I'll come pick you up." He rattled off a phone number, and Becca input it in her phone.

Then she turned, negotiated the fence and started for the creek.

"Hey!"

She turned at Wilkes's call. "Yes, sir?"

"You watch your back. This land you're on? It ain't mine any more. Belongs to that scumsucker Murphy."

A little tremor of fear rattled through her. She

squared her shoulders and nodded her head. "Yes, sir. Thanks for reminding me. I'll be back in an hour and a half or so—or I'll call."

"You do that. I'm gonna see to those hogs of mine. Blamed pests. Oughta turn the lot of 'em into pork chops."

He turned and made his way back to his pickup, and Becca was suddenly left alone.

THE WALK, despite the thick cotton plants, wasn't a bad one. Mostly it was downhill and she could feel breezes blowing up from the creek. As Becca came to the edge of the field, she saw a well-worn path leading into the woods. Farther along, if she squinted, she could make out a narrow track of road. That had to be the access by car.

She settled on the path, figuring it was the shortest route. Sure enough, about five minutes later she stood at a clearing.

It looked like something out of a third-world country. Old tumbledown mobile homes, more rusted-out hulks than anything, leaned on shaky stacks of concrete blocks. Corrugated tin augmented what she suspected were leaky roofs. Doors stood wide-open, windows—the ones that weren't broken—thrown open.

In the bare sand clearing, a gaggle of little girls were playing in the dirt near a still-smoking campfire. An old man dozed on, of all things, a brand-new garden bench. The scent of cumin and chili pepper emanated from the various mobile homes, and it smelled as good as any Mexican cantina Becca had ever patronized. Her stomach rumbled in protest.

The little girls had spotted her. They gaped open-mouthed at her. She approached them, knelt down in the sand.

"*Hola,*" Becca greeted them. Dusting off her rusty Spanish, she asked them what they were playing.

They answered cautiously, then one of them reached out and touched her hair. The dark-eyed girl giggled. "It's so soft!" she rattled off in Spanish to her friends.

Soon all of them were touching Becca's hair. Becca figured out that they all thought it would feel differently than their own dark straight hair. She cadged a seat on a broken cinder block and let them explore to their heart's content. One girl was expertly braiding Becca's hair, and Becca decided it felt cooler that way.

"Hey!"

The girls scattered, retreating to far corners of the yard. Becca looked up to see a woman glaring down at her.

CHAPTER ELEVEN

IN SPANISH, the woman demanded, "What do you want? Who are you?"

Becca held her hands out and stood up. Her introduction and explanations did little to ease the glower from the woman's face. Finally, the only thing that moved her was an assurance that Becca wasn't from immigration and that all she wanted was to speak to someone in charge.

The "take me to your leader" request got a bit of head scratching in response. The woman told her in no uncertain terms to stay put, then retreated to a nearby hulk. A moment later, a worried-looking older woman came across the clearing, wiping her hands on a towel wrapped around her waist.

This wasn't the leader. No, in a Hispanic settlement like this, it would have to be a man.

Becca started her pitch anyway, laced liberally with solemn oaths that she wasn't from USCIS.

The Hispanic woman pursed her lips thoughtfully. Then she glanced over at the old man still dozing on the bench.

But he wasn't dozing, not anymore. He was

surveying Becca and the woman with lazy, half-open eyes.

Of course. He was the one in charge here. The garden bench—the best thing in the whole place—should have tipped her off.

With a slow lift of his hand, which could have been mistaken for him shooing a fly, the old man waved off the woman.

"Go talk to Antonio. He wants to talk to you," the woman told her.

The girls cautiously resumed their playing. Becca closed the gap between her and the garden bench. She waited for Antonio to pat the seat in invitation before she sat down.

Once settled, she started speaking again, but he interrupted her in Spanish.

"I'm only an old man, but I heard you. You come here after something. So what is it?"

"Murphy."

"Pah!" He spat in the sand. "What about him?"

"I'm investigating him. He's stealing money from an insurance company." She phrased it as a known fact in hopes that her certainty would draw him out.

"I'm not surprised. He likes money. But what man doesn't? Why are we here, after all?"

"I think he may have used some of your men to transport a vine from Texas."

Antonio narrowed his eyes. "No. This I would

know, even if it were done by some of the young
hotheads. Besides, we didn't come here from
Texas. We follow the crops. Onions in the spring,
and before that, we worked citrus. Most of our
group has already moved on. But we—" he indicated the rag-tag bunch of trailers "—have our
papers, so Murphy keeps us on. That vine—
dodder vine, yes? That came after we were already here. So it was not us."

"So some of your men didn't plant the dodder
vine? Say, in various farmers' fields?"

He didn't answer. Instead he asked her, "Why
should we care to get involved in business between gringos? So one gringo steals from another? What's it to us?"

"Don't you want to see Murphy punished? I
mean, look at what he has you living in." Becca
indicated the hovel with a swoop of her hand.

Antonio shrugged impassively. "This isn't
so different from Mexico. But at least here we
all have jobs. In Mexico, there are no jobs. Not
since free trade. They promised us factory work,
but what they did was make it impossible for an
honest farmer to earn a living in my country.
There are only so many factory jobs."

"But you could earn so much more—do so
much better—than this. These living conditions
are shameful!"

Again he shrugged. "Who would hire us? Only gringos like Murphy who want cheap labor."

She thought about Wilkes toting food and other necessities down to them. She thought about Ryan, the person she'd come to know through their electronic correspondence. "Not everybody is like Murphy. Is it true you have to pay part of your wages in rent?"

"*Sí,* of course. In cash."

Becca's stomach rumbled loudly. Antonio raised his eyebrows in question.

"Past time for lunch," she told him. She thought wistfully of Ryan and his invitation. But no, Mee-Maw would have put away the food by now, and Ryan would have headed back for the fields.

"Maria!" Antonio snapped his fingers at the oldest child. "Fetch something for the lady to eat."

She scampered off to the trailer the older woman had disappeared into. In a moment, the child came down wobbly metal steps, a giant burrito in her hand.

Antonio indicated that Becca should take it. "Go ahead. Eat. A skinny woman like you—you need your strength."

Hesitant, she bit into the flatbread and the vegetables, finding chicken tucked underneath. A flood of Tex-Mex heaven showered over her taste buds. With greedy bites, she made short order of the meal.

Antonio looked pleased. "You go now," he told her in heavily accented English. "Come back again and I will find out if any of my young *tontos* planted your dodder vine, or if they know anything about who did."

Becca noisily licked her fingers. "I'm sorry—I was just so hungry, and this was the best Mexican food I've eaten in a long time—"

"Say no more. I could tell you were a good woman by the way you let the *chicas* play with your hair. But we have work to do—water to bring up from the creek, wood to gather—all that before the men come in. A few years ago, I'd be out there myself. Now look. Bossing the women around—when they don't need it—that's all an old one like me is good for, I guess."

She could tell a dismissal when she heard one. Becca stood up, extended her hand, which he gallantly took and grazed the knuckles with a kiss. She waved goodbye to the little girls and headed the way she'd come.

IT WAS MIDAFTERNOON by the time Becca made her way back to Wilkes's fence and to the farm proper. The old man fussed over her as much as he had his porcine pets earlier.

"I was just a-fore comin' after you. Got busy with somethin' I needed to do, and the time, it just slipped away from me. And you walkin' all that way. Have you had any dinner?"

"They gave me a supersized burrito back there. It filled me up."

"Well, I can offer you a glass of water or some iced tea."

"Thanks, I believe I'll take you up on that," she said.

A few moments later, Becca tipped up a glass of iced water as she sat on a swing under a big pecan tree. As hot as she felt, the water tasted like nectar.

"I know you have to be a country girl if you didn't turn and run from a few hogs and you can appreciate good cold water," Jake Wilkes told her.

"Yes, sir." Becca thought back to the summers she'd spent with her grandparents.

"So did you find out anything that'll help you take down ol' Murphy?" The old man's face sharpened with eager inquisitiveness.

"Well…they filled in some blanks for me, but they also created a few more. I guess I'll just have to keep digging."

"Anything you need, you just let me know. That old son of a—uh, gun, he robbed me of half my farm. Now I'm pretty much down to just messing around. It's something to do, more than anything else."

Becca set the glass down on a rusty table by the

swing. "I'll be sure to let you know if there's some way you can help. But honestly, you've been a big help already."

"Thank ye kindly."

She stood up. Off in the distance, she heard a squeal of hogs. "Sounds like your hogs are already plotting their next derring-do."

"Probably right. Blamed ol' things. Don't know why I don't turn the whole lot of 'em into pork chops."

"They seem to like you. Maybe they're just doing it for the attention. You know, pigs are smarter than dogs."

"See now? I knew you were quality, but that there just goes to show I was right. Most folks get put off by the smell, but you got it spot-on. Them jokers are smarter 'n any hound I've ever had. You're probably right about them just wantin' some attention." He beamed at her. "I'll remember that next time and not yell at 'em so."

Becca managed to keep her face straight until she got in the car, then she indulged herself in a burst of laughter. She backed around and headed toward the main road.

The call of Ryan's farm beckoned to her as she came to the turnoff for it.

Oh, I can at least apologize for not coming to lunch. Maybe he knows more about Murphy's fiddle with labor costs.

She regretted her impulsiveness when she saw several cars and trucks parked in Mee-Maw's yard. Becca at once concluded that family had gathered for some purpose. She would have turned around and quietly gone on her way, but Mee-Maw spotted her.

The old woman straightened up stiffly in her garden. A broad smile lit her face when she recognized the car. She gestured with her hand for Becca to get out and join her.

Nothing to do but obey. Well, she'd only stay for a minute.

"Now, that's what I call timing!" Mee-Maw told her. "I was just thinking I needed a hand with this. I cut all this okra yesterday, and Ryan helped me with the tomatoes and the cucumbers—but will you look at it!"

Becca wasn't fooled. From the number of cars parked on the grass, Mee-Maw had a whole houseful of people to help her, just a call away. In spite of that knowledge, Mee-Maw's welcome warmed her.

Becca bent beside Mee-Maw and went to work. Together they gathered the day's harvest in companionable silence. The big baskets held okra, cucumbers, bell peppers, a couple of good-sized chili and jalepeño peppers, eggplants, some straightneck squash and, atop all that, firm red tomatoes.

The only times Becca hesitated were when she came to a spot where a plant had been yanked. To her satisfaction, however, she didn't see any sign of dodder vine.

"What about the peas and beans, Mee-Maw? Should I go ahead and pick them for you?"

"No, no…I pick those in the mornings before it gets so hot. This little bit of peas—well, it's nothing to the acre I used to grow. Ryan refused—flat refused—to put in anything more than this garden for me. Said I'd kill myself with heat exhaustion. I tell you! Young people are just getting so—so uppity these days. I wouldn't have dared dream of tellin' my grandmother she was too long in the tooth to grow a good-sized pea patch."

Becca hid a smile. She could see Mee-Maw bossing around her grandmother. She was glad Ryan had put his foot down, though, because she could tell from the old woman's labored breathing how tired Mee-Maw was.

"I, uh, started not to stop. Not when I saw all the cars."

"Oh, that." Mee-Maw waved her concern away. "Emily's birthday supper. That's Jack's youngest daughter. We got a whole houseful in there. Tell you the truth, I came out here to give myself a bit of a rest."

"Here I've interrupted that."

"Nope. You don't chatter on. You work. You

understand that a garden is a sacred place." Mee-Maw gave her an approving look. "I like that about you."

Again, Mee-Maw's words drenched Becca in a warm wash of love. Becca felt far differently with Mee-Maw than with her father. Her father made her, even now, feel prickly and uncertain, off-balance. He seemed to be always looking out for Becca's next mistake—while Mee-Maw never expected anything but good.

"Well, let's get these baskets in, shall we? I've got supper to finish up—though Ryan was going to put chicken on the grill to save me some trouble. That is a good boy. You could do worse than him, you know?"

Becca's stomach did a triple somersault at Mee-Maw's words. The memory of the almost-kiss came back to her. Was her attraction to Ryan so palpable that she hid it from no one? "Mee-Maw, are you trying to fix Ryan up?"

"No'm. I'm trying to fix you up. A handsome boy like Ryan? He'll be off the marriage mart before you can say whist." She winked. "I just don't want to see you miss a good deal."

Becca laughed, taking the joke for what it was. She hefted the heaviest basket. "I'll just get these in for you, and then I'll be on my way. I won't interfere—"

"Becca!"

Another little seismic jolt shot through her as she heard Ryan's pleased voice. She looked up to see Ryan on the back porch, smiling. "Hey," she called back, feeling shy at his obvious pleasure at seeing her. What was it about this family that enveloped her in warmth?

"You stood us up at dinnertime."

"Um, well, I was way off in the woods near the creek. But I did get a very nice burrito."

Mee-Maw clucked her tongue. "You must have gone down to talk to those Mexicans Murphy keeps in near servitude. Ain't nothing more than keepin' slaves, you ask me. The whole lot of 'em is afraid to say boo to a ghost."

Ryan loped across the backyard and took the heavy basket from Becca. "Here, I'll take this. You get the lighter one."

"And what will I tote?" Mee-Maw protested.

"You grew all this," Ryan told her. "You just tote yourself."

"I had some help." But she went on in, leaving the two of them alone.

"So—" Ryan shifted the basket in his hands "—did Jake help you?"

"When I could pull his attention away from his hogs, he was very helpful."

Ryan grinned. "Man loves his pigs. He's had 'em for years, Mee-Maw says." His expression grew more serious. "Was Mee-Maw right? Did you go down to Murphy's Little Mexico?"

"Yep. The conditions are awful, aren't they?"

He nodded. "Some of those guys are really talented farmers. We'd be lucky to hire them, but Murphy pretty well has the Keep Off The Grass sign up all the time. I tried to get one or two men to come help me after Gramps died and J.T. took off—no dice."

His comments triggered a flood of questions Becca wanted to ask. But they had reached the back porch, and the screen door swung open for them.

Ryan's cousin, Jack, stood there, balancing on his one good leg. His smile turned sour as he recognized her.

"What's she doing here?"

CHAPTER TWELVE

MEE-MAW SAVED BECCA from feeling awkward with her scolding, "Jack! Hush, now! Mind your manners! Becca's just stopped in for a spell. She helped me gather those vegetables. You go on now and light that grill for Ryan, else we'll be eatin' at dark o'clock. That broke leg of yours won't prevent you from scratching a match."

Jack looked from Ryan to Becca and then back to Ryan. He started to say something. Then, with an expression that shouted "We'll talk about this later" he pushed past them and headed for the barrel grill on the porch.

"Er…should I leave?" Becca asked Ryan.

Ryan scowled. "No. I just— Well, Jack and I just have some talking to do. I haven't really had a chance to explain to him…" He slid the basket of produce onto the kitchen counter. "Well, about how you—"

"Weren't a forked-tail, horned she-devil out for blood?"

Ryan gave her a crooked grin. "Yeah. Put it that way, it makes me sound bad, but what was I to expect, anyway? You come sashayin' down here on Ag-Sure's orders, I guess I just expected the worst, that's all. But…"

"Yes?" Her insides tingled with anticipation.

"You're just…you fit in. You fit right in. That's all. You're so different than what I expected. I feel like I've known you forever. Sounds crazy, doesn't it?"

Guilt tempered Becca's pleasure at the compliment. She wanted to tell him the truth. She glanced over her shoulder to see family approaching, no doubt expecting an introduction to this strange nonkin addition to the party. No, now wasn't the time. Maybe later if she got the chance alone with him.

So when will be the time? Aren't you just putting off the inevitable?

Becca quelled the inner chiding. "I'm glad I fit in, Ryan." She reached over and squeezed his hand. He responded by clasping her fingers in his and not letting go.

Then he turned back to the family members—his sister-in-law, Marla, all of Jack's brood, the entire extended family crowding into the kitchen. "Hey, y'all, I'd like to introduce you to someone who'll be staying for supper."

RYAN KNEW from the bangs outside on the porch that Jack was communicating his not-so-silent displeasure at Becca's presence.

Or maybe Jack really was having trouble lighting the grill?

Another wham, this one still louder.

Scratch that last thought.

Nodding at Mee-Maw, Ryan jerked his eyes first to Becca and then to the direction of the porch.

Mee-Maw gave an ever-so-slight nod of understanding. She'd look after Becca while he dealt with Jack. "Becca, girl, you come in the living room so I can show you pictures of how cute Ryan looked when he was a baby."

Ryan groaned at the ruse Mee-Maw chose, but he was glad to see his grandmother shepherding Becca away from the kitchen and the back porch.

A hot breeze that did nothing to cool off the afternoon kicked up Ryan's hair as he pushed open the screen.

"Hmm…" He glanced over at the darkening horizon. "Looks like—"

"Don't start prattling on about the weather. Of course it looks like thunderstorms—it's August. We have one every day nearly, even if they don't produce squat when it comes to rain." Jack collapsed onto the lime-green metal glider that Mee-Maw had used for as long as Ryan could remember, stretching out his leg and its cast on the seat. "If you want to talk, talk about this sudden change of heart you've had."

Ryan didn't even attempt to deny that his heart had changed. "Maybe we've jumped to conclusions." He dropped into the glider's matching chair.

"I don't get it. I thought you and I were on the same page. But now you're cozying up to this investigator? Inviting her to my daughter's birthday party?"

"Like I said, maybe we jumped to conclusions. She's honestly trying to figure out what's going on—"

"That's the point. Do we really want her to know what's going on? Huh?"

Ryan considered the ramifications of just that happening. He tried one more time to plead his case with Jack.

"It's not as if I actually planted the stupid stuff—"

"No, you didn't. And you didn't bring it in or hire someone to bring it in. But do we want her to know who did? And more importantly, who might have told that person to disappear?"

After Jack's pointed statement, the two men lapsed into a thoughtful silence.

"She's on our side, Jack. I don't know why...and I sure don't know how to convince you of that, but I feel it. Who's to say she won't dig up some dirt on Murphy and make the whole problem go away? Who's to say Ag-Sure's not just gunning for Murphy in the first place?"

"Right, and real life always has happily-ever-afters. We don't know…" Jack looked pained. "Look, as bad as I'd hate for you to take the fall for something you didn't do, I'd hate worse for Mee-Maw's farm to go down the drain as collateral damage."

Ryan's temper bubbled hot. "As if I wouldn't hate seeing Mee-Maw lose this place? Look, cuz, I didn't work hard out here, pulling fourteen-hour days in all kinds of hellish weather, just to see the farm go. I'm not letting it happen—no matter what I have to do."

Jack held up his hand. "Whoa. I'm not minimizing what you've done. I appreciate the sacrifices you've made—no way I could farm this place on my own and run the insurance agency—and no way could I provide for a family with what I'd make. You've done good. I'm just saying, open your eyes. Maybe this woman is baiting you. Sure, you haven't done anything wrong—"

"No, just colluded with a bunch of greedy jerks wanting to scheme a few million out of a federally backed insurance program. No crime there, huh?"

"As I was saying, you haven't done anything

wrong, just, um, turned a blind eye. But we don't know what her investigation will turn up about Gramps…and J.T. More importantly—"

"I know. Mee-Maw."

"If Mee-Maw helped J.T., the fines alone would ruin her. It'd kill her to lose this place, Ryan."

"But I've asked Mee-Maw until I'm blue in the face and she won't tell me squat. I'm tired of skulking around like some guilty piece of—"

"Look at it this way—sure, this Becca could be on your side. Sure, she could be just gunning for Murphy. But does she really, truly have to know all the details about how the vine got here to nail Murphy? Huh? Wouldn't it be better to go on like we decided, least said, easiest mended?"

"I swear, I don't know. If I just knew for sure what happened that day—"

Ryan broke off as he heard a noise through the screen door. He looked up to see Becca's form disappearing back into the house.

"No! That was Becca. Who knows what she'll make of this conversation."

"See? She's skulking around, spying through keyholes, trying to catch you off guard."

"No. No. She is *not* like that."

"And you know this how?" Jack's sarcasm was heavy. "Just because she bats those pretty, long eyelashes at you?"

"All right, so she's pretty. She's beautiful. But inside...she's like us, Jack. She's like us."

"She's from the city. How can she be like us?"

BECCA HADN'T MEANT to eavesdrop, and she hadn't heard much, just the tail end of an extremely suspicious conversation. But the old saying about eavesdroppers hearing highly instructive things was true. Her appetite—and the pleasure in the evening—had vanished when she'd heard Jack say enough to convince her that the two men knew or suspected how the vine had made the trip from Texas.

The only consolation she'd taken from the snippet she'd heard was Ryan's obvious reluctance. Whatever this deal was, whatever Jack was involved in, Ryan didn't want to be a part of it.

And what was Ryan wondering about "that day" and what had happened? What day?

The time to ask Ryan about it was sooner rather than later—and the first chance she got, she'd definitely demand some answers.

Becca suddenly felt fatigue bone-deep within her, suddenly was aware of how she probably looked. She'd been hiking through cotton fields in the heat of the summer. Her hair was a mess, her little bit of makeup was gone and she felt gritty and exhausted.

And more than a little in the way. Jack's studied indifference to her, as well as the overly polite manners of the rest of the family had a way of eating into the warm acceptance she still felt from Mee-Maw and Ryan.

Becca craved a hot shower and cool, clean sheets. But now that she'd invited herself to this shindig, she was here for the duration until the cake was sliced, served and eaten.

When the German chocolate cake finally was reduced to crumbs, Becca pushed back her chair, paper plate in hand. "Mee-Maw, that's about the best food I've eaten yet. You sure know how to cook. Emily, I'm so glad I could be here to celebrate your birthday with you. But if you guys will excuse me, I'm going to head back into town. I'm more than a little beat."

Ryan rose to his feet. "I'll follow you in."

"No, that's—" An image of that hangman's noose sprang to her mind, as did her earlier determination to ask Ryan about Jack. "Well, I hate to trouble you, but I would appreciate it."

She couldn't miss Jack's eye roll—or Marla's well-placed elbow in his ribs. But Ryan had elected to ignore it. "No problem. It'd make me feel better, what with what happened last night."

Jack frowned. "What happened last night?"

"Someone left her a hangman's noose made out of dodder vine on her door handle."

Jack's face blanched. "That's cold, man. Yeah. You, uh, follow her in. I'll supervise the cleanup."

"Da-ad!" Emily protested. "It's my *birthday*!"

"What? You think just 'cause it's your birthday you get a free ride?" Jack reached over and tugged on Emily's ponytail. "Aw, okay. No dish duty for you."

It occurred to Becca as she watched the banter between Jack and his daughter that the man was someone she would have liked, wanted to still, except for what she'd overheard earlier.

Man. What am I thinking? This whole family had pulled her in a knot. Dad wouldn't have lost his objectivity. He would have marched out here and demanded to know the truth. No, probably he would have had this figured out already.

She worried over how to frame the questions she wanted to ask Ryan as she drove back into town. The flicker of headlights in her rearview mirror served as a constant reminder that he was behind her. It at once comforted her and made her apprehensive about the coming conversation.

The Mini bounced over a pothole or two in the paved parking lot of the motel. The place was dark, blinds drawn. She could see the desk clerk through the wide plate-glass window. He had his feet propped up, and he looked as if he was dozing.

Ryan joined Becca on the breezeway. "Okay

then, just a check in your room." He reached for the doorknob as she unlocked it, their fingers brushing. Becca's heart pounded with the same intensity it would have had they been intending some other, more amorous activity.

Ryan jerked his hand back, his face coloring. "I meant, just to be sure everything's okay. I'll be on my way after that."

"Are you angling to see my etchings?" she teased, trying to break the tension.

He laughed. "Some other time I'd be all over them. But I really need to get back and help Jack."

"Yeah." The mention of Jack's name reminded Becca why she was here. She turned the knob and let Ryan inside.

He looked around, opened the bathroom door, peeked behind the shower curtain, checked the closets and under both beds. That last activity showed her just how well he filled out his Levi's.

As if you needed a second look.

Becca struggled for something to say that would not reveal how attracted she was to him. "Take this bodyguard business seriously, huh?"

"I don't want anything to happen to you, Becca."

Her mouth went dry at the seriousness of his tone. Did he know something she didn't? She squared her shoulders and dived in. "Look, I know you have to get back, okay? But I…I wanted to ask you about Jack. Is he involved in this? Is that who you're protecting?"

"Who says I'm protecting anybody?" The way he folded his arms across his chest and the sudden stillness in his face screamed that he'd shut down.

She crossed the room, touched him on his forearm. "I couldn't help but overhearing you and Jack on the porch. I didn't hear much, but it sounded like Jack…wasn't too thrilled with me digging into this."

"Jack's like me. He doesn't want to see Mee-Maw lose the farm, what with the time it's taking to get the claim settled. Nothing more than that." When Becca didn't reply, his voice softened. "I swear, Becca. He's not involved. I'm not involved."

There was something in his voice, though, that told her he knew more than he was telling.

"But somebody you care about is involved. Somehow…somehow you think Mee-Maw could lose her farm." She pondered the questions, the ifs and hows, running through her head.

"Of course we're worried about the farm. Who knows what Ag-Sure's got up their sleeves, huh? They drag this out, farms like Mee-Maw's will wind up being foreclosed. We just don't have the cushion, the padding. That's why we carry crop insurance, to hedge our bets. If they decide it's fraud, maybe nobody gets paid, even if I didn't plant the vine."

"And you didn't? Tell me. Look me in the eye, Ryan. Tell me, swear to me, that you had nothing to do with that dodder vine getting in that field—in anybody's field." She knew she was close to begging, but she'd be willing to believe anything he said.

He stared down at her, slipped his hands on her shoulders, then down along her back to finally settle on her waist. "I swear. I swear on Gramps's grave I didn't plant it. I didn't bring it in. I wouldn't. It's playing with fire messing with that stuff. Whoever did has no respect for farming, doesn't really, truly understand how to care for land. I swear. I had nothing to do with it. And neither did Jack."

Relief flooded through her. This was what she'd been waiting for, hoping for—his concession that this whole thing wasn't legit, and his solemn assurance that he was clean in all of this.

But that relief was pushed away by something else—the feel of his palms through her shirt. Ryan's face was so earnest, as earnest as a man proposing, she wanted to reach up and kiss the seriousness away from his mouth. She wanted to make him laugh, see his dimples jump.

Instead, Becca remained professional. She settled instead for a smile. "Thank—"

She didn't get it all out. His mouth descended on hers, warm and searching. After a split second's surprise, her body took over, pushing away any common sense she might have brought to bear.

It was Ryan who stepped back first. Becca was a little embarrassed about that. She bit her lip, the lip he'd just thoroughly kissed.

"If I don't get out of here…" he rasped. "What is it about you? Why do I want to just let go, lose it with you?"

Becca didn't have to think up an answer. He pressed another quick kiss to her mouth and bolted for the door, leaving her bereft and confused and wondering what made him jerk away.

He stopped at the door, turned and gave her a look that made her knees go to jelly. In a hoarse voice, he said, "Call me if you need anything. We need to talk…when I can think again."

CHAPTER THIRTEEN

KISSES LIKE Ryan's had a way of creating a monster case of insomnia.

Becca's body practically hummed with energy, even after she'd showered off the day's grit and grime. Though she was tired, her brain, filled as it was with all she'd learned that day, wouldn't cooperate.

Mainly, though, one jubilant thought pulsed through her: *He kissed me! He really, really kissed me!*

Another thought like an accompaniment chord twanged in the background: *He's not involved in this scam with the vine!*

Becca had no doubt that when they did talk again, she'd get the full story. She could write her summary report for Ag-Sure, a report that would absolve Ryan of all guilt or suspicion, and she could confess to him about being Sunny.

It wasn't such a horrible secret, was it? No way he could get mad about that, right?

Right?

Mee-Maw was hauling out dodder vines, clipping them into short sections, saying, "Now, see, we can batter-fry them up like okra and they'll sell like hotcakes. Aren't you glad I planted them, Becca?"

Suddenly Becca felt a vine wrap around her throat, constricting her breathing. It came alive, turned into a boa constrictor, hissing in her ear.

"Wake up!"

Becca struggled to leave the dream behind, but woke to find that something really was wrapped around her throat, her mouth. She stared up, terrified, feeling a heavy knee in her chest.

"Shh. Shh. Easy. You be quiet, listen, and I'll be on my way."

Hard eyes glittered out from the holes of a ski mask. There was no mouth, and somehow that terrified Becca even more.

In response to her gurgle, the hands tightened more.

Quickly, she managed to nod, to mouth *okay*. She needed him to let his guard down if she was ever going to have a chance against his solid weight.

The rough southern voice hissed in her ear again. "Smart girl. Now, you be even smarter and get out. Just pack your bags and forget you was even here. What's that money to a rich insurance company? Nothin'."

Was it Murphy? Too thin to be Murphy, and besides, Murphy wasn't the type to break in to a motel room.

"Just go on back to Daddy, or else you'll be sorry." The voice singsonged like some sort of twisted grade-school chant. He pulled her into a half-sitting position. His thumb, in rough work gloves, slid along her jaw. "A shame I got orders not to leave any marks."

She held still, squeezed her eyes shut.

He moved away from her. "Half of me's hopin' you will stick around. 'Cause they won't care what I do to you if they tell me to finish you off. But for now...I got orders. So later, babe."

In a flash, he dropped her. For a dizzying moment she was falling backward. Her head hit the cheap motel headboard with a sick clunk.

She forced herself to open her eyes. One moment he stood at the door, silhouetted in the light from outside. The next, he was gone, and the door slammed shut.

Becca stumbled out of bed for the window, making it just as a beat-up pickup truck with the tailgate down burned rubber out of the parking lot. She tried to register the make and model of the vehicle he was driving in the brief glimpse she'd had, but all she could see was a dark blur and a streak of taillights.

Her convulsive trembling hadn't stopped. She

leaned, gasping, against the cool plate-glass window, then backtracked for the phone.

When the 9-1-1 operator asked her what her emergency was, Becca burst into tears.

SHE SAT IN THE BACK of an ambulance, a rough blanket thrown around her shoulders, impatient with the E.M.T.

"Let's just go on to the hospital, get you checked out…" the female E.M.T wheedled once more.

Through gritted teeth, Becca rasped, "No. I'm fine."

The woman touched Becca's neck. "Well, he sure left you with some bruises."

Just then, Becca heard raised voices.

"Where is she? I want to know, is she okay? Where is she?"

Ryan. Her heart flooded with joy and relief. A separate, almost detached part of Becca's brain wondered at how he could make her feel safe by his very presence.

"Easy, easy…they're checking her out. She's okay…" Brandon Wilkes trailed off awkwardly. "Before you start your inquisition, she didn't get a good description. She didn't get the make and model of the truck. She got squat. But she's alive and she's pretty much in one piece, so I think that makes her a winner, okay? It just leaves us little to work on."

"Ryan!" Becca's voice came out ragged and croaky, thanks to her assailant's handiwork.

"You want him in here?" Without waiting for an answer, the E.M.T. stuck her head out of the doors. "We're done here. She says she doesn't want to go to the hospital, and there's not a whole bunch we can do for her throat. She wants Ryan whoever-it-is."

Ryan pushed into the back of the ambulance. His arms went round Becca. To her shame, she nearly cried again, trembling much as she had right after the attack.

"I feel so stupid," she muttered. "Just so stupid. I should have—"

"What would you have done, honey? You against a grown man? You did the smart thing, and you're here. And I'm here. I'm here. Shh. Shh. It's gonna be okay." He pulled her against him. The embrace was an awkward one as her arms were still under the blanket, but she didn't care. She just wanted to get warm again, feel safe.

"If anybody should feel stupid, it's me. I should have never let you come back here."

"How—how'd you find out?" she asked him.

"Brandon called me on his cell phone."

The deputy propped one foot on the bumper of the ambulance. "Hope you don't mind, Miss Becca. But I figured you'd need somewhere to stay tonight."

"Oh, I do, don't I? Because I am never going back in that motel again."

"Do you know if anything was missing?"

Becca shook her head. "He—he didn't touch anything but—but me."

"The reason I ask is that… Well, it's strange that it was just a warning. I mean, I first thought maybe you had got hold of something they didn't want you to have. Maybe some pictures you took? Or something someone gave you?"

She considered Wilkes's question. "No," she said finally. "No. I think they wanted to scare me into giving up on the investigation."

"And…well, not to put too fine a point on it, but have they?" Wilkes asked her.

"Honestly, I don't know. Nothing like this has ever happened to me. But…but my dad always says never to make a decision when you're upset." She groaned and put her fingers to her throat. Already she could tell it would hurt, but it would be nothing compared to the chewing out she could expect from her dad. He would point out in excruciating detail all the security lapses she'd made. "My dad. I need to call him. He's gonna be livid."

"Well, now, if you want me to talk to him and assure him that we are going to put all our resources behind this—"

"No. I mean, he's going to be livid with me.

He's…" She didn't want to confess what a screwup her dad sometimes accused her of being.

"No, ma'am, I don't think so," Wilkes assured her. "Really, this wasn't any bit your fault. You didn't— Don't fall into the trap—" He broke off, obviously unaccustomed to offering solace or advice on matters like this.

Ryan picked up where the deputy had left off. "He won't be mad. How could he be mad? He'll be worried, sure. But Brandon's right. This wasn't your fault, Becca. You did nothing to make this happen."

She wasn't convinced. She could think of a million things—well, at least a good half dozen—she could have done to have made this harder for her attacker. Her dad would say she'd not watched her back, been unaware of her surroundings, shown incompetence. Her dad had never been the touchy-feely type. Scraped knees and skinned elbows were completely her mother's—and after her mom passed away, her aunt's—domain.

Should she get the call to her dad over and done with, or put it off until daylight?

Heads you win, tails I lose.

"What about this? While the E.M.T.s are packing up, I'll go get your stuff. You call your dad. Tell him you're staying with me and Mee-Maw." Ryan patted her arm and headed out the way he'd come.

Right. Dad will be doubly thrilled that I'm stay-ing with the target of an investigation. Whoopee. More great news.

But Becca had no desire to stay in another motel room. It would be a long, long time before she'd ever want even to try. In any event, she had no choice but to stay with Ryan.

She was still dickering with herself about whether to call now or later when Ryan came back with her cell phone. "Here. We'll clear out, give you a little privacy. Remember—no dad is going to be mad that his daughter is safe."

Becca regarded the phone in her hand with all the warmth she'd display for a scorpion. Sighing, she punched in her dad's speed-dial number and waited for him to pick up.

Despite the early morning hour, he answered with crisp alertness, a legacy of his time in the military.

"Yes?"

Her story spilled out. She tried to keep it bare-bones, no emotion. Her voice, though croaky, held steady, and for that, she was proud of herself.

A long silence followed. Finally, he said, "So you're okay?"

"Except for my throat, I'm okay."

"When I find out who he is, I'll rip him apart. I'm getting in the car now to put an end to this mess. I'll be there in—"

Mortification sluiced over her. "No, Dad! You don't have to come. I'm okay."

"Obviously you're in over your head, sweetheart. I need to handle this myself."

Not me. The investigation. The job. A pang shot through her. One day maybe she and her dad could carry on a conversation like two equals, or at least with mutual respect. But that day wouldn't be tonight.

"No. No, you don't have to come."

"Look, I put you in harm's way, and I shouldn't have. Clearly, we both miscalculated."

Did he really mean that, or was he just trying to soothe her?

"Dad. Can we talk about this in the morning? That will be soon enough. I'm fine. I'm not hurt, not permanently anyway. I'm making headway on this job. There's no need for you to leave now. Get some rest and we'll talk tomorrow morning."

Her logic seemed to make him hesitate. "You're sure?"

"Yes. Yes, sir."

"Where will you stay?"

Becca swallowed, the action painful in her sore, battered throat. "I'll be staying with one of the farmers. Ryan MacIntosh and his grandmother. They've offered to put me up for the night."

"Becca, don't you have sense even to come in

out of the rain? How do you know it wasn't this MacIntosh that attacked you?"

At that moment, Ryan appeared at the open doors of the ambulance. He held up her one small suitcase and smiled in a reassuring way.

Becca smiled back. To her father, she said, "I just know, Dad. The phone number to the Mac-Intosh farm should be in the file. Call me in the morning. I'm going to try to get some sleep now."

With that, she clicked the phone shut. She shrugged off the blanket and stepped down into Ryan's embrace.

CHAPTER FOURTEEN

FURY LIKE HE'D NEVER experienced before made it nearly impossible for Ryan to speak on the way out to the farm. He glanced at Becca sitting beside him in his truck. Her face was drawn and pale; the bruises on her neck stood out in stark contrast.

The jerk. He'd kill Tate—it had to be Tate who sent the creep in. And he'd kill Murphy for setting all this in motion. Didn't he have any clue what could have happened, or did Murphy just not even care?

Becca cleared her throat. "It was nice of the deputy to call in a buddy to take my car out to the farm. I don't think I could have driven tonight."

"Save your voice. Remember? The E.M.T.s said to treat it like laryngitis—easy on the talking, plenty of warm liquids."

Ryan tightened his grip on the wheel. He could have lost her. He could have lost her even before he'd had a chance to really get to know her. Now that he had this second chance, what was he doing? Nurse-maiding. She probably wanted to slap him.

But Becca smiled at him. He would have killed for that smile. It gave him hope that she was okay, that things between them would be fine.

This is all my fault. If I'd just gone to Ag-Sure from the get-go with what I knew—or even what I suspected...

Another voice niggled at him—maybe Jack's voice.

Yeah, but what about Gramps? And Mee-Maw?

Ryan hated this feeling of being caught in the middle. Whatever he did—or didn't do—people he cared about were bound to get hurt.

"Mee-Maw's making you some hot tea—I called her before we left. You feel up to talking when we get there? We really need to, Becca."

For a moment, he saw weariness flash across her face, but she nodded. "Yeah. I probably won't sleep very well anyway."

"We're going to put you in the house tonight. Tomorrow, if you want, we can move you out to the pond house. You'll have more privacy there. But for tonight...I want you just down the hall from me, okay?"

She nodded again. "That sounds great."

"Good." He made the turn onto Mee-Maw's rutted drive and stifled a yawn. 3:00 a.m. Wasn't long before he'd have to be up feeding the cows and the chickens and getting on with the day. Might as well not even try going back to bed.

Wilbur thumped his tail at the back door as Ryan led Becca in. Mee-Maw waited for them just inside the kitchen.

"Becca, Becca, girl, come here! Let me see you! Let me be sure you're okay!"

Ryan watched as Becca collapsed into the older woman's embrace. He wouldn't blame Becca if she did pack up her few things and head for Atlanta when day broke.

Mee-Maw fussed over her, pouring her a cup of steaming tea and fixing her a piece of toast with homemade strawberry preserves. Ryan recalled picking those strawberries for his grandmother—it seemed like a completely different lifetime. Had he really been that optimistic? That energetic? That sure he could save this farm for Mee-Maw?

Yes. With Becca's help, he could do it again.

Fine thing for you to do, asking a woman to rescue you after she's been nearly killed because you kept your trap shut.

The thought reminded him of Jack's warning. He left Becca in Mee-Maw's care, stepped out onto the back porch and used his cell phone to dial Jack's.

Marla answered the phone with the waspish grouch of the awakened and promptly handed the phone over to Jack.

"What is—"

"Somebody broke into Becca's motel room, roughed her up, scared her to death. Still think least said's easiest mended?"

"What?" Jack seemed more alert. "Hold on. Let me go into the kitchen."

A minute later, Jack was back on the line with a volley of questions. Ryan filled him in, then waited for his reply.

"What did you tell Brandon? Did you tell him about Tate?"

"I started to. But…I've got no proof. Just something he could blow off. Look, I don't know what to do. We can't continue to keep our mouths shut if somebody—Tate or whoever it was who sent that goon—is that desperate and dumb. This changes things."

"Man…you're right. Of course she's gonna dig in her heels now."

For a moment, Ryan was irritated with Jack's apparent self-serving interest. "Well, *she* is here. At the farm. No way was I gonna let her stay there."

"I don't like it… Murphy's gonna crap a brick when he finds out." Before Ryan could say anything, Jack continued, "But at least she's safe there with you. And you've got the room—I got every bed filled here with our crew. Just…try to talk her out of anything rash before we can decide what to do, okay? And don't go thinking confession is good for the soul. Think of Mee-Maw. For now, we watch out for Becca, but we keep our mouths shut until…until we decide what to say."

Ryan felt like it was a fair enough deal. He ended the call and slipped back inside. He was pleased to see the tea and toast had bucked up Becca. If there was one thing Mee-Maw knew how to do, it was mothering.

When Ryan went to double-check the locks on the doors, Mee-Maw followed him. She whispered, "Is this because of that investigation? That infernal vine?"

Ryan dipped his head in confirmation. "Yes, ma'am."

Her lips thinned and her face tightened. "That Murphy has a special place in hell. I'll believe to my dying day he had something to do with it."

Ryan hesitated. "Murphy's too smart for that. He'd know it would attract suspicion. But I wouldn't put it past dumb lugs like Tate or Oliver."

"Well? What are you going to do about it, young man? Are you going to help her? Isn't that what she came to you for?"

"I— Yes, ma'am," he repeated. Sometimes that's all that was really wise to say to a woman like Mee-Maw.

"Well, then." She looked satisfied. "I'll go on to bed. Leave you two to talk. I expect…I expect

184

she might talk more to you than to me. I have her bed ready. You holler if you need me."

He followed her back to the kitchen table, where Mee-Maw gave Becca a peck on the cheek. "You get some rest now. In the morning, you sleep as late as you like. I'll fix you some nice hot grits that'll be soothing to your throat, okay?"

Alone with Becca, Ryan sat down in the ladder-backed dining chair next to her. He folded a hand over hers. "Becca…I'm so sorry about all this. I feel like so much of it is my fault."

"It wasn't you who didn't make sure the door was barricaded with a handy dresser."

"But I should have known how sorry the locks were on those motel doors—Brandon said the guy used a credit card or a knife, then used bolt cutters on the chain. I could have at least told you to stay with us. You could have."

"It's going to be okay, Ryan. Eventually. I'll be okay. I won't lie—it scared the life out of me. I thought…" She looked as though she might cry again. She went on, though, with calm deliberation. "My dad…my dad wants to come down here and take over the investigation."

"Maybe that's the wise thing to do."

She shrugged her shoulders. "Yeah. Maybe. But that will be two failures back to back on my part. Besides…"

Becca's face pinched with misery. She wanted

to say something else, something that pained her, he could tell. Whatever it was, she didn't reveal it. She simply shook her head as if to clear it.

"You don't want to let him down."

"No. But more importantly—and this is really stupid of me, you know—I don't want to let *myself* down. I can do this. I can figure out what's going on here. I already have a bunch of it figured out. If I can just get some proof, hard evidence."

"I'll help you. I don't—" Ryan closed his eyes and thought about Mee-Maw. He made a decision. Looking Becca straight in the face, he said, "I don't know what I can do, what I'm able to do—even what I'm willing to do. But whatever I can, I'll do it. Okay?"

She smiled again, and the sheer megawatt power of that smile dazzled him. Whatever it took to make her smile like that, he'd do. Whatever it took to keep her safe—keep his whole family safe—he'd do.

Or die trying.

BECCA CAME AWAKE in a jolt. The rising sun shone pink and gold through white eyelet curtains, spilling onto a wedding-ring quilt.

Safe. She was safe.

She traced the pattern of the interlocking rings on the quilt and wondered idly if Mee-Maw had stitched it.

The rings were like this problem Becca faced now. Pull one and the whole thing jangled. You just had to figure out which was the loose one.

Think. Go back to the basics.

Her father's voice again, this time from tenth-grade geometry when he sat beside her, trying to get her to grasp how to do proofs. "What do you know? What can you postulate from that?" he'd ask her.

She knew that last night's attack would be enough to make the insurance company tie up the settlements until future lawsuits could decide how it would all turn out.

But Ag-Sure was after more. They wanted the smoking gun—enough to prevent any lawsuit from even being filed in the first place. That's what they'd hoped for with the case she'd blown.

What do you know?

The vine just hadn't hopped across the Mississippi. It had help. Help that the Hispanic workers hadn't provided.

Somebody had planted it. Somebody had allowed it to take root and spread.

And it had spread. In the early days, it would have been small enough to go unnoticed, but surely herbicides would have—

Her finger paused in its trace around a lavender ring. Another plan of attack occurred to her.

She'd need to follow up on the threads she'd

unraveled, yes, but this one might be enough to satisfy Ag-Sure…or at the least, pry information loose that could be used for more leverage.

The only thing—she'd need Ryan's help. So, was his promise good? Would this be one of those things he'd be willing to do?

She had the day to convince him—and to convince her father that she had a Plan B.

Assuming, of course, that her dad wasn't already halfway down I-75.

Becca padded along cool heart-pine flooring to her suitcase. She pulled on some clothes and rummaged until she found where Ryan had stuck her toothbrush and toothpaste the night before. Time to get moving.

Ryan startled her as he stole out of the bathroom on tiptoe. She couldn't help the small shriek she made.

"Are you— We were planning on letting you sleep." He frowned. "Are you okay? Did you need something?"

She took in his damp hair, the steam wafting out of the bathroom and the way his T-shirt clung to his chest. She stammered, "Um…I couldn't sleep anymore."

"I wish I could sleep a little longer. I made the mistake of thinking I could catch an hour or so and now I've slept late. But Mee-Maw's got some breakfast done. How's your throat?"

Becca put a hand to it. "Sore. But pain's...pain's definitely better than the alternative, right?"

"Definitely. Well, uh, I'll see you in a few minutes."

She closed the door to the bathroom and looked in the mirror. The bruises on her throat looked like a vile necklace. Her hair was a mess because she'd gone to bed with it wet. No way she could have slept without scrubbing off every vestige of her attacker's touch.

A part of Becca still wanted to stand under a stream of the hottest water possible until she felt cleansed. But soap and water wouldn't wash away the memory. Only putting the people responsible behind bars would help.

Teeth brushed, hair pulled back into a ponytail, Becca started for the kitchen.

Mee-Maw glanced up from the pot she was stirring and did a double-take. "Child, you didn't have to get up. You could have slept on. But since you're up and dressed, you might as well come get you some of these grits." She banged the spoon on the rim of the pot and covered it with a lid.

Becca helped herself to a cup of steaming coffee and a plate of grits and bacon. As she found her chair—amazing, she already thought of this place at the table as *her* chair—Mee-Maw added, "I'll fry you an egg, too—won't take but a minute."

"No, ma'am. This is fine, thank you."

"I was planning on making some cream biscuits, but I just slept too late this morning. Guess we all had a night of it. 'Specially you."

Ryan settled beside her, his own plate loaded down. "I put some toast on, Mee-Maw. C'mon, dip your plate and rest. I'll get the toast when it's done." To Becca he said, "Did the phone ringing in here wake you?"

"Phone?"

"Yeah. Your dad called. He was checking on you. Sounds fierce."

"He was in the marines. Pulled two tours in Vietnam. So, yeah, he is pretty fierce."

"I told him you were sleeping. He was worried when he couldn't get you on your cell phone."

"I—I'll call him after breakfast."

They ate in silence for a few moments. Becca stewed over the coming phone call and hoped it would go better than the previous night's conversation.

"I sure appreciate you letting me stay here last night."

Mee-Maw and Ryan made aw-shucks noises. Becca put up a hand. "No, really. I was—I was in such a state that I don't know what I would have done."

"'Tain't right, what happened to you. I hope they find whoever the garbage is and string him up," Mee-Maw said.

"I'd like to help out here a little today. Whatever you guys think I can do."

"You don't have to, Becca," Ryan told her. "Trust me, I was glad to do what little I did last night for you. Don't you need to rest?"

She shook her head decisively. "No. I think I need to be busy. I want to talk to my dad, but for today… Well, I think maybe the best thing is just to lay low. I certainly poked some sort of hornet's nest yesterday to get that kind of reaction. What I need to do is figure out exactly what I did to… well…"

"What did you find out yesterday? I never got a chance to talk with you about it last night."

No, but we did something else. The memory of his kiss came back full throttle, stirring up a slew of butterflies in her stomach. She was glad that the attacker had not destroyed the pleasure of that kiss.

Ryan must have realized what she was thinking, because his expression turned sheepish. Then he grinned.

"I'm mighty curious, too," Mee-Maw interjected.

Becca gave them a quick rundown of what she'd learned from Jake Wilkes and Antonio. "I don't know whether Antonio has any answers for me, but I'll need to go back and see him."

"You shouldn't go alone. I'll go with you."

Becca didn't protest Ryan's offer. She was hoping his protective mode would continue and he'd agree to help her with the project she wanted to tackle after sundown.

"I think, if you guys don't mind, I'll go call my dad now." She stood with her plate and took it to the sink.

"Just leave it, Becca. I'll get it."

"No, ma'am. It won't take a minute." As Becca scrubbed the plate, she glanced out the window at the chicken coop. "Want me to collect the morning eggs for you?"

"Well…"

Becca didn't turn and look, but she had a feeling that Mee-Maw and Ryan were holding a silent conversation behind her back.

"If you really think a little work'll get your mind off last night, far be it from me to turn down free labor. Yes, ma'am, you can gather the eggs for me."

Mee-Maw joined her at the sink. "Watch out for Henrietta—she's the black one with the red chest. That gal flat refuses to lay her eggs in her nest. You'll most likely find 'em in a corner. The scratch is by the door, but they'll need some chicken feed, too. Don't give 'em too much scratch, mind—won't be long before they're molting, and I'd like to get what eggs I can out of 'em before then."

"Yes, ma'am. Let me just make this call and then I'll go."

A few minutes later, Becca sat on the bed and punched her father's speed-dial button on her cell phone. He answered on the first ring.

"You okay?"

"Yes, sir."

"Give me one reason why I shouldn't be on my way down there."

"I halfway figured you already were."

He sighed. "I started to. But…you seemed so… adamant about not wanting me there."

"Oh, Dad." She'd never heard him sound so wounded before, at least not about her. "It's not that I don't want you here. It's that…I want to do this myself."

"I still think these guys are too rough for you, Becca. I sent you down to what I assumed was a quiet little insurance fiddle and I forgot the cardinal rule."

"What's that?"

"It's all about the money. People go crazy over money. Either they think it will pry them out of a hole or they think it will keep them from sliding into one."

She thought about Murphy and his Early Banker decor. "Yeah. They do."

"Tell me what you know."

Becca gave him a more detailed report than the

thumbnail sketch she'd given to Ryan and Mee-Maw. He harrumphed, asked a few pointed questions that Becca was glad she'd already thought of herself and said, "Well. You, ahem, sound like you've got some good leads. I like the one about the ex-con hired hand—J.T.? I haven't found him yet, but I'm still looking."

Her heart filled with a fragile joy. It was the first time she could remember her dad ever complimenting her.

"But listen, Becca. These people aren't playing. They're serious. I'm giving you three more days before I come down there. And you'd better report in twice a day—make that three. I don't hear from you or I can't get you on your cell phone, I'm down there like a shot. Got it?"

Becca gripped the phone. Three days. But it was more latitude than her dad had ever given her before. He was really trying to trust her instincts.

"Got it, Dad. And…thanks."

"You trust this Ryan? If you do, be sure you take him with you. Don't go off alone anymore. Give him my cell number in case—" Her father broke off, leaving her marveling at the completeness of his shift in perspective. When he continued, his voice was crisp to the point of harshness. "Remember—morning, noon and night reports. Don't do anything stupid. Three days."

CHAPTER FIFTEEN

EGGS COLLECTED, chickens fed, Becca grabbed a pan and joined Mee-Maw on the back porch where she was shelling peas. What she needed to do now was some serious thinking—and catch Murphy and his crew unawares after dark. If Becca were lucky, she might even manage to pry details out of the ever-evasive Mee-Maw.

The rhythmic thump of pea hulls landing in the bucket spurred Becca on to shell faster to keep up with Mee-Maw. Still, the physical labor seemed to free up her brain to think. While she shelled peas, she considered the investigation from all angles.

No, she hadn't missed anything. She just hoped that Ryan would go along with her plans—and that Antonio's own detective work would produce a harvest. Should she risk seeing Antonio today, or give him one more day to find out what he could?

They had enough peas for lunch, put them on to cook and shelled on. Again, Becca had a moment to think. This time, though, she thought of Ryan. The personality he'd revealed in his six months of e-mails had been consistent with the real Ryan. He may not have shared with her the fearsome battle he'd waged with either the dodder vine or the big-shot farmers like Murphy, but he had been honest and open with the things that mattered most. As his e-mails had indicated, he was a hard worker, with a sense of humor and a great big heart.

But electronic messages had failed to convey how attractive he was. Truly, it was the cherry on top as far as Becca was concerned, and maybe her own undoing.

Becca had introduced herself to the online community as a farmer's daughter, not a private investigator. It had been a whim on her part, after lurking there for weeks. At the time, not telling Ryan what she did for a living hadn't seemed like a big lie. After all, she'd figured, he probably was hiding things, too.

Well, he was. He could have told you about the scam, and you could have helped him solve the problem when it was little. You could have helped him go to Ag-Sure, tell them his suspicions.

So why hadn't he? What was keeping him from going to Ag-Sure now? She knew he still kept something from her. She knew he'd been privy to conversations and plans that Murphy had done.

So why had a man so honest and so open not spoken up?

It didn't jibe. The conspiracy had to involve family—maybe somehow Gramps had been involved.

But to Becca, what with all she'd heard about Gramps, that theory didn't make sense, either.

Talk to me, Ryan. Tell me what is going on.

DUSTY AND TIRED from working in the fields, Ryan trudged toward the house. Last night's lack of sleep was telling on him. If he moved any slower, he was liable to fall off the tractor. His only hope was that lunch and a rest would revive him.

But the sight that greeted him on the porch sent a surge of energy through him.

There were Mee-Maw and Becca, rocking and shelling peas together. They didn't see him; they were deep into some conversation. The slightest of hot breezes carried Becca's sudden trill of laughter out to him. At the sound of such music, Ryan's throat tightened.

How could he help the one without hurting the other?

Becca spotted him then and she waved for him to join them.

He leaned against the railing to watch them. "Wow. You ladies got a lot done."

"Yep." Mee-Maw nailed the bucket with another long pea hull. "Who would have thought we would have had this good a crop this late in the season? Guess all those afternoon thunderstorms are really paying off, huh?"

"Not to mention those soaker hoses I ran for you. Puts the water right down where it won't evaporate off. And you thought they'd be too new-fangled."

Mee-Maw made a face and rocked on. "I did have to oblige myself to watch out for them early on when I was hoeing. But I have to admit, they work better than the old spray sprinkler. I've never had a prettier pea patch. Which is a good thing, as you sure do eat a plenty of them," Mee-Maw teased.

"Every one you cook, I'll eat, yes, ma'am." He shifted his weight. "Speaking of eating…what's for lunch?"

"Dinner's on the stove. I was just about to ring the dinner bell for you. We got peas and fried ham and some more tomatoes, and there's some rice and onions for you. Plus, I fried some of that okra I cut yesterday. I would have batter-fried eggplant instead, but it was just too hot. Air-conditioning can barely keep up today."

"This house needs a boatload of insulation—not to mention rewiring, replumbing and a better foundation."

"House'll be here when we're long gone, young man," Mee-Maw told him in a tart voice. "Mac built this house himself, and he didn't cut any corners."

Ryan exchanged a knowing glance with Becca. It felt good to have someone his age around— someone who wouldn't fight him on small improvements like dishwashers and more energy-efficient hot-water heaters and insulation.

Mee-Maw set aside her dishpan full of shelled peas. "I know you're itching to get back out there and I hear we may have some bad weather moving in this afternoon. So I reckon I'd better stop here and get our dinner."

ABOUT THREE O'CLOCK, Ryan saw the first sharp spear of lightning cut through the sky. A loud boom of thunder reverberated around him.

He didn't have to be told twice. He turned his tractor around and headed for the barn. Halfway there, hard raindrops splatted down on the tractor's canopy. The sky was a curious gray-green that spelled trouble to Ryan's experienced eye.

Tornadoes. Just what they needed to contend with now.

The sky suddenly darkened as if to confirm his prediction. As soon as he nosed the tractor into the safety of the barn, Ryan heard the telltale clanging of ice on the metal roof.

Sure enough, Ping-Pong-ball-sized hail rained down in sheets. He rushed for the house to find

Becca and Mee-Maw yanking out tarps from a cabinet on the back porch.

"What are you doing?" he yelled over the noise of the storm.

"My tomatoes! My kitchen garden! I can't lose it! These'll help protect them—we've got to hurry!" Mee-Maw hollered back.

"Let it go! It's not worth it!"

"No! We can do this!" Becca told him. "I'll help you!"

Together they wrestled the tarps over the tomato vines and the rest of the garden. Ryan could see that some hail had already struck the plump tomatoes, leaving holes and gashes in them.

Hail beat into his back as he crouched down to secure the edges of the tarp with heavy bricks and rocks. He had to hand it to Becca. She hung right in there, racing for more weights to hold down her end of the tarp. They covered the little garden and made a beeline for the back porch.

"Well," shouted Mee-Maw, "we've done all we can do. Let's get out of this infernal weather."

The lights went out a few minutes later. They sat around the kitchen table while they waited for the storm to pass and the electricity to be restored.

"I sure hope this doesn't last past dark," Becca muttered.

"It probably won't. Why? Are you afraid of storms?" Ryan asked her.

"No…I had…I had something I wanted you to help me do."

Ryan couldn't help grinning.

She blushed. "Um, I wanted to do a little recon work. And I'd promised my dad I wouldn't go off by myself."

His interest was piqued now.

"What kind of recon work?"

"Remember that farmer you said had tried herbicides without any success?"

"Yeah. The kinds he used should have worked, theoretically. They're common enough, but they're pricey. I was going to try them, but when he told me not to bother, I didn't see any reason to lay out capital for something like that."

"This farmer—is he like Murphy or the other ones you'd mentioned? Tate or Oliver?"

"Hmm, I wouldn't put him in the same class as that. He usually doesn't pal around with Murphy. No, Martin's always seemed on the up-and-up to me."

"Ralph Martin?" Mee-Maw harrumphed. "Not so up-and-up. Mac rented him some land some years ago, and Ralph was mighty slow in paying him. Made all manner of excuses, but I sure saw him driving a brand-new shiny truck. Man can't pay his bills, that's one thing—we've all had hard times. But a man who *won't* pay his bills?"

"I've not heard any talk of him being in financial trouble, though, Mee-Maw. At least not recently." Ryan scratched his chin thoughtfully. "But I didn't know that he stiffed Gramps out of rent money. You've never mentioned it to me before."

"He *tried* to stiff Mac on rent money. Your granddaddy got it eventually. As for me not bringing it up before, well… No point in bringing it up if there's no cause to, now, is there?"

Becca broke in. "I wanted to go to Martin's farm—see if he has any leftover herbicide. Don't you keep leftovers?"

"Sure, if they won't expire before you use them again. Are you saying that you don't think he put it out?"

"Exactly. It's been done before—one of the more common insurance fiddles is just not to spray your crops. You save money on the front end by not buying the herbicide or insecticide, and the bugs and the weeds take care of creating the disaster."

"But I saw his men applying it. I saw the canisters on the back of his tractor with my own eyes. Mind you, now, I didn't get close enough to see what was coming out of the sprayers. I just… Man, I took him at his word. He's not usually cozy with Murphy and I had no reason to think…and at that point, honestly, I didn't suspect anything."

Becca frowned. "That vine had to gain a foothold somehow. When it was small and green it should have been killed off by whatever you put out."

"True. Once it gets bigger, then you have to kill the host plant, which is sort of like killing the goose with the golden egg. You get rid of the problem, surely, but you have no crop remaining."

"I'll bet that Martin's infestation came later, right?"

"Yeah. He swore it spread from my field and Jake Wilkes's."

Mee-Maw scoffed, "Right. That farm of his is six miles by way of the crow. Like that vine really jumped a state highway and hippety-hopped over to his place."

Becca regarded Ryan for a long moment, weighing her decision to involve him in her next move. She trusted him. She knew him. And she believed him when he said he wasn't a part of this scam.

She took the plunge. "I want to go there. Tonight. After dark. If Martin were on the up-and-up, he'd still have the containers."

Ryan stared at Becca for a moment. "You want to break in to his barn? His outbuildings? How is that going to help you get evidence?"

"Well…it won't, not anything that would stand up in court," Becca admitted, "but if I found something for the police to get a search warrant on, I could, ahem, fib a bit and say an informant gave me the heads-up. Ag-Sure would press criminal charges, but I can't go to them without confirming it first, though. If they went in and didn't find anything, it would be a PR nightmare."

"Becca, I don't know..." He hated his indecision, but this was breaking and entering.

"If I were ten years younger, I'd load up and go," Mee-Maw told Becca. "In a New York minute. Too bad I'm an old broke-down woman."

Mee-Maw looked meaningfully at him. "But Ryan here..."

Ryan put his hand to his face to shut out the I-mean-business light in Mee-Maw's eyes—and the pleading one in Becca's.

"Oh, all right," he groused. "I can't fight you both. Tag-team effort. What am I getting myself into?"

CHAPTER SIXTEEN

Two hours later, Ryan's agreeing to go with Becca looked like a moot point. Though the worst of the thunder and lightning had passed, the rain still came down in sheets and the lights still weren't on.

Becca thought she'd go stir-crazy cooped up in the house. She could hear the ticking of the clock in her head: one day almost all gone. She kicked herself for not tackling the Martin farm head-on earlier in the day, but she had wanted to scope it out first, then ambush Martin with whatever she'd found out.

Finally she gave in, closed her laptop with its perilously low battery and slipped outside on the front porch with a crocheted throw.

Becca stopped short when she saw Ryan stretched out on the front porch swing. He cracked one eye open, the screen door's squeaky hinge obviously heralding her arrival.

"Hey." Ryan's sleepy smile stretched wide. "Want to join me?"

He'd changed out of the jeans he'd worn earlier in the day, and now had on a pair of shorts.

"I didn't know you were out here. I just—"

"Brought a blanket, too. C'mere." He sat up then, the swing rocking under his weight. "There's room. I don't bite."

He smiled again, teeth flashing in the dimness. *Get hold of yourself. You don't need to do this now. You have an investigation to finish.*

"C'mon. You're not disturbing me."

Ah, but you're disturbing me. Another little battle played out in her head. *You are all grown up. Responsible. Professional. Surely you can sit on a swing beside an attractive man without losing it.*

Ryan stood up, crossed the wide porch planks and took her hand in his. He led her to the swing. "See? You have your side. I have mine."

But it was a snug fit and she was keenly aware of him. She remembered the kiss the night before—and the assurance she'd made to her dad earlier that she was not involved with Ryan.

Okay, so she'd fibbed. But what was one little kiss in the scope of things?

To fill the silence and avoid looking like a complete twit, Becca asked, "Does the sky look any lighter?"

"Wishful thinking. If anything, it's getting darker."

"But the storm's passed."

"Uh-huh." Ryan lay back against the corner of the swing and stretched out his arm across the back of it. "You look tired. Put your head on my shoulder. You can prop your feet on the arm of the swing there."

Without thinking, she did—and then realized that the feel of his muscled bicep along her nape was not sleep-inducing in the slightest.

Then he moved and the throw whooshed above her as Ryan spread it over her. His fingers tucked the crocheted cotton around her.

Keep things professional, remember? she told herself.

He leaned back so that she could settle once again against him. The swing swayed to and fro, and she closed her eyes and listened to the drumming of the rain on the tin roof.

Becca could almost persuade herself that nothing existed beyond this front porch, no investigation, no dodder vine. And if those obstacles weren't in her way, she'd reach up and give Ryan a—

And then, as if reading her thoughts, he kissed her, slow and sweet.

Just as suddenly they were showered in the blue-white fluorescent light of the yard's security light. They broke apart, startled, the spell broken.

"Well. Looks like our linemen have got us

juiced," Ryan commented, running a hand that she was glad to see trembled through his hair.

"The rain—it's slowed down to a drizzle."

Ryan chuckled. "Honey, just now, the whole world slowed to a crawl."

She didn't know what to say to that. An emotional connection crackled between them.

Sudden bumps and bangs drifted through the screen door—sounds of Mee-Maw up from her own nap and starting preparations for supper.

Becca felt suddenly shy and sheepish about what the kiss meant. She stood up and busied herself folding the blanket.

"So—" Ryan joined her and grabbed one end of the throw "—you still fired up about spying on Martin's chemical stash?"

The sudden change of topic made her hesitate for a moment. "Yes. If you'll go with me. Do you know where he keeps his herbicides?"

"Sure. In his back barn. I've helped him prep the containers for recycling."

"Is there a back way in?"

"Yeah…if you don't mind tramping through muddy grain sorghum. He grows it for food for the chickens he has."

"I'm game if you are. Mud will wash off."

"So why the 007 approach? Why not just go ask him?"

"He's under no obligation to show them to me.

I'm a private investigator, so I'm supposed to have permission to inspect. He can stall, delay, and all I can do is back off and give him time to dispose of whatever it is he's hiding. I probably won't find anything, but it's worth a shot."

"And if you find something interesting, you call up Ag-Sure, tell 'em you've…"

"I'd embroider the truth a bit. I'd tell them I had an informant who says there's evidence of fraud, Ag-Sure files charges, the local boys in blue execute a search warrant."

"You do this sort of thing often?"

She bit her lip as she laid the blanket down on the swing. "No. I don't usually break the law to close a case. My dad…now he's really more the 007 type."

Ryan looked doubtful. "I admit I'm not thrilled about this. At the best, we could get shot at with a double-barreled shotgun. At the worst, we might both end up in the clink."

"But you'll do it? You'll go with me?"

"I'll do it. We're outta there, though, at the first sign of trouble."

"Uh…I FORGOT TO ASK," Becca started in a nervous voice. "He doesn't have guard dogs, does he?"

They had paused at Martin's back fence, which they'd accessed by using a dirt track that ran along the edge of Jake Wilkes's property and alongside Martin's.

"What?" Ryan teased. "You afraid of a little ol' Rottweiler?"

"Are you kidding?" She froze, then made a decisive turn for Ryan's truck.

"Yes, I'm kidding. The only dog he's got is one that makes Wilbur look like he needs Ritalin. I would have talked you out of it if he'd had a dog like that."

"Okay. This is the field of sorghum you talked about? Where's the barn from here?"

"See that glint of light?" He pointed. "There. It's right between two fields. He uses it to store his chemicals so he doesn't have to haul 'em so far on his tractor."

"Let's go, then."

Ryan helped her over the fence, then walked beside her. "We could go a lot faster on the edge of the field," he said.

"Well, yes, but with all this rain, we'd leave tracks. They're not going to find footprints as easily in this sorghum."

"True enough. Shall we?" He offered his arm, and off they went, high-stepping it through the tall, grassy sorghum.

The kiss was still fresh in her mind. His touch still had the power to fluster her. For a moment it seemed as if they were two kids, bent on a little mischief, maybe a little kissing…

But then they came closer to the barn and Becca sobered. This was it. Right now she was only trespassing, but if the barn were locked, she'd commit breaking and entering.

Ryan halted her, put a finger to his lips. He leaned over and breathed in her ear, "I hear voices."

She strained to hear what he did. Scraps of a quarrel floated back to her. "Can we get closer?" she whispered.

They eased slowly through the grain. Once they'd cleared the slight rise in the middle of the field, Becca could see lights on in the barn and a truck backed up to the open double doors.

How close could she and Ryan get and not be seen? They had little cover in the sorghum field. The inky darkness had been their best camouflage so far.

She dared to go a couple of rows closer. Ryan tugged at her with an insistent hand and pointed to an outcropping of chinaberry trees along the fence bordering the field. She followed him, hoping that if they left tracks, later showers might erase their trail.

Here, they were close enough to make out more of the squabble—especially when a tall, lanky man came stomping out of the barn, followed by the unmistakable potbellied profile of Murphy.

"That's Martin," Ryan whispered.

Becca nodded and concentrated on the argument.

"I still don't know why we have to do this ourselves—and tonight," Martin was protesting. "I could have a couple of them Mexicans do it for me tomorrow. They ain't gonna tell anybody."

"No, they've screwed up enough already—they planted the vines too regular. It was fine with just the adjustor—I had him paid off and now he's retired. But then that Reynolds woman came sniffing around—it won't take her long to start checking everybody's backstock of herbicide. You're the only fool who bragged that nothing could kill the mess."

"Well, what was I supposed to say? MacIntosh was wanting to borrow from my supply—he'd seen my men spraying it. I knew plain water in those jugs wouldn't fool Ryan a minute if he got close to them—he used to sell the stuff."

Becca could feel Ryan stiffen beside her. His anger was palpable. He'd been played a fool, and he was mad about it. She lay a hand on his arm.

Her warning served its purpose. He nodded, though his jaw was hard and tight.

"It don't matter," Murphy was telling Martin. "What matters is that we've got to pour out every bit of water in these jugs and stack 'em up like you didn't get around to recyclin' 'em. Why'd you fill so many jugs anyway?"

"Because!" Martin shook his fist. "Because it seemed like a pretty good idea at the time—the water was free and I was using last year's jugs and I didn't want to run out and have somebody go hightailing it off to the feed store and ordering more of the real stuff. And you make all this talk about 'we' got to pour all the water out of the jugs, but I don't see you breaking a sweat. What's the big deal if someone finds water in last year's jugs anyway?"

"It looks suspicious. Just do it. I want to go home and go to bed. I don't dare leave until you get this mess cleaned up because you're liable to say forget it. And then tomorrow she'll waltz right in here."

"I thought Tate said he'd taken care of her."

"Tate! I told him to let me handle her. She ain't left yet. She's holed up at MacIntosh's farm. Found that out this morning."

Just then, something moved at Becca's feet. She tried to suppress a yelp of surprise as she jumped away from whatever it was. She reached up to steady herself on a low tree branch.

Raindrops showered down on them, and the wet leaves rat-a-tatted off one another in a louder than expected spatter.

Ryan put his finger to his lips and pointed. It was a scared little rabbit hopping off into the rows of grain that had startled her.

Becca's heart settled into a more sedate rhythm. But then Murphy said in a sharp voice, "Quiet! You hear that?"

He strode from the truck to the edge of the field, coming straight toward Becca and Ryan.

CHAPTER SEVENTEEN

MURPHY STOOD silhouetted on the edge of the field, watching, waiting. He shifted something in one hand that, Ryan saw, gleamed in the light streaming from the barn.

A gun.

Ryan's fingers ached to wrap around the trigger of a nice, comfy double-barrel shotgun. Here he and Becca were, spying on someone who had a million-plus bucks to lose—and they were caught without any cover between them and the truck.

Stupid. The whole escapade had been stupid— enlightening, sure. At least now Becca knew pretty much the whole score without Ryan having to tell her.

Well, not quite the whole score, but enough to get Mee-Maw out of hot water.

So, if they could get out of here alive, maybe this venture hadn't been so stupid after all.

The rabbit that had started the whole mess long-legged it across a couple of tufts of weeds. Ryan eased down to the ground. He scooped up a pebble or two and skipped them through the ankle-deep grass, just close enough to the rabbit to startle him.

It had the desired effect. The bunny bounced off, leaving behind him a shower of spattering raindrops off the sorghums.

To Ryan's relief, the tension in Murphy's frame dissipated.

"Rabbit or some other critter, I guess," Murphy hollered back.

But, apparently ever the cautious type, Murphy fired a warning shot off into the night sky. "That'll scare off whatever's out there." Then he turned and headed back to the barn. "C'mon. Let's get this show on the road. I want to get home."

Martin still grumbling, the two men disappeared into the barn. Ryan tapped Becca's shoulder.

"They won't stay out of sight forever. Let's get outta here."

HE DIDN'T FEEL SAFE until he had Becca over the fence and in the truck. The pickup bounced over potholes he couldn't see in the dark, but there was no way he was going to risk using headlights until he was well down the dirt road.

Once he flicked the lights on, it seemed to signal the same feeling of relief to Becca. She let out a huge sigh.

"Whew! That was a close one!"

"But you learned a lot, right?"

Becca grinned at him. "And I thought you'd fuss at me for dragging us out there. I was all set for a scolding."

"It was an incredibly dumb thing to do."

She became serious. "You're right. And it was pretty much in vain."

"What?"

"No way I can get Ag-Sure to move quickly enough to stop them from draining those herbicide containers. I didn't expect them to be here tonight. I was crossing my fingers that getting rid of the empty containers wouldn't occur to them for another couple of days. My intent was to scope out the place, get enough info to get a warrant and then go in there the right way."

"But we were there. We saw them—we could testify—"

"Yeah. And we were trespassing, too, something the defendant's counsel will be only too glad to point out. Fruit of the poisoned tree and all that."

Ryan slammed his fist down on the steering wheel in frustration. "But you know now that—" he ground out. "You're right. What was the point?"

She shook her head. "It was useful for me. It confirmed my theory, and that does a world of good for my confidence. I agree, it's frustrating to know they've already guessed my next move. I'd hoped to use Martin as leverage."

"Can't you still do that?"

"With the right pry bar and the perfect spot, I can move the world. But I'm fresh out of pry bars." Becca lolled her head back on the seat and closed her eyes. "Don't worry. I'm not giving up. They haven't emptied my entire bag of tricks. That was just the easiest one, the one most likely to work."

Ryan eased onto the paved road and turned the truck in the direction of home.

"Hey." Becca spoke up from the passenger side. "Where are you headed?"

"Home. Why? Is there some other mad dash you want to make through a sorghum patch?"

She laughed. "No. I, uh, just thought you and I could talk for a little. In private."

Ryan couldn't suppress the thrill that coursed through him at the prospect of having Becca all to himself. Juvenile of him, he knew, but still...

"Talk, huh?"

Again Becca laughed. This time, he was gratified to hear it had a nervous edge to it. "Yeah. Talk. Just talk. Although I have to admit I was enjoying our rain-delay activities."

"Did you now? It so happens—" Ryan turned the wheel of the truck and left the paved road "—that I know of a little place."

He parked the truck on the far edge of one of his fields, careful not to stop in any mud. He switched off the ignition and twisted in the seat to face her. Enough moonlight streamed through the windshield to illuminate her small, nervous smile.

"Come here often?" she asked.

"Not been since, let's see…high school? Maybe college."

"With a girl."

"Several different ones…at different times, of course. You?"

"Different field," she bantered. "If I'd known what a great kisser you were, I would have ditched the Hayseed Hank I had and moved over here."

"I'd have kept the truck warm for you, but I wasn't much to write home about."

"Oh, I think you were."

At her words, Ryan pulled her to him over the bench seat. "Well, I can always use more practice." He lowered his mouth to hers, kissed her.

He could kiss her for hours—well, maybe not hours, but longer than he'd ever wanted to kiss any other woman.

Ryan finally pulled back, broke the kiss.

"Wow." Becca's breath came fast and shallow. "I didn't… This wasn't what I intended. I really did just…"

She slid back to lean against the passenger door.

"That's your side of the truck. This—" she pro-scribed a circle with her arm "—is my side."

"I'll try to be good."

"I'm so disappointed to hear that."

"I said try. I might fail."

"Be still, my heart." Becca's face took on a more serious look. "I really did need to talk with you. It's hard, what I need to say, what I need to talk to you about, around Mee-Maw."

The switch in topics got Ryan's attention. "What could be hard to say around Mee-Maw?"

"I needed to talk with you about…J.T. And… your grandfather."

A wash of acid drenched his gut. "J.T.?"

"Yeah. Your grandfather's hired hand."

"Not just a hired hand." Ryan looked away from her, staring out through the windshield.

The cotton field stretched on for a country mile. He'd planted that cotton. It had been backbreaking work, long hours on a tractor from sunup to sundown and sometimes working past dark.

"Okay, so he was what? The farm's operations manager?"

Now Ryan longed for Mee-Maw—or something—to come along and interrupt them. But nothing that convenient intervened and he was forced to answer.

"You could say that. It's a fancy way of saying he was Gramps's right arm."

"Yeah. That's kind of what I thought. And J.T. just left. Just took off?"

"Why do you need to know about J.T.? He was gone long before that dodder vine ever sprouted."

"Was he?"

"Sure. Yeah. Didn't you know? He left the day after Gramps's funeral."

"What reason did he give—"

"Look, I don't know. I didn't talk to him, okay? He just…was there one night and gone the next morning. He didn't even bother to leave a note."

"Hey, Ryan. Easy. Don't get so worked up."

He struggled to get his agitation under control. "Sorry. I just—" Ryan cast about for some plausible explanation as to why the subject rattled him. "He cut out at the worst possible time. He left Mee-Maw without any help, okay?"

"Did you ever think maybe he did have something to do with this? Those dodder vines had to be transported into Georgia some way. And according to Charlotte, J.T. was from the part of Texas where they were having the most trouble with the dodder vine."

"I tell you—he was long gone. I planted that cotton. By myself, thanks to J.T. cutting out when he did."

"Charlotte said he had a criminal record. Grand theft auto."

"Charlotte talks too much."

"Why are you so angry?"

"I'm not angry. I just don't like to talk about him." Even to Ryan, it sounded lame.

"Look, nobody except Charlotte—not you, not Mee-Maw, not anybody on any of the neighboring farms—will talk about J.T. Every time I bring up the subject, nobody wants to talk about him. They don't know where he went. They don't know why. I think it's too big of a coincidence that a man with a criminal record vamoosed right before a plant explodes—a plant, mind you, that was abundant where he came from—a short time after he left. I'm like my dad, Ryan. I don't like coincidences. J.T. may have nothing at all to do with it. But a man doesn't run if he doesn't have something to run from."

Ryan worked this problem. How much to say to Becca without saying too much?

Before he could decide she continued with her questions. "It just makes me curious—the fact no one wants to talk about him. Did he leave on bad terms? Did he feel shorted in some way? Could he have come back and planted the vine as revenge?"

"Boy, you're sure into conspiracy theories. I'd love to hang all this on J.T., and the way you say it, it even makes sense. But believe me. He's not been back. He's gone. He's been gone. Leave it alone. Trust me, he had nothing to do with this."

"You can't be sure of that—unless you know

something you're not telling me. If you've been up front with me, if neither you nor Jack had anything to do with that vine being planted, then it has to be someone with easy access to your land. J.T. fits that bill, and you know it. Even if he didn't plant it, he could have seen something. He's the key. At least, I think so. But I can't be sure until I talk to him. We need to find him," Becca pleaded. "He may well be the link between Murphy and the vine."

"He could be wasted away in some bar, where he's been dead drunk for months, with no clue as to anything that's gone on here since he left."

Becca's mouth twisted with impatience. "I'm looking for him. You ought to know that. I told my dad that we needed to find this man, but it's hard to find a Texan with the initials J.T. when you don't know what they stand for! So help me out, won't you?"

"I don't know what they stand for. I barely knew the man."

"So you let an ex-con work with your elderly grandfather, live on the same property with your grandmother and you didn't know zip about him beyond that?" She laughed. "Right. Like I can believe that."

"Believe it or not. Gramps ran this farm. Not me. I asked him about J.T. when he hired him, and he assured me that J.T. was an honest, hard worker who did more than his share. Beyond that, Gramps didn't care."

"Ryan!" She touched his arm and he jerked away.

"Becca…you are so barking up the wrong tree here. Just leave it alone, okay. Leave it alone."

"I can't. And you know I can't. Ryan, when will you get it through your skull that I'm trying to help you? You've got some piece of information tucked inside you, and you are wrapped around it as tightly as any mama bear around her cub. Let it go…please. Trust me. I know what I'm doing."

He rubbed the bridge of his nose, felt weary down to the soles of his feet. He was so tired of carrying around this doubt, this fear.

He could tell her. He could tell her everything. Every suspicion he had. Every worry.

But it would be selfish. He wouldn't be thinking in Mee-Maw's best interest. He'd be doing it just to transfer the burden from his shoulders to Becca's.

And what could she do? She worked for an insurance company; she had to follow Ag-Sure's best interests. Not those of a widow who had spent nearly every waking day on this farm for well over half a century.

When he thought about it like that, it was an easy decision to make. With jerky movements, he fired up the pickup and slammed the transmission into gear.

"If you want to find J.T., then I expect you will. You're the expert. But all it will do is bring a world of pain down on Mee-Maw, so you can do it without my help. And I'd be obliged if you'd not bring up that man's name to Mee-Maw. Ever."

CHAPTER EIGHTEEN

HIGH-HANDED, stubborn...

Becca fumed inwardly, thinking of a thousand things she'd like to shout at Ryan, but he'd closed up as tight as a bank on Sunday.

Her phone vibrated in her pocket. With a groan, she remembered that she'd neglected to do her evening report to her dad.

In lieu of a greeting, she answered the call with, "I'm okay. I was just in the middle of something and—"

"Well, just get *out* of the middle of whatever it is and follow directions," her dad snapped. "Do you know where I am? In the front seat of the car, with the keys in my hand."

"Everything's...fine, Dad." She shot a glance at Ryan. For the first time this evening, she wished for some privacy so she could tell her dad the predicament she was in.

"What was so all-fired-up important that you took off a good five years of my life?"

She related what she and Ryan had just seen. Her dad made the expected growls about how foolish a risk they'd taken. "Good idea, though. A shame it didn't work out."

"I agree. Listen…about that hired hand…" She sensed Ryan stiffen behind the wheel. "Any luck?"

"No, not yet. But I've got a few strings left to pull if you think it's worth the trouble. J.T. was long gone before any of this unfolded. What makes you so sure he has something to do with this?"

"I-I can't give you all the details now, Dad. Can't you just trust me on this?"

He made an impatient noise in reply. "All right. I'll start doing a serious search for this guy. But we're going to have to justify it to Ag-Sure, or the head honchos over there will accuse us of running up billable hours, so you'd better get something to me in writing fast. E-mail me that and I need a full name and a social, or it's going to be hard going. Why can't you just get it from the MacIntoshes?"

"Uh…" How much could she say without Ryan understanding why she was talking about him? Zilch. "Tried that and failed."

"What? Then we really do need to turn up this guy."

"I'm going with Plan B in the morning."

"Didn't you say he had a girlfriend?"

"That's my Plan B."

"Good. Check her out. Any small thing might be the key, you know that."

Becca felt guilty about letting her dad loose on the hunt for J.T., but Ryan could have made it easier.

And he hadn't.

His reasons didn't hold one droplet of water. She knew he was hiding something—had every reason to suspect that it was J.T. behind the infestation and for some reason the townspeople were protecting him.

But why?

Ryan pulled up near Mee-Maw's back porch. He turned off the truck and slung himself out of it. Becca watched as he stalked across the backyard and up the steps.

Her heart twisted with regret. She was asking him to trust her, but wasn't he asking her to do the same for him when it came to J.T.? And wasn't she refusing?

Didn't he understand that she had to?

THE NEXT MORNING, Ryan still hadn't unbent himself out of whatever pretzel he was in over her questions about J.T.

Ryan's silence—and his refusal to meet her eyes over the cups of coffee they drank—worried her. Just when she'd convinced herself Ryan had truly been caught in a simple bad spot, he was deliberately obstructing her investigation.

Why?

"I'm going into town to talk to Charlotte," she announced over the grits she'd barely touched.

Mee-Maw nodded. "Good timing. I need a few things from town," she told Becca.

Ryan ignored Mee-Maw and gave Becca a less sanguine reply. "You're what? No, you're not. I can't spare time away to go with you, and you're sure not going alone."

"Why not? Murphy's not going to risk something in broad-open daylight. Both times he's tried something, it was at night."

Becca didn't want to admit how rattled she was at the prospect of braving the trip by herself, but a part of her was glad Ryan couldn't go. She'd figured—rightly it had seemed—that he'd need to catch up on his work and inspect the damage from the storm. What she needed was to talk to Charlotte—alone.

"Didn't you hear what I said, Ryan? I *said* I needed a few things," Mee-Maw interrupted as Ryan started to protest. "I'll be going along."

Becca suppressed a groan. Just what she needed. She genuinely liked Mee-Maw, but right now, more than anything, Becca needed to ask Charlotte some questions. Without Ryan. Without Mee-Maw. She needed the time to stare Charlotte down and make her cough up every suspicion she had about J.T.

Becca most certainly did not need to be chauffering Mee-Maw to the grocery store.

"Oh, all right," Ryan ground out. "No need in Mee-Maw getting caught in any cross fire meant for you. I'll take you."

For a moment, Becca was too angry to speak. Did he really think she'd let his grandmother wander into harm's way? Did he think Becca was some kind of Disaster Doris that brought hell raining down on anyone unlucky enough to be close to her?

Maybe he just doesn't want me to have time alone with Mee-Maw where he can't monitor the situation.

Mee-Maw drew herself up to her considerable full height. "No, sir, young man. You will hit those fields. Becca and I will get ready and head for town. If we don't dawdle, we'll be back for lunch. I'm too old to get on a tractor—which is why you're going to do that, and I'm going to do what I'm still able to do."

Then she rose from the table and carried her plate to the sink. The subject was clearly closed to further discussion.

I've got to learn how to do that, Becca decided. *When I do, the first guy I'll try it on is my dad.*

Her heart did a funny little skip as she added

to herself, *The second guy will be Ryan, so he'll tell me what he's hiding.*

MEE-MAW DID NOT CARE one whit for Becca's Mini Cooper. She sniffed as she arranged herself and yanked on her seat belt.

"Got to be one of them imports. Pshaw, they couldn't even figure out where the gauges go in the dashboard. Why would you buy something defective anyway? Or did you get it for a good deal?"

Becca's lips twitched, but she smothered the urge to laugh. She suspected that Mee-Maw was a lot worldlier than she let on. Probably the old woman simply pretended to be a country bumpkin to make sure people routinely underestimated her.

Something Becca had long since stopped doing.

She drew in a deep breath as she turned the car toward town. While she had Mee-Maw captive, she might as well dive in feetfirst.

"Mee-Maw, I really need to know some more about J.T."

Mee-Maw ceased her under-the-breath grumbling about the Mini Cooper's shortcomings. "J.T. again. Honestly, I believe you're a tad bit obsessed with that man, though I don't understand why. Is that what you and Ryan were in such a twist about last night? Land sakes, my screen door can't handle such door slammings as Ryan did when he came in. Knocked me clear out of a sound sleep, it did."

Becca resisted the urge to be sidetracked by Mee-Maw's evasive measures. She focused on the topic at hand. She needed some answers.

Gripping the steering wheel a little tighter, she said, "I'm not obsessed about J.T., but I think he might be vital to the investigation. I have to find him. You guys may not get your insurance money until—and unless—I do."

"Young people don't fight fair, you know."

For a moment, Becca was nonplussed by Mee-Maw's response. How was she not fighting fair?

But then Mee-Maw went on, "Don't let the sun go down on your anger, that's what we always lived by when I was comin' up. Me and Mac, we never went to bed before we worked out whatever problem was worryin' us. No sense in it, anyway. Wasn't like anybody was going to get any sleep. Ryan didn't, either, not last night. I could hear those springs of that ol' bed just a creakin' as he tried to get settled."

Becca pictured Ryan tossing and turning. A lump formed in her throat. Had he been upset over their fight? Or was he trying to figure out how to keep whatever secret he held from her?

If he'd just tell me—

Her frustration made her speak more sharply

to Mee-Maw than she should have. "Mee-Maw! Listen! Aren't you hearing me? I want to help! I want to, but I need—"

"I know, I know. Find J.T. What good it will do you, I don't know."

"Let's just say I have a theory that a man convicted of grand theft auto would be the type to make a quick buck."

"I'll just bet you're full of theories, a girl like yourself. I was at your age. I had life all figured out. But people ain't what they seem—and neither is life. Sometimes…sometimes you just gotta take second chances when you can get 'em."

Becca frowned at Mee-Maw's cryptic words. Had J.T. left to take a second chance? Or was she telling Becca that she was missing an opportunity for a second chance herself?

"I need his full name and his social-security number. You have that, don't you? You had to pay his social-security taxes, right?"

Mee-Maw slumped down in the seat. She closed her eyes. "That's a good boy, that J.T. He got in a scrape of trouble when he was younger. Some of his buddies stole a car, told him it was a new one that one of the gang had just bought. So they all went for a ride. It was J.T.'s turn to drive— they were all taking a turn behind the wheel, see. Only…when the police pulled 'im over, those so-called friends of his…well, they said it was all J.T.'s idea."

Becca had heard that sort of story before, but she supposed it could have happened that way.

Mee-Maw went on, "Can't get a real good job when you've served time in prison, so J.T. bounced around a bit. Found his way to us. He was good help. Really liked farming, had a talent for it. I didn't expect him to stay forever."

"Mee-Maw…"

"John Thomas. I got his social-security number at the house. But I can tell you, that boy knows how not to be found. If he don't want you to find him, you'll have to look mighty hard until you do sniff him out."

BECCA MANAGED to mute her protests—albeit with gritted teeth—as she pushed the buggy down the aisles of the grocery store behind Mee-Maw.

Mee-Maw poked, that was the only way to describe it. She'd pick things up, turn them over in her hands, make a comment about the products under inspection, then gently replace them on the shelves—label facing out, top dusted off.

She even troubled herself to straighten out a couple of little messes the stock boys had left.

It drove Becca insane. Ordinarily it wouldn't. Ordinarily she would have been charmed by Mee-Maw's shopping style.

Ordinarily Becca's dad wasn't packing up this very minute to come and take over the investigation.

Becca was resigned to the fact that her dad would, indeed, come south. But she didn't have to be happy about it—and she wasn't. She wanted to present him with good solid leads, a way of saying "See? I didn't need you after all. You could have stayed in Atlanta."

Mee-Maw managed to choose a suitable chicken to buy after she'd fussed over the conditions of the fryers in the meat case—much to the dismay of the market manager, who seemed to know her well. She sent a stock boy to get her an undented can of Crisco. She hefted a bag of flour into her cart. A few items later, she stopped at the dairy section, dropped a carton of whipping cream into her cart, inspected the eggs with a sniff of disdain.

Becca ground her teeth some more as she waited for Mee-Maw to dicker with the frozen-foods manager to see whether he would like some farm-fresh eggs—he would—and what price he'd be willing to pay for them—not enough, in Mee-Maw's opinion.

At the checkout, she waited still longer for Mee-Maw to carefully glance at her register tape to make sure the total had been tallied correctly. Becca refrained from tapping her foot while the store manager came and cleared up a small discrepancy in the bill.

Outside, after the bag boy had carefully stowed the groceries in the car and admired the import, Mee-Maw settled herself back in the passenger seat.

"Well, now. That didn't take too long, did it?"

Becca decided her aunt's advice—not to say anything if you couldn't say something nice—was appropriate for the situation.

Mee-Maw didn't seem to notice Becca's continued attack of muteness. "I expect," the old lady said, "you want to talk to Charlotte. She ought to be just getting off—I think I timed it just right. That Nell Evans—she owns the diner—don't like people chatting up the help on the clock."

Becca twisted in the seat, her hand on the gearshift. She gaped at Mee-Maw. She'd poked in the grocery store so that Becca could have time to talk with Charlotte?

Mee-Maw's face split into a wide grin. "Had you goin', didn't I? I called Charlotte right before we left. She said to meet her at the diner after she got off this morning."

She closed her eyes, still smiling. "Being that you didn't blow up on me during all that shopping, I can tell you'd be right-good granddaughter-in-law material if that's what you were after. But no matter…time will tell on that subject. Still, if you can learn how to make my cream biscuits and a proper fried chicken for that stubborn ol' grandson of mine, I expect you'll get whatever help you need out of Ryan. Now, hurry up. Charlotte's not going to hang around forever, and I don't want my milk to sour."

CHAPTER NINETEEN

CHARLOTTE HOOKS MET THEM in the diner's parking lot. She wore her white poplin uniform and a worried expression on her face.

She didn't wait for Becca to even close the car door before she asked, "Is J.T. in trouble? Is he okay?"

Becca and Mee-Maw had pulled up to the rear of the diner, where the help used the back door for access. A battered old picnic table and a smoker's urn beside it had been left as a designated smoking area.

Mee-Maw got out of the car stiffly and made her way to the table's bench.

Terrific, Becca thought, *I've got an eighty-four-year-old sidekick who might just have an interest in making sure I don't find J.T.*

Charlotte still peppered Becca with more questions. Obviously she'd misunderstood Mee-Maw on the phone and thought they knew J.T.'s whereabouts.

"Whoa. Wait." Becca held up a hand to halt Charlotte's onslaught of questions. "I haven't found J.T.—not yet—but I'm looking for him. I was hoping that you could help me with that."

"Finally!" Charlotte plopped down beside Mee-Maw. "I've been worried sick about him and nobody seemed to be concerned. He wouldn't have run off without telling me where he was going—or at least, that he was going."

"He didn't tell you?"

"No. He…he left me a note. That's all. Said that he had to go off for a while and that he'd try to get back. Said it might be some time before he could call. Not to worry. *Not to worry!* How could I do anything but worry?"

"So he came by your house? Or here? When? The day after Mr. Mac's funeral?"

"No. He must have left sometime during the night, after they buried Mr. Mac. He left the note with Mee-Maw."

Mee-Maw nodded. "Yes, indeedy. Had Charlotte's name on it, so I called her after I found it and gave it to her."

"And no warning? No hints about it beforehand?"

Charlotte chewed on a hangnail on her thumb. "Well, he'd been plenty preoccupied about something for a while before Mr. Mac passed. J.T. wasn't much to share his troubles. Some guys, you know, they're like that."

Boy, do I ever. J.T. and Ryan must be cut from the same cloth.

"You don't know what he'd been worried about?"

Charlotte shook her head. "I thought maybe Mr. Mac had gotten sick or something. But all I know is that J.T. finally got so worked up, he had to drive out to Texas and he was gone a week. He said that would take care of it, but it didn't. He just got more and more worried."

"Family, I suspect," Mee-Maw butted in again. "J.T. had family near Odessa. Good place, Odessa. My cousin's people moved out there. Made a little money. 'Course, Maisey never saw 'em much, but that's one reason Mac hired J.T.—he could check him out with a couple of calls. Maisey's folks out there knew J.T.'s people."

Becca drew a different conclusion. A week would barely give him time to get to Texas, then turn around and drive back. He went to pick up something.

Three guesses what that was.

"Did he bring anything back with him? Any plants? Any seedlings? Any dirt, maybe?"

Charlotte shrugged. "Can't help you there. He came in late one night, and I didn't see him until the next day. Mee-Maw might be able to tell you."

Mee-Maw got a mild look of surprise on her face. "I certainly didn't inspect J.T.'s belongings.

If he brought anything like that back from Texas, he didn't tell me. Oh, wait…he did bring me something." She beamed. "He brought me some cornmeal that had been ground at a little mill near where he grew up. Fine cornmeal in an old-fashioned cloth bag. Made some good muffins from that meal. J.T. ate all but one."

"Do you still have the bag?" Becca asked her.

"Lord, no. It's been many a year since I had to save cornmeal and flour sacks. Don't rightly recall what the name of the meal was, either. The ol' brain's not what she used to be."

Becca turned back to Charlotte. She quizzed her on what sort of truck J.T. drove, what her memories of him were, asked for a picture of him.

Charlotte rooted around in her purse until she found her wallet. She flipped it open and pulled out a tiny strip of photos.

"J.T. took me up to Macon one Saturday." The waitress let a finger slide over the images. "Took me to the Olive Garden, let me wander all around that mall up there. There was a picture booth." She looked up at Becca. Her eyes were full of tears. "Can I get this back? It's the only picture I have of him… Of us."

"Sure. I'll get duplicates made somewhere and get it back to you." Becca held out her hand for the pictures, excited to get her first glimpse of the mysterious J.T.

But Charlotte held on to the photos. She stared at the images until one tear slid down her cheek. "He was the best thing that ever happened to me. We had plans, you know. He was gonna save up some money, maybe see about buying a little piece of Mr. Mac's land for our own farm one day. He was happy. He said I made him happy. He said after you'd been in prison, you didn't take happiness for granted anymore. That's—that's why I know he didn't just take off."

"I'll find him, Charlotte. If he's in trouble, I'll do what I can to help him, okay? That picture will be a big help."

Charlotte nodded. She sighed, caressed the photo one last time and handed it over to Becca.

The man in the photos smiled broadly in one image. In the next one, he was glancing down with clear affection at Charlotte—who was grinning into the lens. The last photo showed them cheek to cheek, looking very much in love.

Either he was a good actor, or this guy hadn't planned on leaving the happiness he'd found. Charlotte's and Mee-Maw's description of him had shattered any preconceptions Becca might have held—or that her father certainly held— that J.T. had been a no-good con who skulked around waiting for a chance at mischief. Becca kicked herself for her earlier cynicism. The first time she'd heard Charlotte say the phrase, *served time,* Becca had stereotyped J.T.

A truck drove past on the highway that ran alongside the diner. The driver braked abruptly and cut the wheel sharply to make a late turn into the parking lot. Gravel sprayed up, bouncing off the door of the truck—a door that read, Murphy Farms—Not For Hire.

The truck came to a sudden, shuddering stop and the driver's door flung open. Murphy's boots—still crisp and new with no trace of mud on them—hit the gravel. He came toward them.

"Miss Reynolds. I thought that was you. I'm surprised you're still around after what I heard happened to you at the motel."

Becca's stomach lurched. She managed to compose her face so that hopefully it wouldn't reveal exactly what she thought of the scum before her. "It takes a lot to scare me off an investigation, Mr. Murphy."

"I do like a woman who's dedicated to her work." The words and his tone seemed to contradict each other. "But I fear you're just wasting everybody's time. And by the way, I don't want you on my property talking to my tenants again, not without my permission. I'm particular about what happens on my land, Miss Reynolds. I don't appreciate you sneaking around."

"I had permission from the…tenants, sir. I'm not required to get a landlord's permission."

"You are if you want to use a private access road—or cross a field of mine. If you know what's good for you, you'll stay well clear."

"With threats like that, you're not helping your case, Mr. Murphy."

"I don't care what I'm doing. There is no case. I want my money. Now. I want you to get on the phone with Ag-Sure and tell them to start cutting my check or I'll sue. I'll sue Ag-Sure and I'll sue you…you know how that feels, don't you, Miss Reynolds? You know how that goes, huh?"

Her stomach rolled and pitched again. "Do what you must. I'm just doing my job."

"Come here, Miss Reynolds." He beckoned with one fat, stubby finger. "I've got something to show you."

She exchanged looks with the other two women, then crossed the gravel halfway to the still-rumbling truck.

Murphy reached in for a file folder on the passenger seat, then met her where she'd stopped. "Flip that open. Go on. Look at it."

She did as she was told. Inside, there was a past-due tax notice from several years previous on the property of one Hiram G. MacIntosh.

The amount due, with penalty and interest accrued: just over eleven thousand dollars.

"Mac MacIntosh didn't always pay his bills as you can see. That's the house—the one you're staying in, if I'm not wrong. Mrs. MacIntosh doesn't know about Mac letting this one slide. He worked it out on the sly with the county tax commissioner when ol' Mac couldn't pay both his fertilizer bill and his taxes. Right now the county's been looking the other way about this bill on account of Mrs. MacIntosh and her age, and the fact that Mac just passed not too long ago. That's the reason I wanted to have a word with you in private," Murphy said. He inclined his head toward the women, who sat out of earshot with concerned expressions marring their faces. "No need to worry Mrs. MacIntosh. Yet."

Becca hated the way the papers shook in her hands. She tried to protest that her own financial research on the farm had turned up nothing like this, but Murphy lobbed another guided missile her way.

"You'd better take a gander at the rest of what's in there, Miss Reynolds."

She did. The next thick stack was the transcript from the libel lawsuit. She felt ill at the memory of the humiliating cross-examination she'd endured at the hands of the plaintiff's attorney. Who knew why that jury had returned a verdict in her favor.

"You libeled a man, didn't you?" Murphy asked. "Got a story all wrong. You and your dad have kept this quiet, haven't you? Ag-Sure doesn't know about this. I'll just bet Ag-Sure's gonna believe your word over mine. Go home, Miss Reynolds. Pack up your bags and get out of this county. Or else you and your daddy are gonna lose your biggest customer…and Mee-Maw over there is gonna be crying when her farm is sold off on the courthouse steps."

IN THE CAR, Becca refused to tell Mee-Maw what Murphy had shown her. She needed to talk to Ryan first, see if he knew anything about the tax debt. Surely he would have some clue.

In her financial research, Becca had turned up the old tax lien, but it had been canceled. She'd been sure of that. If Mee-Maw hadn't been with her, she would have been on the phone with her dad, getting him to double-check the financials.

The whole episode with Murphy had left her as nauseous as she'd been right after the man had assaulted her in her motel room—Murphy had that same smug arrogance that he could have his way.

Charlotte had scuttled to her beat-up little compact the moment Murphy had slammed the truck door shut. "I need this job," she'd said. "And Murphy and the owner are in real, real tight, if you know what I mean. One word to her and I'm history. If you…if you find J.T., tell him that I love him—and that I still believe in him, okay?"

Becca helped Mee-Maw unload the groceries. Her brain was frantic in its attempt to work out how Murphy had managed to resurrect an old tax bill for leverage—never mind how he'd dug up her old skeletons. True, the trial was public record, but the transcript was available on file only at the Fulton County clerk's office. Murphy had gone to a lot of trouble.

She shoved milk and butter and cream, along with the chicken Mee-Maw had fussed over so, in the fridge.

"Mee-Maw, I need to make some phone calls, okay?"

Mee-Maw nodded, uncharacteristically quiet. Her own face seemed shadowed. "I was planning on showing you how to fry that chicken—unless you already know how."

"I'd like that, Mee-Maw, but later, okay? Maybe for supper?"

"Sure, child. I think—I think I'll just go lie down for a bit."

Out on the porch, Becca dialed her dad's cell-phone number. She spilled the story about Murphy to him.

"Already I hate this man," he told her. "I'm going to take him down if it's the last thing I do. He wants to play hardball? Well, he'd best bring his lunch."

"Dad, you've got to do some research on that tax bill—"

"It's not there. I know. I just went back over the financials—I, uh, was afraid you might have missed something."

"What?"

"Well…you seem pretty soft on this MacIntosh fella. I didn't… I just did a thorough checking over, okay?"

Becca was too overjoyed that Murphy had been bluffing to be angry. After all, what her father had done had been no more than what she had called to ask him to do. The fact that he hadn't completely trusted her stung a little—she could admit that. But knowing Murphy had been lying more than took away that sting.

"Good. I was afraid I was turning an old woman out of her house."

"Any more information on this J.T. fella?"

Becca relayed all that Charlotte and Mee-Maw had told her. "I've still got to get J.T.'s social-security number out of Mee-Maw."

"No matter, I can chase him down with this, though the social would be good. Get it to me later today, okay? I'll see you sometime tomorrow. You're still staying on the MacIntosh farm?"

"Yes, sir…I, uh, think they wouldn't mind you—"

"I got us rooms at the Holiday Inn in Dublin.

It's not far, and we've got a good Internet connection there."

Regret at this being her last night with Ryan surged through Becca. She couldn't stay without arousing her dad's suspicions that she was more than just a little "soft on this MacIntosh fella." Maybe Mee-Maw's irresistible hospitality would swamp her dad and pull him in.

No. Not likely. Unlike Becca, her dad was all business.

She rang off the conversation with her dad in time to see Ryan stalking across the fields.

He came to a stop a few yards from her. "I just got off the phone with Murphy. He called me. On my cell phone."

"Yes?"

"He's holding a tax lien over my head, do you know that? An old tax bill that Gramps didn't pay. I guess you turned it up, huh? Well, Murphy's saying either you go, or he'll force a foreclosure on the farm."

"No, Ryan, my dad says he's bluffing—it's not on your financials. I just double-checked."

"It doesn't matter. Murphy's brother-in-law is the tax commissioner. He's pulled a stunt like this before when Murphy's set his eye on a piece of property—that's what happened to Jake Wilkes's land. Suddenly this old tax bill comes out of nowhere, and just as suddenly you find yourself having to scrape up the money or see your place auctioned off. And guess…just guess who is, oh-so-willing to buy your land to ease your tax troubles?"

"Murphy," she whispered.

"Oh, yeah."

"But he can't do that, Ryan—"

"Oh, yes, he can. He *has*. That's what I'm telling you, Becca, what I've been trying to tell you. Things don't work here like they do in the big, bad city. Things happen to you here if you don't get along with your neighbors."

"But can't you prove—"

"I can't. No. I've torn this house upside down, inside out trying to find proof of payment for that tax bill and I can't. I know Gramps paid it—I know he did—but sometimes, when he got into a tight, he'd pay half of it and then pay the rest later. You could do that before everything was computerized. He probably paid the rest in cash."

"Can't you pay the tax bill? Borrow the money and—"

Ryan snorted in disbelief. "Bank's not going to loan me that money. Murphy's on the board of directors. Besides, it's their policy not to loan money to pay past-due debt."

He shook his head in disgust, his tall frame rigid with anger and frustration. "Neat, isn't it? Nice trap Murphy's got me in. I understand you're just doing your job and all, but it's putting me in a bad spot. So, Becca, you got a cool eleven grand I can borrow? 'Cause it's either that, or you need to hit the road."

With that, he turned and headed back to the fields.

CHAPTER TWENTY

YOUR LAST DAY. This is your last day.

The thought circled in Becca's brain like a hungry piranha, gobbling up all rational thought. This *was* her last day—her last day of solo investigation and her last day with Ryan.

One thing that had to be done, with Ryan or without: she had to search out Antonio, the "mayor" of Murphy's Little Mexico, as Ryan called it. She had to know what Antonio knew. It didn't take a rocket scientist to figure out that whatever he'd discovered about the dodder vine was what had launched Murphy into action.

In lieu of lunch, she wrapped a piece of bread around a slice of cheese and headed for her car. Yes, by going off without a bodyguard and planning to cut across the back way to where Murphy housed his workers, she was practically double-dog daring Murphy to jump her.

But she couldn't take a chance on him conveniently running off anyone with any answers. Migrant workers would not stick around if moving down the road would behoove them.

She parked the Mini Cooper in Jake Wilkes's yard and scouted the horizon for the hog farmer. His hogs were happily rooting in the mud of the pigpen, but Jake wasn't anywhere to be found.

Maybe that was good. Maybe he would find it easier to forgive her than to give her permission to tackle Murphy head-on.

Squaring her shoulders, she headed for the back fence. Today was as good as any to declare open war on Murphy.

A yell behind her halted Becca in her progress across Jake's field. She turned to see the old man waving her down.

They met halfway, near an old tobacco barn that looked as shabby and as run-down as the rest of Jake's farm. Her heart wrenched at the prospect of Mee-Maw and Ryan's place looking this run-down.

"Missy, you got your mind set on something, that's for sure," Jake told her between pants. "Didn't hear me until I hollered loud enough to wake up the dead."

"Sorry, I was just using your field as a cut-through to talk to Antonio—"

He nodded. "I figured. But you don't have to. Antonio sent one of them young'uns up here with a note for you. Said not to go back there, make it too hard on the lot of 'em."

The last little bit of hope within Becca shriveled, guilt swamping her. "Oh. I take it Murphy wasn't pleased about my last foray?"

"Nope, not a whit. Antonio said Murphy nearly turned 'em all out, but he settled on just upping their rent."

Becca compressed her lips. *What a jerk.*

"I don't suppose Antonio included anything in the message besides a warning?"

Jake shrugged his bony shoulders. "Wouldn't know. Don't read a word of Spanish 'sides *adios, amigo,* but it was a pretty long note. I just got it this morning—figured I'd call you when I went in to get me a bite to eat. Had to look after the hogs. Geraldine is feeling a mite poorly today, bless 'er heart."

Becca's hope soared again. "A long note, you say? Can I get it?"

"Sure. I got it put in the house. I'll just go get it."

A few minutes later, Becca smoothed out the yellow-and-blue-lined paper. It was filled with cramped hand-writing, all in Spanish with spotty grammar. She made a quick scan of it, translating it in her head as she went.

Senorita Reynolds, don't come back again. It is not safe, not for you, not for us. The boss has made it difficult for us after the conversa-

tion we had and after a few of my idiots decided not to listen to an old man's counsel.

Here he'd written something she couldn't quite
make out—possibly some idiomatic expression
about young people. She read on.

   The man you want is not here anymore.
A gringo brought the vines. We had nothing
to do with bringing it here. But a couple of
good-for-nothings of mine did the planting.
They are not here anymore. Naturally such
lazy men wouldn't want to do an honest day's
labor. The gringo did not work for my boss,
so I do not know him, but I think he is gone,
as well. This is not so helpful, I know. If the
two men who planted this vine were here, I
would...

Here again Antonio's cramped handwriting,
combined with his idiomatic Spanish, made it
impossible to be certain what his promise was
to those men. But Becca assumed that whatever
it was, it wouldn't be pleasant, not from his em-
phatic "and then they would surely tell you what
you needed to know."
He ended with another plea for her to leave
them alone, unless and until, Murphy could no
longer coerce them, but at that point, she knew

the whole bunch of Antonio's people would have moved on.

Would Murphy really turn out the migrant workers right before the last of the farm's big push to harvest?

Of course he would. He never meant to harvest that crop anyway. For a million bucks in insurance money, he was the type to turn out his own mother. To him, what was a few migrant workers who live in substandard housing? The bulk of the migrants had already moved on, anyway.

"Any help?" Jake asked.

"Some. It confirms a few things for me. I just wish…"

"Aw, now. I can see it. You want to go talk to Antonio. Let me tell you, you won't find a peep of a living creature down there if they don't want you to. 'T'ain't no good in it. 'Sides, you're just askin' to meet up with the wrong end of a shotgun— Murphy's shotgun. He done warned me not to be letting people onto his land. Now, I don't take orders from no man, but some things, they're just flat foolish. If Antonio can help you some more, he will. You can count on it."

Becca bit her lip, considering. Her instinct was to agree with Jake. If she didn't push Antonio, depending on his immigration status, the old man might be a really good witness if this thing ever went to trial—civil or criminal.

But she had to take Murphy down first.

That meant finding J.T.

And whatever else Ryan might be hiding from her.

She glanced at her watch. Half past one. She had a good half day left...with no good leads that her dad hadn't already started pursuing.

She'd spend the remaining part of the day trying to convince Ryan to trust her.

Or if he couldn't find it in his heart to trust her...

Then saying goodbye.

"THAT'S RIGHT, that's right...salt and pepper. You dip that chicken into them eggs. Then the buttermilk. Right, right...now you dredge it in the flour."

Mee-Maw supervised from a spot at the kitchen table while Becca tried to follow her directions.

"Mee-Maw, this is a lot of work for fried chicken," Becca complained.

She was elbow-deep in flour, a platter of raw chicken still waiting to be double-dipped and dredged in the stuff. A huge cast-iron frying pan filled with shortening was heating on the stove.

"This ain't *any* chicken, honey. This here is my say-I-love-you chicken. This is what got me out of every bit of hot water I ever got into with Mac.

He had a mighty stubborn way of holding on to grudges, my Mac did."

Say-I-love-you chicken. Do I love Ryan? It's not like I've just met him. I know him—the parts of him he'll let me know. So I love the parts I know— and I'll take a chance on the rest...if he'll take a chance on me.

Focusing on the project at hand, Becca started the complicated and onerous battering process with a short thigh. "So...your husband was stubborn? Like Ryan?"

"I see a lot of my Mac in Ryan. Course, Ryan's more progressive-thinking. Mac was a good man, but he'd never trouble himself to wash a dish or change a single solitary one of my babies' diapers. Still, I'll eat my best gardening hat if Ryan won't soften up with this chicken."

"Guess it must have hurt to lose him, huh? Mr. Mac, I mean?"

The light in Mee-Maw's face faded. "Nobody's got a clue how much. I thought I was prepared— you don't get to be my age and not think about how you might be in tomorrow's obits. But when J.T. came up that afternoon with Mac in the back of the truck...I knew. I knew when I saw that truck coming up before sundown. But I wasn't... prepared, you might say."

The old woman sagged in her chair at the kitchen table and rubbed at an imaginary speck on the vinyl tablecloth. "I wake up every morning and it's always this awful jolt of surprise that Mac's not there beside me. No, you don't ever..." She shook her head. "Jack tried to get me to sell this place after J.T. left. Wanted me to move into town. Town! Maybe I would get a ton of money for this place if I sold it to the likes of Murphy, but I'd never be happy anywhere but here. Mac worked this place out for me, gave me anything I ever wanted—he was a good man, a good husband. No, that's my one comfort. I can look at everything here, and everything I see...it's something that Mac loved."

How would it be, Becca wondered, to be with the love of your life all your life?

Was the love of *her* life out in the very fields that Mee-Maw's love had tended and wrestled into productivity for the first time over sixty years ago?

MEE-MAW HELPED her pack up a big picnic basket of the fried chicken, potato salad, butter beans and the biscuits they'd baked. After she'd tucked in a jug of tea and a stack of paper plates and plastic forks, Becca hefted the basket up in one hand.

"I never thought I'd be toting a picnic to a guy," Becca said.

"And what's wrong with it? 'Tain't nothing. It's not like you're gonna turn into a meek little doormat who'll be fetching his tea and taking off his shoes. Pshaw! I can't see you doing *that* for no man. Now, go on. Sun's setting and that man had not two bites of lunch today. He's probably hungry."

So Becca left Mee-Maw munching on her own chicken and headed for the barn. The tractor, though, was tucked into its usual spot.

Underneath it, jean-clad legs stuck out—along with a hand fumbling for a socket wrench. Wilbur looked up from where he was curled up nearby and thumped his tail.

"Ryan?"

Ryan froze, then slipped out from under the tractor. His icy-blue eyes regarded her in silence.

Becca swallowed past the lump in her throat. "Hey. I cooked you some supper."

She indicated the basket.

Ryan didn't say anything for a long moment. "Becca…look, maybe I could have said things differently today—"

She held up her hand. "Wait. Let's…let's call a truce, okay? Let's not talk about Murphy. Or that dodder vine. Or the investigation. Let's just find a spot to eat this…and talk."

"Talk, huh?" Some of the wariness faded from his expression. "I was just finishing up here. The tractor broke down on me. It's been awhile since

I've had a picnic, but I could do with a break. What's in there?"

Becca felt herself blush. "Mee-Maw's fried chicken."

Ryan raised his brows. "Mee-Maw makes two kinds of fried chicken. So, which recipe did you use?"

Her face heated up even more. "Um, she didn't…it was the one with the eggs and all."

"And you don't remember what she called it?" The corners of his eyes crinkled.

"Hey, you want this chicken or not?"

"Sure. But I want to hear you say it. The name."

"I don't recall," she mumbled, still blushing furiously. "Happy now?"

"I'd be happy with KFC…but I've died and gone to heaven with Mee-Maw's chicken."

Wilbur, too, looked interested in the chicken. He snuffled at the basket, ignoring Becca's attempts to keep it out of sniffing range.

As Ryan washed up in the barn's rough sink, Becca said, "I thought we'd go down by the pond, spread out a blanket."

"What do you say to pulling up a nice bale of hay, instead?" he asked, drying his hands.

"Here?"

He pointed to the dim recesses of the barn's rafters and grinned. "Unless I put Wilbur in the house, he's going to drive us crazy with begging.

Besides, where else is a good old boy going to take his date down on the farm? Won't you step into my hayloft, ma'am?"

Becca chuckled. "Looks mighty full of hay."

"The hay's just a cover. Living here with Mee-Maw took some getting used to. This is my thinking place. When I need to worry over something or think something through, I just climb up there and wait until the answer comes."

"I'm in need of a few answers." That lump in her throat had come back. "Will your thinking place work for me?"

"Only one way to find out. Here. Let me take that." Ryan relieved her of the picnic basket, then negotiated his way up the hayloft's ladder with the basket. Becca followed him.

"Well? What do you think?"

She looked around the hayloft before answering. A big tattered blanket covered a thick layer of hay on the loft's floor. A stack of books and an old pillow were by a bale of hay.

Becca shook a mock-stern finger at Ryan. "So this is where you've been hiding out when we've been thinking you were hard at work," she teased.

"Nope, scout's honor. So…that chicken? You about ready to eat?"

"Possessed with a one-track mind, aren't you?" She grinned.

"More like a one-track stomach. I can't believe you fried me chicken."

"Well, I don't know how good it's going to be. Save any compliments until you taste it."

They settled down on the blanket, the basket between them. Ryan dug out the containers of food. "Wish I could offer better than a hayloft—"

"No, no…it fits. Really. This *is* your special thinking place, after all, not just any hayloft."

Ryan paused in spooning vegetables on Becca's plate, his expression full of amazement. "You really don't mind, do you? That's what I like about you. You understand my way of thinking."

"I know you love this place. This farm."

"I do." Ryan finished up with Becca's plate, topping it off with a biscuit. He handed it to her. Their fingers brushed and Becca felt her face heat again.

He picked up his plate and frowned. "I never knew," he said, "how stifled I was until I came back here. A suit and a tie—even a button-down shirt, are just too restrictive. But here I'm free. I'm not lying, now. It's hard work, and I worry a lot, but I love what I do. I don't mind getting up in the morning. It's what I've wanted to do since I was six years old. I never want to work anywhere else again."

They ate in silence, except for Ryan's appreciative mumbles over the chicken and the potato salad and the beans.

"So, did you want to grow up to be an investigator?" Ryan asked.

The question caught her off guard. "What?"

"It's your turn, remember? This—" he indicated the supper and the hayloft with a sweep of his hand "—was supposed to be like a date, right? So I want to know about you. All about you."

Becca's supper suddenly transformed itself into a heavy brick in her stomach. What if she said something to Ryan that would reveal he knew her alter ego?

CHAPTER TWENTY-ONE

"DID YOU HAVE the magnifying glass and the little-kid detective kit when you were six? Back when I was tooling around on a toy tractor?" Ryan didn't seem to realize that she had tensed at his questions.

"Uh, no. I didn't know what I wanted to be. An astronaut, I remember that. And, um, let's see…a doctor who discovered the cure for cancer."

"Aimed high, didn't you?"

"I guess. I wound up going to college and majoring in journalism. So I guess I wanted to be the next Woodward or Bernstein. But…it didn't happen."

"No?" Ryan took another bite of chicken.

"I worked at the *Atlanta Journal-Constitution* for a while, and then with the Associated Press for a bit longer—loved the travel—but then I started my own magazine. I'd been at it for maybe two years and was making some real headway in my initial loan when—" She broke off. The memory of the lawsuit and the misery it had brought down on her still stung.

"Yeah?"

"A guy didn't like a profile I'd done. Said he thought it was supposed to be a puff piece, but…it was part of an investigative series, you see. I was really good at investigative journalism. He sued me. It took me two years to fight it, but I won. I even won a countersuit for defamation—a half million dollars."

"So why are you working with your dad?"

"Advertisers started dropping like, well, like flies. The judgment I won is tied up in appeals courts. I couldn't pay the staff, couldn't pay the rent. Couldn't pay much of anything there at the end. I had to shut the doors and file for bankruptcy. Hardest thing I ever had to do. Lost pretty much everything."

"Then that's how you know."

"What?"

"You…I've wondered from the start why you seemed so determined to help us. I've known investigators in the past—I mean, investigators from insurance firms—and they're nothing like you."

"You make it sound like a compliment."

"I meant it like that."

"My dad…" She put her plate down and pushed it aside. "My dad wouldn't."

Ryan reached over, touched her face. "Just because you have a heart and a sense of compassion doesn't mean you're not good at your job.

You're very good…at everything. Including frying chicken."

Over the basket, he met her lips in a kiss. Then he sat back, a dazed look in his eyes.

"Whew," Becca murmured. "Mee-Maw's say-I-love-you chicken really does work as advertised."

"Thought you didn't know what she called it," he teased. "As good as the food is, it's the company, not the menu."

Becca didn't answer. She couldn't help thinking how things would change tomorrow. She knew that with her father around, she'd have to protect her heart a bit more. Her dad would frown on the way she was so free with Ryan. Never let your guard down around a target, her father had told her.

She'd let her guard down, all right. She'd let Ryan steal away with her heart.

"Hey," Ryan said, "are you afraid of the dark? I want to show you something, but I have to switch off the lights to do it. Will you be okay?"

Becca smiled. "I trust you." She stowed the rest of the dishes in the picnic basket and moved it to one side.

Ryan scooted down the ladder. "Here goes!" he warned from below.

With a loud click, the barn went black. She heard Ryan come back up the ladder. "Wait just a bit for your eyes to adjust," he said, "and let me unlatch this… No, close your eyes."

"This must be some sort of whamdoozler of a surprise," she commented, but she closed her eyes anyway.

A moment later, she felt the night air on her face. "Can I open them? What are you doing?"

"Okay, you can look."

Becca opened her eyes to see an open access panel, and beyond it, stars studded the evening sky, which seemed to stretch on forever.

"Oh, my. Oh, my…that is so beautiful."

"I can't afford to give you the real thing, but a sky like this, well, it's a country boy's diamonds."

The Atlanta skies were never this clear, this bright with stars. She couldn't remember the last time she'd seen a night full of constellations glittering down at her.

"See? There's Casseiopea. That's the first constellation I could ever find. And see the Big Dipper? And the Little Dipper, too." Ryan held up her hand, tracing out the pattern the stars had made. "And there's the North Star."

"I always thought the North Star was supposed to be this huge bright star. I have to admit, I was a little disappointed to find it was such a dinky thing."

Ryan, his profile lit by starlight, shook his head. "The North Star's special because it stays in one spot. You can count on it being there to guide you. It stays true."

"So…who's been your North Star, Ryan?"

"Gramps, I guess. And Mee-Maw. My parents are great, don't get me wrong. But I always felt like I was born in the wrong generation. My dad couldn't wait to leave the farm behind—I never could figure out what his hurry was. The closest he ever got to a farm was teaching agricultural courses at Abraham Baldwin. My mom was a city girl. They're perfectly happy cooped up inside the city limits of Tifton. I guess one reason that Gramps would be my North Star is that…he did stay true. He did—"

Something broke in Ryan's voice then and he fell silent. Becca chose not to push any harder on something that seemed so raw within him.

"What about you?" Ryan asked finally.

"I guess…my aunt Mala. She had her own way of doing things, but she practically raised me. My dad loved me as best he could, but he didn't count on being left with a little girl to bring up on his own."

"What about your mom?"

A pang of sadness tore through Becca. "She… died when I was five. I barely remember her— just, little fragments, you know? She was…happy. I remember her being so full of life. It freaks me out to think that I'm older than she was when she died. My Aunt Mala, Dad's sister, came to live with us after that."

"Well, your aunt Mala did a fine job."

"Of what?"

"Bringing you up. You...you could be a North Star for me."

Becca's mouth went dry. She wasn't sure what to say. She closed her hand over Ryan's fingers. "Why do you say that?" she whispered.

"Because...my heart keeps telling my brain that you understand a guy like me. Maybe it's the way you don't seem to mind being on a farm. City girls, you tell 'em about the seven-day work-weeks and the long hours, let 'em get a whiff of diesel fuel and they're outta there. Even a lot of country girls—they're so ready to hit the big city they'll grab on to the first guy on his way out of town. But you..." He looked her full in the face now, his fingers sliding up into her hair. Without asking, he loosened the ponytail she wore. "You seem to fit here. You don't even mind Mee-Maw."

"I love Mee-Maw. And I..." She couldn't get the words out. She was afraid saying what she felt would break the spell. Instead, she satisfied herself with, "I love it here. I love the rhythm of country life."

"See? Who else would get that?"

Somewhere close by, an owl hooted, its lonesome call punctuating the feelings overflowing in Becca's heart. Whoooo. Whoooo.

Who else but Ryan would I feel this comfortable with? Who else would I belong with?

CHAPTER TWENTY-TWO

BECCA DIDN'T START to worry the next morning until she realized that Ryan wasn't at breakfast—and that the tractor was still in the barn.

They'd parted with a sweet kiss at her bedroom door. She'd felt sixteen again, slipping in past curfew. Maybe that's what she liked most about Ryan—he made her feel as if she had a fresh, clean start on life.

But this morning, with no Ryan at the breakfast table and a tractor still cold in the barn, she wondered if perhaps he'd had second thoughts. She even went so far as to peek into Ryan's "thinking place."

The hayloft was empty.

Even Mee-Maw looked worried. Becca brought in the basket of eggs from the chicken coop to find her on the porch, scanning the horizon for some sign of Ryan.

"Y'all didn't fight any more, did you?" Mee-Maw asked Becca. Then she waved away the question. "Listen at me, soundin' like some ol' busybody gossip. I don't need to know that."

"No, Mee-Maw…we, um, we had a really good talk."

"He must have his mind on something. I hope he's not off moping at Mac's grave."

A chill went through Becca at Mee-Maw's anxious speculation. "Is that bad? Does he do that often?"

"When he needs to work something out in his head or when he's fretting about something."

"Wh-where…"

Mee-Maw stretched out one gnarled hand and pointed. "See up there? That rise with the thicket of trees? That's the family plot. You might find him up there."

Becca hesitated. "What if he doesn't want me to butt in?"

"You can always leave him alone, right? But I'd sure like to know he's okay."

Becca nodded and started down the steps. "Me, too, Mee-Maw."

The morning air was soft and cool but with a hint of the heat that would come. Becca trekked up the rutted dirt track leading up the hill that Mee-Maw had indicated.

She slowed when she came to the first of the trees. A bit farther, Becca stopped at a low brick wall, within which crumbling headstones stood silent. The only sound was a sassy mockingbird high up in a gigantic live oak tree. Its broad branches sweeping low and wide, the tree stood like a guardian over the cemetery, casting a dim shadow over the area.

Becca swept her eyes over the markers and graves. She saw no hint of Ryan from where she stood. Seeing an open gate in the wall farther down, she took a few steps toward it.

Now she could hear something—someone had started speaking.

Ryan.

Becca picked her way through the graves and around the oak tree. Ryan crouched ahead of her at the end of a grave in a newer part of the cemetery. The hill, she could see, dropped off sharply. From this vantage point, the farm's acreage spread out in a panorama of morning sun, in stark contrast to the family plot.

Her breath caught at the peacefulness of that view, and the way Ryan was kneeling.

Part of her wanted to turn and walk away. She didn't belong here, not now. She felt guilty for intruding on this moment. Surely, though, he'd heard her.

If he had, he gave no sign. He went on talking in an almost conversational way.

"—don't want to let you down, Gramps. I need to do right by Mee-Maw, but…I don't want to do this by myself anymore. I think maybe you'd tell me it was okay." Ryan's shoulders and taut back muscles moved under his T-shirt as Becca saw him drag in a deep breath. "I'm thinking Jack's wrong and we should tell her. What do you think?"

Ryan fell silent.

For a moment, Becca almost expected to hear a response—crazy, she knew. Still, the way Ryan had spoken, it was as if he'd been talking to a real live flesh-and-blood person.

Only that sassy mockingbird sang a reply, though.

Then Ryan rose to his feet, his back still to her, and spoke again. "I still miss him. Still can't believe he's gone. I expect you think I'm a nut job, Becca, talking to a dead man like he'll answer back."

She jumped at the sound of her name. So he had known she was there all along.

Becca joined him. She stared down at the smooth granite. then closed her fingers around Ryan's. "Did he?"

"Hmm?" Ryan met her eyes and reached over to tuck a strand of hair behind her ear. "Answer, you mean?" He shook his head. "Nope. Not that I could hear. But that's just like Gramps. He liked you to figure things out for yourself."

Becca thought of her dad, who had a similar outlook on life. "I know a guy like that."

"I pretty well had my mind made up before I came up here. I just needed…to talk it through."

"Okay, then." Becca's heart thrummed in her ears. She gave Ryan's fingers an encouraging squeeze. "I'm ready to listen."

"I figured you already had it sussed out. You know about the tax bill. You know that J.T. was from Texas. And you know…you know that I worked for an ag-chemical company."

"I've been trying to fit the puzzle pieces together for a while, Ryan, and I'm still missing a piece or two."

He let go of her hand and crossed over to the brick wall before sitting down heavily. "Well, I started the whole mess."

Becca went still for a moment, her mouth dry, her brain focusing on Ryan's words. A tremor of doubt quaked through her.

Her feet moved of their own accord, closing the gap between them. Ryan grasped her hand and pulled her down to sit beside him.

For another moment, Becca couldn't force out the words. It was all she could do to inhale a breath of the damp, mossy air.

"How?" she asked. "How did you start it?"

Please, don't let him have come up with the idea, please, please—

"Stupid. I was a stupid idiot. I'd come home for a visit—I'd been out to Texas, consulting with some of the farmers who were dealing with the vine out there. Gramps and I were at the feed store, and somebody was bellyaching about how slow the drought disaster-relief money was coming in."

Becca stayed quiet and waited for Ryan to continue.

He traced one of the gaping cracks in the mortar with his finger, picked up an acorn and used the point to doodle first a heart, then savagely cross it out. "I told 'em, 'be glad you weren't like those folks out in Texas. Sure, they had checks in their hands overnight, but they were at a complete loss about how to even plant next year's crop.' I said—" Ryan closed his eyes as if in pain "—I said, 'You want a slam-dunk insurance settlement? You just find a few dodder vines in your field.'"

Relief pulsed through Becca—and a little shame at doubting Ryan. Her heart settled into a less painful rhythm as she waited for Ryan to divulge the rest of his story.

"So the next day or so, Murphy comes schmoozing up to me at a Rotary meeting Gramps had dragged me off to—Gramps liked to show me off. I was the boy who'd gone off to college and done him proud, you know? He was proud of his grandsons, me and Jack." Ryan's mouth twisted.

"Yes?" she prompted when he didn't go on.

"Murphy was full of questions about the vine. I thought he was just…making conversation. He asked me, wasn't J.T. from that area of Texas? I told him I thought so."

Ryan shook his head, a disgusted look on his face. "I gave it to him all—the means, the method…even told him who knew where to get it."

"But you didn't mean to, Ryan. You had no idea that he'd twist what he learned—"

"It didn't matter. I shouldn't have trusted Murphy. I just, well, he looked successful, and he was always talking about how farmers had to move with the times."

Ryan shook his head again. He slapped his palms down on the wall in frustration. "Can't be undone. Guess I can't waste time worrying about it, can I?"

"So that's the big secret? That's what you've been worried about? That the federal government will haul you off to the federal pen because you mentioned the dodder vine to Murphy?"

"No."

Ryan rose to his feet and paced restlessly. He kicked at a half-buried rock in the grass until it came free. Then he picked it up and hurled it over the wall and down the hill.

"Then…what?" Becca guarded her heart. No more doubt. She would not doubt him anymore.

She knew this man. She knew him better than she knew most any person on this planet.

"For one thing, I kept my mouth shut, Becca. That has to make me complicit, right? When I saw that dodder vine…well, at first, I thought it was some sort of horrible coincidence. But then…it was too convenient. You saw it—I mean, it practically screams *scam* at you."

"Okay, I agree, it doesn't look good. But if you come forward with what you know…if you help me find J.T.—"

"If I help you find J.T., Mee-Maw may finish out her days in that federal prison you were just talking about."

"What?" The word came out strangled, harsh, even to Becca's ears. "What do you mean? What does Mee-Maw have to do with this?"

"Gramps is dead. So… This is scary. Telling you. Jack is going to kill me."

"What about Jack? Does he—"

"No. I told you…just…I know I'm slow telling this, but just let me get it out. And then…well, then you can decide what to do."

Becca nodded. "Sorry. I… Well, go on."

He didn't for a long moment. Ryan compressed his lips and looked as though he was trying to figure out just what to say.

"When I first spotted the vine, I called all the farmers around, notifying them. I wanted to report it then—you know, through the usual channels so that other farmers in the area would have a jump on it. Murphy came out to see me. I thought he was dropping by for some fatherly type advice. I was still pretty new at everything, even though I'd helped Gramps for years." He stopped, a sick expression on his face.

"I take it Murphy had something else in mind."

"Oh, yeah. Like telling me that Gramps had agreed to send J.T. back to Texas to bring the vine to Georgia. He has pictures. Took 'em on his cell phone. Gramps. J.T. By J.T.'s truck—with J.T. holding the vines up. That's when Murphy told me that Mee-Maw had paid off J.T. to become scarce."

"You don't honestly believe that—"

"I didn't. Not until I found a canceled check Mee-Maw had written to J.T. for five thousand dollars."

A wave of nausea swept through Becca. "Did you ask her about it?"

"Didn't do any good. What did you get out of Mee-Maw every time you asked her about J.T.?"

"Well—" Becca hesitated "—not much," she admitted. "She did finally tell me his full name and offered to give me his social-security number. But…she didn't want to talk about him."

"See? Same problem I had."

"We can't put it off any longer, though, Ryan.

She has to tell us what that money was for. This isn't just an insurance scam…this is an attempt to defraud the government."

"Don't I know that?" he snapped. He closed his eyes again. "Sorry. I'm— I don't mean… I know you're right. But honestly, I'm afraid of the answer she might give us. If she knew Gramps had something to do with that vine… Murphy said Gramps brought the vine in to pay off the tax debt. That I gave Gramps the idea…a slam-dunk insurance scam."

"We have only Murphy's word about it. He is surely not the most trustworthy soul."

Ryan shrugged, resigned and defeated. "He knew about the check. How did he know about the check unless she—"

"I don't know. But one thing I do know is that you can't keep guessing about that money. Do you— You didn't destroy the check, did you?"

"I'm stupid, but I'm not that stupid," Ryan told her. "First, destroying that check would put me on a slippery slope. Plus, even if I could have squared what I'd done somehow with myself, I know enough about banking to know that it wouldn't make any difference. There's a copy somewhere in some bank's database."

"Well, I hope you have the original document handy. We can tell a lot about where J.T. cashed it by routing numbers and other info on it. If Mee-Maw won't tell us where to find J.T.—"

"She honestly may not know," he protested.

"If she won't tell us, then we'll find him."

Ryan blew out a breath. "I'm trusting you. You've told me that I can. I think…after last night, that you really care. You do, right? Jack would tell me that this was all some elaborate scheme of yours to worm your way into my affections—"

"No. *No.*" She wrapped her arms around him and hugged him. "Ryan, I promise you. I will do what I can for Mee-Maw. I will do what I can for J.T. But we cannot keep concealing knowledge—or even possible knowledge—of a federal crime. I could lose my P.I. license…and we could both end up on the wrong end of a federal indictment as coconspirators."

He pressed her into him. "How do you know it will work out?"

She tightened her hold for a moment, then stepped back so she could stare him full in the face. "I don't. Even if Mee-Maw had the best of intentions, she could still be charged with accessory after the fact. She aided and abetted a person involved in a conspiracy to defraud the government." Becca yanked her train of thought from going in that direction. "No. We can't think like that. We have to know the truth and deal with it, the sooner the better. So, I think it's time for a meeting with Mee-Maw."

CHAPTER TWENTY-THREE

THE CORNERS OF Mee-Maw's mouth pulled down in a frown. She turned away from Becca and Ryan, busying herself with the pot of peas she had on the stove.

"I don't know why you are so set on hunting down J.T. That boy has had a rough enough time, and if he'd wanted to stay in touch, he would have called or wrote or sent up smoke signals."

Becca exchanged a look with Ryan.

"Mee-Maw," Ryan started in a resolute voice, "that check you wrote to J.T. before he left—"

"I done told you about that." She slammed the lid down on the peas and marched over to the refrigerator. Mee-Maw occupied herself for a few minutes, shifting the contents around. "Need to throw half of this stuff away. Can't find nothing in this refrigerator."

"Why did you write him a check for five thousand dollars, Mee-Maw?" Becca pressed.

"Wages owed, of course. And expenses. Mac hadn't got around to paying him back for a few things."

"Five thousand dollars?" Ryan's voice was full of disbelief. "J.T. waited on five thousand dollars' worth of pay and reimbursements? Mee-Maw, I've told you before—"

She closed the refrigerator door with a thud and turned around. "He wasn't ever that interested in money. Why did he need money, anyway? He stayed out in the pond house, we provided him with lights and water and he ate what we ate, when we ate. What did he need, except a little spending money for taking Charlotte out on the town? He didn't do that very often. That boy was a worker. If you'd known him better, Ryan…"

"Maybe you didn't know him as well as you thought you did, Mee-Maw—"

"Hush your mouth, Ryan! For a while there, that boy ate at my table more 'n you did, and I didn't get this many wrinkles and gray hairs without a decent judge of character to go along with them. Whatever he did—or didn't do—he did the best he thought at the time. And I for one think you should stop hounding him."

"Well…what about that social-security number, Mee-Maw? You did say you'd get it for me?" Becca asked.

"I did, didn't I? Well, I shouldn't have. I should have stuck to my guns and let you and Ryan figure it all out, since you young folks think you're smarter 'n me. Me doin' it thataway would have at least let J.T. have peace for a little longer."

Mee-Maw set her mouth and refused to answer any of their other questions.

Frustrated, Becca stepped out on the back porch. Ryan followed her out, slamming the screen door behind him.

"See? That's how it always is with her. She gets her back up, and there's just no reasoning with her. She thinks—she honestly thinks—J.T. is going to get hurt or in trouble if we find him."

Becca dropped into a chair and put her fingers to her temples. "We need that social-security number and that check. Dad said he'd work on tracking him down without the number, but it will eliminate duplicate names and we can start to work on piecing his financial info together. The check, depending on where it was cashed, could give us a lead on his current whereabouts."

"I'll get the check. It's in Gramps' office. I put it away so it would be safe. If I can't lay my hands on any of J.T.'s tax info, our CPA ought to be able to dig up the social-security number." Ryan shook his head. "I just wish I didn't have to do it this way. I wish she'd understand why we need to do this."

"She does, Ryan. But for some reason, it's not worth it to her. Or else, she knows something that would make losing the farm more of a certainty if J.T. is found than if he stays gone."

"Her refusal to explain anything about J.T. is really what makes me think Gramps did have something to do with that dodder vine."

Becca stood up and crossed the porch to Ryan. She took his hands in hers. "From everything that you knew about him, would he do something like this?"

A spasm crossed Ryan's face. "A year ago, I wouldn't have answered that question with anything but a 'No!' But then…a year ago, I wouldn't have thought Mee-Maw would have written out a check for five grand to a hired hand the day he left—the day we buried Gramps. That's a huge severance package J.T. got. Becca, I'm so confused, I don't know which way is up. But I want some answers. At least, I think I do."

A dull rumble in the distance broke into the stillness of the morning. Ryan frowned, but Becca recognized the sound. She stepped off the porch and shaded her eyes with her hand.

Sure enough, a motorcycle rider was dodging potholes in the drive up to the house.

"My dad," Becca told Ryan. "He rode the Harley down. I should have guessed he'd be here by now."

Her father pulled up on the bike, dropping the

kickstand and silencing the beast beneath him. He pulled off his helmet.

For a moment Becca was afraid to meet her father's eyes. Would she see disappointment in them? Resignation that, yet again, he had to come rescue his daughter?

Before she could brave those eyes, her father pulled her into a rough embrace, then set her back from him. "I thought you said the bruises were almost gone."

"Well, they are. I'm better. Really."

Ryan had joined Becca and her father. He stuck out his hand. "Ryan MacIntosh."

Her father hesitated before accepting the hand. Becca knew in that instant, her father had sized up Ryan and come to a conclusion that would be hard to shake.

The devil of it was, her father was usually pretty accurate in his assessments.

"Matt Reynolds."

"Glad to meet you." Ryan's greeting was pure politeness, nothing more. After a beat, Ryan tagged on, "Sir."

Becca's stomach tensed as she registered the stiffness between the two men. It would have been a funny show of machismo if she didn't care about both of them.

She decided to cut short their mutual sizing-

SEEDS OF TRUST

up of each other. "Ryan, could you go dig up that check?"

Ryan must have recognized the hint for what it was. He gave a quick mock salute and turned toward the house.

"Dad, did you find anything on J.T.?"

"Nope. Not a trace. I tracked down his hometown from what you told me, found some family who says they haven't heard from him since before he left south Georgia. They don't have a clue as to where he might be. I could use that social-security number. There's got to be a thousand John Thomas Griggses in this country."

"We may have a lead on where he headed after he left here." Becca paused. She wanted her dad to meet Mee-Maw before she told him everything. She wanted him to see how loveable Mee-Maw was, how unlikely a player she was in this scam.

But Mee-Maw *was* a player, no matter what Becca and Ryan wanted. Becca had no doubt that Murphy was growing more and more determined to make a move to protect his position. How on earth he thought he could get away with this, she had no clue, but he obviously did.

"A lead? Good. Fill me in."

So she did. By the time she was finished, Ryan had rejoined them, a cancelled check and a slip of paper in his hand.

"Sir, my grandmother swears it was back wages."

"Mighty convenient to have such a nice round number as the total. Any chance J.T. might be blackmailing your grandmother?"

Ryan shook his head, but doubt pulled his features taut. "I don't know. She won't hear anything bad against him. I can't imagine what he could possibly hold over her. My grandparents valued good morals over making money."

Matt Reynolds didn't look convinced. "Morals can take a beating when the family homeplace is at stake—or when an old woman doesn't want her late husband's name dragged through the mud."

"I just—I know it looks bad. But I cannot picture Mee-Maw doing something that she knows is illegal. Or even condoning it."

Becca's father took the check that Ryan had extended to him with a grudging hand. Examining it, Matt Reynolds pursed his lips. "Cashed in a bank in Arkansas. Looks like it cleared three weeks after it was written."

"Well, that delay could have been because Mee-Maw had to move money from the savings account to the checking. If J.T. had cashed it the day it was written, it would have bounced. That's something else I can't understand—she's never written a check without sufficient funds. If the money wasn't there, she didn't write the check, simple as that. But this…" More pain etched into Ryan's face.

"Any more checks like this?" Becca's dad asked. "Maybe smaller amounts? Especially since J.T. has been gone."

Ryan shook his head. "No, sir. Just the one."

"Well, if ol' J.T. was extorting money, I can't see why he stopped at such a small amount. Never saw a blackmailer who wasn't greedy." Her father turned to Becca. "You've been sitting on this?"

"No, sir! I would have told you—"

"Sir, it's my fault," Ryan interrupted. "I told her just this morning. I—I kept thinking that I would tumble onto a reasonable explanation." Ryan toed the dew-covered grass with his workboot, but then lifted his head and met her father's eyes. "Finally I figured…maybe there wasn't one."

"We'll be able to find him—at least his trail to this—if you have his social-security number."

"Yeah. Here." Now Ryan surrendered the slip of paper. "I found the number while I was pulling out the check."

"Good." Her dad tucked the number into his jacket pocket. "You don't have Internet access by any chance?"

"We have dial-up, if that will do."

"Well, okay. It will be slow, but what can you do? Lead the way."

The three of them entered the house. Becca's

throat tightened when she saw Mee-Maw at the kitchen table, her head in her hands. When Mee-Maw glanced up, she looked as though she'd aged another ten years.

But her prickles still showed in her voice. "Ryan? Who's this?"

"Mee-Maw, this is Becca's father—"

Becca's father didn't wait for the formal introductions. He crossed the room to where Mee-Maw sat and extended his hand. "Ma'am. Matt Reynolds."

Mee-Maw grouched in response, then apparently remembered her manners. "'Scuse me." She stood up, bracing herself with a hand to the tabletop. "These young'uns have been worrying me a bit this morning."

Becca's father's face twitched with more than a little amusement. "So I gather. They're just trying to help you."

"So they say." Mee-Maw didn't seem convinced. "Will you be staying with us, too?"

"No, ma'am, but thank you. I've reserved rooms for Becca and me in Dublin."

"I'm sure sorry to be losing Becca. She's mighty good help with the chickens and all. But y'all will stay for dinner?"

Becca felt her face flush as her father wheeled his gaze to her. "Chickens? I sent you down to investigate a fraud case, and you've been helping with chickens?"

"Some of my best thinking is done in the chicken coop, Dad," she told him tartly. "You ought to try it."

Her father expelled a long, overly patient breath. "What I ought to try is that dial-up connection. I need to make some phone calls, too. I want to find J.T. before the close of business day."

Ryan led the way to the office, her father trailing behind. Becca stood there for a moment, feeling a bit superfluous as she stared after them, but when she turned, she saw that Mee-Maw's face had blanched and she had sat down heavily in her chair.

"Mee-Maw? Mee-Maw, is there something you need to tell me about J.T.?"

Mee-Maw put her head in her hands again. "The better question is, child, is there something I'm *able* to tell you about J.T.? And the answer is no."

A FEW FRUSTRATED HOURS later, Becca's father had come up with nothing.

"I don't get it. The man has to work somewhere, but my contacts with the Social Security Administration, the IRS and the Arkansas state revenue department say no taxes have been withheld on that social-security number," her father told them as they sat together in Gramps's office.

"So?" Ryan let the question drag out.

"It means he's working on a cash basis…if he's alive," Becca said.

Her father gave her an appreciative look. "Got it in one."

"He does farm labor for a living, working as day labor or even for room and board—wouldn't be that hard to do," Ryan mused. "He could literally be anywhere."

"My bet is Arkansas," her dad told Ryan. "Is there any connection between Arkansas and your grandmother? Because I've looked, and there's no connection between J.T. and Arkansas other than this check. Why would he cash a check there? Five thousand dollars wouldn't keep him all these months if he's on the run, so he's got to have some stream of income."

Ryan frowned as he pondered the question. "We don't have family in Arkansas, if that's what you mean. I've been there a time or two for work, mainly to Little Rock. But Mee-Maw or Gramps…neither one of them had ever visited Arkansas."

"I'll keep digging, see what I can find. It's just going to take longer than I'd like. If I'd had this information days ago—"

Becca stared at her hands, feeling miserable and

incompetent. She should have dug this up sooner, but her dad had been right on the money: he'd sent her down to investigate, and she'd been feeding chickens.

In the middle of her self-recriminations, a knock sounded on the door frame. She looked up to see Mee-Maw, still tired and tense, standing there.

"I sure hate to break up your powwow in here," Mee-Maw said, "but, Ryan, Brandon Wilkes is on the back porch. He says he needs to talk to you urgentlike. Says it can't wait."

CHAPTER TWENTY-FOUR

"MAN, YOU'VE REALLY stirred up a hornet's nest now," Brandon Wilkes told Ryan the minute the screen door closed behind him. "Murphy's in high gear. You know my brother's girlfriend works at the paper, right?"

A lump of dread coalesced in Ryan's gut. "Yeah. What's that got to do with Murphy?"

Brandon dug out a folded sheet of paper stuck in his sheriff's uniform shirt pocket. "Here. It's a forced-sale notice. Melton over at the tax office faxed it over to the newspaper, told 'em he'd pay double to get it in this week's legal notices. Said he should have put it in with the others but it was an oversight."

Ryan took the official foreclosure notice from Brandon. "Melton's nothing but a stooge for Murphy."

"I know that, man, but take a look at it. It's on your farm. Murphy's putting the same squeeze on you that he did on Uncle Jake."

Nausea roiled up within Ryan. For a moment, his brain refused to wrap around what Brandon was telling him. Becca had assured Ryan that it was a bluff, that there was no lien on the property.

So had she been wrong? Or would Murphy and his brother-in-law dare to create a tax debt out of thin air?

One look at the Latin phrase, *fieri facias,* told him all he needed to know. The words that followed, like *on the courthouse steps* didn't get put in the paper unless the county was willing to go forward with a sheriff's sale.

"I'm sure sorry, Ryan. Soon as I found out, I figured you would want to know." The expression on Brandon's face mirrored what Ryan was feeling. "This the first time you've heard about it?"

"Murphy's been beating me over the head with an old debt of Gramps's…I know Gramps paid it, though. He would never have let the county have a chance at his land. I just can't…"

Brandon raised one eyebrow. "Prove it?" He shook his head. "I don't know what to tell you to do about it if you can't prove it's bogus."

"First, I've got to talk to that sorry scum of the earth Melton. And then…let's just say I'm not going to take this lying down."

Brandon regarded him with a wry look. "He deserves to be pumped full of birdshot, but I'm afraid that in my official capacity I can't let you do that. So don't make my job any harder, okay?"

"Don't worry, Brandon. I won't take my shotgun to Murphy—it's too merciful for what that jerk deserves. But I can tell you, I've never felt more like putting a man six feet under." The sick sensation in Ryan's stomach had turned itself into resolution.

The screen door pushed open behind them. Becca asked, "Ryan? What's wrong?"

He hesitated. "Where's Mee-Maw?"

"She's lying down. Said she needed some rest."

Ryan ran his fingers through his hair. Guilt and worry twined in an uneasy knot within him.

"Murphy's put the wheels in motion to foreclose on the farm. Do *not* tell Mee-Maw. She'd have a heart attack. Let me handle this."

"Ryan…" Becca had that let's-try-it-my-way look on her face. "I thought Mee-Maw knew about that tax bill. Maybe you *should* tell her. Maybe she ought to know what the stakes are here. It might make her tell us where J.T. is."

"No!" Ryan exploded. "I will not have her worried! It's my job to look after her now that Gramps is gone. Gramps always told me he took care of things. He didn't let her stew over things he could fix."

Becca rolled her eyes. "Oh, come on! You don't seriously buy into that? That woman's tough as a lightered knot, and you know it. You don't stay married to a farmer for as many years as she did without knowing the worries of a farm."

"I think she's right, Ryan," Brandon said. "Mee-Maw deserves to know the farm's at risk—"

"She's my grandmother, and I know what Gramps told me. She's…she's gone down a lot since Gramps died. I don't want her worried unnecessarily. Maybe I can fix this and she'll never have to know." Ryan wasn't sure he knew how to even start to undo the damage that Murphy had created, but Becca and Brandon hadn't been here day in, day out with Mee-Maw. They hadn't seen how frail Mee-Maw had been just after Gramps's funeral. She'd only in the past few months begun to seem like her old self.

Impatient with Becca and Brandon and impatient with himself, Ryan didn't take the time now to explain all that. They'd just have to trust him.

"I'm going to Murphy's. On the way, I'll call Melton at the tax office, see what he has to say. You're the one, Becca, who kept telling me that if you just had a social-security number you could find J.T. Well, you've got it. You look for J.T., and I'll see what I can get out of Murphy. And don't tell Mee-Maw. Let me be the one to tell her."

"But you will tell her?" Becca pleaded.

"I don't even know if this is official yet. It could be—let's hope it is—just some elaborate barrel Murphy's constructed to put me over. Once I know what the situation is, yeah, sure, I'll have to tell Mee-Maw. But I'm not going in there half-cocked with a bunch of theories and speculations."

With that, he left Becca and Brandon and headed for his truck.

HE FOUND Murphy leaned against an impractical white-rail fence running along the edge of the Murphy farm. Throwing open the truck door, Ryan stalked over to him.

"Just tell me what you mean, pulling a stunt like this?"

Murphy gave him a look of mild interest, took in the sheet of paper Ryan was shaking at him, then turned his attention back to the fields of cotton in front of him.

"News travels fast. To be expected, I guess. What did you think I'd do? Stand by and let you cost me a million bucks?"

"This bill is paid, Murphy, and you know it."

Murphy shrugged. "Prove it. Take Melton the cancelled check and show him it's paid in full."

The metallic taste of frustration and fear welled up in the back of Ryan's mouth. "You know I can't. Gramps paid part of that debt in cash."

"Then maybe you're up to working something out, huh?"

"What are you talking about,'work something out?'"

Murphy shifted, putting one foot on the lower

rail and leaving a dark stain from his boot on the pristine white wood. "Simple. Ag-Sure wants a fall guy. Leave J.T. wherever he is. Tell that Reynolds girl that Mac was the one who came up with the scheme." He turned his attention back to Ryan. "That's all there is to it. Ag-Sure won't pay you guys…but they'll give the rest of us a partial settlement most likely, especially if you tell 'em Mac was the one who planted the vine on our land. Cheaper than taking the lot of us to court."

Ryan barely resisted the urge to slug Murphy in the jaw. "And how will that solve all our problems?"

"Your granddaddy's dead. Ag-Sure can't press charges against a man already in the ground. You get to keep the farm, your grandmother has a place to call home."

"So that tax bill…"

"Computer glitch. You know, that brother-in-law of mine ain't the brightest bulb in the pack." Murphy winked. His face grew more serious. "First thing, though, is to call off the hunt for J.T. He's not going to help at all, just muddy the waters."

"Sounds like he's alive and kicking out there somewhere, and full of news to spill about you."

"News that won't help you save your farm from a sheriff's sale. Like I said, simple. But if you need me to make it plainer for you, how about this? How about I go to Ag-Sure, tell 'em that you and your granddaddy cooked this whole thing up, and you've been covering it up by planting vines in everybody else's fields? I got pictures of your granddaddy and J.T., and there's that check your grandma wrote. It don't look good, Ryan, not for you."

Murphy's cell phone buzzed then. "'Scuse me." He reached in his pocket. He spoke into the phone with a quiet voice, glanced up at Ryan and said, "Gotta take this." He wandered off a few yards out of Ryan's earshot.

The interruption was just as well. Ryan couldn't speak. Disgust and fear and worry all combined to paralyze him where he stood. Did Murphy really think he'd trade Gramps's memory and reputation for Mee-Maw's homeplace?

Then sick resignation pooled in the place of the disgust.

Did Ryan really have much of a choice?

BECCA STOOD outside, the heat from the Holiday Inn's asphalt parking lot shimmering up in scorching waves. On the phone, Ryan had sounded…hard. That's the only way she knew how to describe it. His voice had seemed as unyielding as granite when he'd told her he needed to talk with her immediately—not on the phone, but face to face.

So she'd told him that she and her dad were in Dublin, and she'd come outside to wait for Ryan. In case her dad didn't need to hear whatever Ryan had to say.

Ryan's old truck rolled up a few minutes later. He parked, got out and slammed the door. One look told her his news wasn't good.

"Ryan—" she started to say as he drew closer.

"I don't know how they did it, but the notice is official. They've put this thing on the fast track. That auction is moving forward."

Becca closed her eyes. "I am so sorry. Murphy—we'll get him. Just as soon as we find J.T., we'll put Murphy in so much hot water, he'll—"

"You haven't found J.T. yet?"

She shook her head. "No. Dad's still looking. He's got some leads, though—"

"Tell me. Honestly. Can you guys run him down by this weekend?"

"This weekend? Ryan, I don't know. Today's Wednesday, and it's practically gone already—" His expression silenced her for a moment. "Surely even if the tax commissioner is moving ahead with the foreclosure, it will take a while to do the sale. We have time, Ryan."

"No, we don't. According to Melton, I've been served with all the necessary paperwork. That legal ad is the last step, Becca. He's saying I've been given adequate notice. Sheriff's sale is on Friday."

"Friday?"

"Last day of the month. That's why Melton rushed to get this notice in, so that it could be lumped in with the rest of the month's sales. Sheriff's sales are expensive for the county, especially if you have only one or two properties to get rid of. Sometimes there will be a span of months where you don't have any sales."

"He can't—"

"Yes, he can. I keep telling you, Becca, and you just won't hear me. Things are done differently around here. Somebody with pull wants your property? Well, forget due process. They just phony up an unpaid tax bill and ram it through the barest of notices."

"So go to court, file an injunction—do *something,* Ryan."

"That takes time. Time I don't have." Ryan shook his head. "I could make all this go away. All I have to do is say Gramps was the one who did all this."

"But, Ryan—that doesn't even make sense. If Mac did it, then how did those vines get in the fields?" She lay a hand on his shoulder, but he shook it off. "Think about it. Ag-Sure won't believe it for a minute—"

"They will if you go along with it."

Becca stepped back. "No. I can't. Not even for you, Ryan. You're upset. You're not thinking clearly. Calm down, think this through. We'll figure something out."

"I'm calm. All you have to do is buy me some time. Just…go away for a little. You can still look for J.T. But make it look like you're packing up, going home. Let Murphy think that and he'll call off the dogs."

"Ryan! You don't know that. You have nothing but a scammer's word that he'll tell Melton to cancel that sale. Why should he? Why would he? You know Murphy. You know what he's like."

"I might have the chance to scrape up the money, Becca, to pay that tax bill. If I go up there with eleven grand, with a witness, then Melton won't have any hold on me—and neither will Murphy."

"You'd pay eleven thousand dollars in money you don't owe to get Murphy off your back?"

"Yes, I would!" Ryan's jaw tightened and he clenched and unclenched his fist. "Don't you get it, Becca? These people are playing for keeps!"

"So who's to say they won't go back and dummy up another bill?"

"I'll take my chances."

"But you need me—and Dad—to make this work. You need us to make we-quit noises." Sick disappointment ate at Becca. "Ryan, you have to trust us. Get a lawyer *today,* and start trying to stop that sale. Buy us some time to find J.T. We have contacts in Arkansas—"

"You won't do it? You won't help me?" Ryan gaped at her. "You're just trying to clear this case, aren't you? You just want to hand Murphy to Ag-Sure."

"This isn't the Ryan MacIntosh that I know. Not if you're willing to even bend a tiny fraction of an inch to an extortionist's demands. You have to stand on principle, Ryan. You have to fight, I know that, but you have to fight the right way. You give in to Murphy now…"

They stood there, eyeing each other. Becca's heart pounded as she prayed for what she said to sink into Ryan.

"You don't know me then. That farm—and Mee-Maw—that's my priority. No lawyer's going to be able to do anything in the short time I've got—no lawyer's going to go against the county on this, anyway. I should know, I've already asked. I'm not saying, Becca, that I want Murphy to get off, but can't you see—"

"No. No, I can't. And when you're calmer, when you're thinking more rationally, you'll agree."

He swore. "It *is* about the case. You just want— oh, I don't know. Principle's fine, Becca. It's fine and dandy until you see the land that's been in the family for over a century sold on the courthouse steps. It would be different if I knew you could find J.T. and if I knew for certain he had some answers. I'm grasping at straws here, Becca, and you don't act like you understand. If I knew you understood, I'd—"

"I do. I know. I know you, Ryan."

"No, I don't think you do. What's land to a city girl?" Now Ryan's Adam's apple jerked in his throat and his words were hoarse with emotion. "You can't know me. Not if you don't—"

She took his hands in hers again, looked up in his eyes. "I do. I've known you for months. Ryan...I was going to wait to tell you this. Until after the investigation was over. But I've got to make you see that I am on your side, that I do know you. I'm Sunny."

"Wh-what?"

"Sunny. Sunny seventy-six."

Ryan's face blanched as her words sank in. He jerked away from her. "You mean...all this time? All these months? You knew I was in this trouble? You were investigating me the whole time?"

"No! No, I didn't know then. It wasn't like you're saying—"

"Maybe you do know me." Ryan shook his head as if to clear it. "But I sure don't know you."

He spun on his heel and walked away. Becca raced after him, trying to stop him, but he wouldn't hear her. He just slammed the door to his grandfather's truck and peeled out of the parking lot.

And he didn't look back.

CHAPTER TWENTY-FIVE

HALFWAY HOME, Ryan's hands were shaking so badly, he had to pull the truck onto the interstate's emergency lane.

He turned the cranky air-conditioning up to full blast, barely making a dent in the August heat. Then, as the cars whizzed by, Ryan sat still.

Whatever calm he was waiting for didn't come. His gut wanted to turn itself inside out. His heart tattooed a double-quick rhythm behind his ribs.

What was worse? Finding out that Murphy had a firm grip on the farm—and Ryan over a barrel? Or that Becca wasn't who she said she was?

No. That last one wasn't strictly accurate. Becca simply hadn't bothered to fill him on minor details—like she'd known who he was from the get-go.

Had anything between them been real? Between him and Sunny? Between him and Becca?

"Well, buddy," he said aloud. "You get off the hook for thinking you're a jerk for liking them both."

Both of the day's news would have been bad enough, but to have it all land together?

Ryan slammed a fist down on the steering wheel. He couldn't afford the luxury of working out the Becca/Sunny problem right now.

He had to figure out a way to save Mee-Maw's home.

Another surge of fury rattled through him. If Becca had just understood what he'd been trying to say—he hadn't wanted Murphy to get out from under this. All they needed was a little time to lull Murphy into a false sense of security.

What harm would have been in that?

But Becca's pleading with him came back full force. *You have nothing but a scammer's word that he'll tell Melton to cancel that sale.*

She was right about that. He was a fool to think that he could salvage anything at this point.

Ryan squeezed his eyes shut, swallowed hard.

If he couldn't count on Becca to help buy more time…then the most logical thing to do next was to talk to Mee-Maw.

RYAN WAS GLAD to see Jack's truck parked by the house when he pulled up. He hadn't been sure, when he'd called Jack on the way, whether his cousin could shut down the insurance office early. Especially when Ryan hadn't gone into detail about what the crisis was.

I'll probably tote a butt-whuppin' for sure after Jack hears what kind of mess I've created. But at least I know he's got my back.

Before he got out of the truck, he smoothed out the printout of the sale notice and examined it. Amazing. This was America and still, with a little help from corrupt hands, someone could take your land and nobody would put up a fight.

One look around made the lump in his throat grow bigger. Mee-Maw's garden, the garden he'd managed to save from both the dodder vine and the hailstorm, was still rich with produce. Off in the distance, that crazy cow Daisy Bell was galloping like a fool horse across the pasture.

And a field white with cotton waited for harvest.

How would he tell her? How would he tell Mee-Maw that he might have lost it all?

Jack met him on the back porch, his face looking grim.

"Brandon called me. Said he couldn't run you down, that you weren't answering your phone, weren't returning messages. I know about the sale, Ryan. What is going on?"

"Same old, same old. It's Murphy up to his old tricks."

"But why? What happened? He'd pretty much promised...we keep our mouths shut, he leaves us alone."

Ryan shrugged. "Guess that's what we get for thinking a scammer will honor his word."

"Nuh-uh, cuz." Jack poked him in the chest. "Word on the street says that Murphy is one angry dude. At you. So what gives?"

Normally Ryan would have floored anybody who'd so much as lay a finger on him. But he was too distracted to care much—and feeling too guilty.

"I guess I didn't put Becca on the road quick enough to suit him. It was J.T. all along, Jack. Murphy as good as told me that today. J.T. must have brought those vines in, and Murphy doesn't want him found."

Some of Jack's belligerence went out of him at Ryan's words. "I was hoping that Murphy was just bluffing with that. So that's what Murphy's hot about? Becca found J.T.?"

"Not yet. You know, by a weird sort of twist, if we did find J.T., it might be the thing that saves us."

"I don't know, Ryan." Jack looked doubtful. "There's still Mee-Maw's check to consider. What if she did pay him off? We've asked her about that thing a thousand times, and she just clams up. What if J.T. comes back into town with the glad news that Gramps and Mee-Maw were part of this mess?"

"You don't honestly believe that, do you? I keep

trying to figure why Mee-Maw would protect J.T., and I can't—except she's always been one to fight for the underdog. But I cannot for the life of me see her breaking the law. It's just not her, Jack, and you know it."

"What I know is that I should have run J.T. off the minute Gramps told me he'd hired him. J.T.'s the cause of all this mess. He brought those vines in knowing what Murphy meant to do with them. Then he left. I didn't like it when he disappeared when he did."

"I should have risked going to Ag-Sure. I should have…" The bitter taste of regret welled up in Ryan's throat. "This is getting us nowhere. What can we do at this point? I have maybe three grand in the bank. Do you have any you can lend me? If we pay this tax bill, they'll have to hunt around for another stick to club us with."

"Man, I'm strapped." Jack shook his head. "Between the car payments and the house payments and the school nickel-and-diming us to death, it's a struggle just to get food on the table and clothes on the kids' backs."

"Any way we can stop this process? Anything a court can do?"

"You've talked to that sorry excuse for a tax commissioner, I guess? What did he say?"

Anger whistled through Ryan again. "Melton's a smarmy jerk, all right. Said he had records to prove he'd mailed out notices that went ignored. Jack, we've got no notices. None. Murphy's been bellyaching about this old tax debt, but every time I'd go to check, Melton would always say something like, 'You're square for now, Ryan.'"

"You know, if Gramps had left a will, it would have had to go through probate and all the old debts would have been addressed then—"

"Don't go blaming Gramps, Jack. He didn't leave a will because he knew it would all go to Mee-Maw anyway, which is what he wanted. He wanted her to have it."

"I'm not blaming— Okay, so I am," Jack admitted. "Can we sell part of the land to raise the money?"

"Sure…to Murphy. Nobody else has either the money or the credit. But, it's worth a try…if Mee-Maw goes along with it."

They looked at each other. Nothing else to do but tell Mee-Maw…and Ryan knew it.

He reached for the pull handle on the screen door. One thing was for certain: if Mee-Maw didn't come up with some answers now, Ryan could pretty much guess what secrets she was bent on keeping.

MEE-MAW DID NOT take the news well.

Her face sagged into wrinkles Ryan had not even realized were there. She slumped in her chair at the head of the table and buried her face in her hands.

"Mee-Maw?" Ryan reached out a hand, lay it on Mee-Maw's thin, bony shoulder. "I am so sorry." Those words sounded about as adequate as a Band-Aid for a cancer tumor to Ryan.

Her frame shook under his hand. He realized she was crying, and he had not a clue what to say or do. Jerking his head toward the bathroom, he muttered to Jack, "Get some tissue or something."

For once Jack didn't argue. Ryan figured that he was as much undone by Mee-Maw's grief as Ryan was.

A moment later, Mee-Maw wrapped her fingers around the tissue Jack had shoved her way. She dabbed at her eyes and blew her nose.

"Mac paid that tax bill," she whispered. Her voice grew stronger. "I know he did. I'm thinking that's the one he had to pay in parts because that sorry Melton and the tax assessor had run up the fair market value on it. He had to, you see, to appeal it. And you can bet he did—he blasted that assessor's board with both barrels, and the next year, our taxes were more reasonablelike. Mac figured Murphy was trying to run us out then. I got no use for that man—either Murphy or Melton."

Hope shot through Ryan. An appeal would

mean that Gramps had to pay it—at least the part the assessor's board had considered fair.

"That might help, Mee-Maw. Do you have any proof of that? I've looked—"

"You know how your granddaddy was, Ryan. He could make a rock grow, but when it came to paperwork…well, that was his weakness. He usually let me handle all of that part, but that one, he got so het up about, he took care of it. I don't know where the papers on it would be if they're not with the other tax papers."

Ryan blew out a breath. "Well, I'll go through the files one more time just in case."

"What does Becca say?" Mee-Maw reached out a hand and folded it over Ryan's. "She's an investigator, knows about the law. Does she say that Murphy can do this?"

Ryan bit his lip. He couldn't answer for a long moment. "Mee-Maw…I don't think we can count on Becca to help. At least, not in the short term."

Some of Mee-Maw's spunk came back in her face. "Not count on her to help? What nonsense is this? Of course you can. She was helping this morning, with her daddy. In her own way, of course, thinkin' that dragging J.T. in the middle of all this would solve our problems."

"It's too complicated to explain—"

"Don't you go treatin' me like I'm an imbecile. You should have already come to me with this tax business, and I would have given that good-for-nothin' Melton a piece of my mind. So you tell me what this talk about Becca not helping is all about."

Ryan shoved his chair back from the table and walked over to the windows, his back to Jack and Mee-Maw. From his vantage point, he could see the barn where he and Becca had gotten closer. Pain ripped through him at the memory. She'd seemed so special, The One even.

And it had all been a lie.

"I found out that Becca had been investigating me for a lot longer than I thought—undercover, sort of. She'd passed herself off as a farmer's daughter on an online community."

"That Internet thing you used to always get on at night?" Mee-Maw asked.

At the same time, Jack said, "Internet? What? Some online-dating site?"

Shame heated through Ryan. "It wasn't an on-line-dating site. It was…just a group where you could talk. You know, to others going through the same thing, dealing with… Jack, it gets lonesome out here. You're married so you've got somebody. But I—I'd just moved up here, didn't know many people my own age, didn't have time to spend with anybody if I did. The computer, well, it offered me a link. I didn't feel so isolated."

"And you told her what? What did you spill

to her to get her interested in this case?" Jack's words were hard.

"Nothing! We didn't even trade details we thought could identify each other. I thought I was so smart. She knew all along."

He turned back around. "Well, that's water under the bridge. It's over now, if there ever was anything beyond the investigation."

Jack looked as if he wanted to say something, but Mee-Maw cut him off.

"Jack, you leave Ryan alone about this. Becca's a good girl, and all she's done is try to help. I truly believe that."

Jack protested anyway. "It's not going to—"

"Jack!" Mee-Maw shot back. "I mean it! This is still my house—for as long as I can keep it, anyway—and I ought to get some measure of respect."

But the bluster went out of Mee-Maw as quickly as it had come. She pursed her lips. "No use trying to pay a tax bill that's already been paid. Even if we had the money, which we don't, either they'll say we hadn't paid it again or they'll just dream up another past-due tax debt. No, sir. Not a bit of good in that. And there ain't no stopping a sheriff's sale once it goes to the paper—not unless the county's got some mighty big egg on its face. So…"

Her face grew even more troubled as she lapsed into silence.

"I called a lawyer I know, but he said the sale pretty well couldn't be stopped if the county had proof of proper notification," Ryan told them.

His cousin snorted. "Yeah, like any lawyer around here's going up against the county." Jack turned to Mee-Maw.

"Mee-Maw...what if we tried it like this?" he asked. "What if we did try to strike a bargain with Murphy? It's not like Gramps is around to complain—"

She drew herself up to her full height. "Hush your mouth! Gramps would rather see this place go up in flames than save it thataway—and so would I. No, sir. I'll have none of that. Besides, you can't trust Murphy. Deal with the devil, that's what you'd be doing." Mee-Maw shook her head. "Only one thing to do. It might be too late, anyway. Plus...I gave him my word, and I do so hate to go back on it."

"Gave who your word, Mee-Maw?" Ryan asked.

"J.T. I gave J.T. my word that nobody would come looking for him. That's why I gave him that five thousand dollars...so he'd have a chance to get away."

Sunny_76@yoohoomail.com: Ryan, you're not answering your phone, you're not answering my e-mails, you're not giving me a chance to explain. So I've explained it all anyway in all the e-mails you've probably just deleted until I'm blue in the face. I know I made a mistake not telling you sooner. But, I swear, I didn't know you were Rooster... not until the willow tree.

I swear, Sunny and I are the same woman. The same person. There was no pretense.

Just remember...you said you didn't want to know. You said you didn't want things to be spoiled. So...I tried not to spoil it. And I wound up making a horrid mess of things. I'm sorry. I am so, so sorry.

CHAPTER TWENTY-SIX

BECCA YAWNED AND rubbed her eyes, which felt as if they had lids made of steel wool. Opening them, she saw the clock: 6:45 a.m. Friday. Auction day.

Resolutely, she went back to tapping away on her keyboard. Since Ryan had stormed off Wednesday afternoon, she'd practically been welded to her laptop, trying one last ditch effort to turn up any electronic trail on the elusive J. T. Griggs. Behind her, the hotel room's adjoining door opened, and her dad stuck his head in.

"You decent? Got some coffee on?"

"I haven't been to bed, so, yeah, I'm as decent as anyone is after an all-nighter. As for the coffee, I think I drank the last of it at around four-thirty this morning."

"Becca! You swore you were going to bed ten minutes after I did, and that was at half past one." The clank of glass and spoons and the rip of sugar packets signaled that her dad was taking care of the morning's java jolt.

She yawned again. "I know, but then I got a

lead on a John Thomas Griggs in western Arkansas. For a while, I really thought I'd found him."

Her father swung a chair around and straddled
it, resting his chin on the back. "Honey, you can't
get so emotionally involved in your cases. You're
going to hear a million sob stories, see a million
wrongs done over the course of your life. That is,
if you stay with the job."

His words brought her up short. She really
looked at him now, met him eye to eye. "I figured after the hash I'd made out of this case, you'd
be ready for me to do anything else."

He shook his head. "You didn't make a hash
out of it. You came down here, verified there was
fraud, found out the extent of that fraud, who was
behind it and pretty much how it was done. You've
also discovered a key witness. Ag-Sure is going
to be very happy."

His words didn't convince her. "None of that
matters. Even with Mee-Maw's information, we
still can't lay our hands on J.T. And without him,
we can't stop Murphy."

"Oh, we will. Just give it time. Murphy's like
those guys you hear about on TV, the ones who
stumble out of a convenience-store robbery and
they don't know they're shot? Well, Murphy has
no clue just how over his scam is. Eventually Mrs.
MacIntosh will get her farm back."

"Eventually! She's eighty-four years old, Dad!

When I went out there to talk to her, after Ryan called to tell me what she knew about J.T., she looked so worn out, so frail."

She tried not to think about how Ryan had looked the last time she'd seen him. When she'd gone to Jack's to talk to Mee-Maw, Ryan had been stone-faced. His cool politeness hurt worse than if he'd yelled at her. He'd made it a point not to touch her, not to sit anywhere near her. He'd just shown her to the kitchen table, said, "I'll let you two talk," and then he'd stomped out the screen door.

Mee-Maw hadn't been able to tell her much, just that she'd sent J.T. off with the five thousand dollars and a note to some Arkansas friends to find him a safe place to work.

Calls and legwork had developed that J.T. had bounced around Arkansas, doing work for a succession of old-time farmers, moving on before too many questions could be asked.

Nobody seemed to know where he might be now.

"Mrs. MacIntosh could have put an end to all this months ago, before it even started, Becca. You know that. People make choices, and when they do, they choose the consequences."

She harrumphed. "Or the consequences choose them."

"Either way, it doesn't matter."

"No, it doesn't." She let out a long, despairing breath. "Today's the sale. Barring a miracle, Mee-Maw's going to be saying goodbye to the only home she's known for nearly sixty years."

"Becca, don't do this to yourself. Don't pin all your hopes on J.T. Don't think you can save the world single-handedly. You remind me—"

"I know. Too much of Aunt Mala."

"No." He shook his head, cupped her cheek. "Too much of the me I used to be."

"Oh, Dad…"

Now tears thickened in her throat. She couldn't get over the pride she saw in his eyes—pride mingled with concern and worry.

Before she could speak, her cell phone buzzed. She yanked it up. "Yes?"

"Found him!" the Little Rock detective told her. "On a farm, working for room and board. It was a friend of a friend of a friend kinda deal. I swear, if I'm ever on the lam, I'll know to use the Old Coots' Farm Underground."

RYAN THOUGHT he'd prepared himself.

But when that gavel came down and the auctioneer yodeled, "Sold!" all Ryan wanted to do was upchuck what little breakfast he'd managed to get down.

Mee-Maw had insisted on coming here today, though he'd asked her not to. Being present for this was like watching an execution of an innocent man. He'd wanted to scream, "No! Don't! Stop!"

But he'd known all that would have done was make him look like a crazy man.

The auctioneer tuned up for the next poor soul's property. Ryan turned, pushing his way through the crowd, Mee-Maw by his side.

Then Becca was there. Ryan's heart almost forgot about the betrayal, the lies, and all he could do was marvel at how beautiful she was.

He willed his heart to behave and to listen impassively at her news.

"We found him! We found J.T.!" she told him. "He's on a plane heading for Savannah now. My dad's rented a car to go pick him up. And we've got the feds involved now, too—"

"Oh, honey. Bless you." Mee-Maw stretched out a hand and patted Becca on the shoulder. "You don't look like you've had a wink of sleep. But I'm afraid…well, honey, it's too late. Murphy just made the final bid on the farm."

Becca staggered at the news. Without thinking, Ryan reached out and braced her.

"I—the auction—" Becca's words were lost in the din of the crowd.

For a moment, her pain was so much that Ryan wanted to fold her up in his arms, tell her it would be all right.

But then he thought about Murphy, busy now

with the paperwork on the farm Gramps had sac-
rificed so much for, and he realized it wouldn't be
all right. It would never be all right.

"I have to get Mee-Maw somewhere. This day
has been too much for her," he said.

The crowd around them suddenly fell silent and
parted. Murphy came out of the cleared path. He
stopped in front of Mee-Maw, gazed coolly at
Ryan and Becca.

"Ma'am. I wish I could extend you a bit more
time, but I'm afraid that wouldn't be good business practice. You'll need to gather up what personal items aren't included in the foreclosure and
be out by the close of business tomorrow."

Ryan moved to deck the sanctimonious jerk, but
Mee-Maw tightened her grip on his arm.

"Come a little closer?" she asked, cupping her
free hand around her ear. "I didn't hear what you
said?"

So Murphy obliged, stepped forward and
started to repeat the despicable order even louder.

But he didn't get three words out before Mee-
Maw spat in Murphy's big, round face.

Then she shook off Ryan's arm and strode off
purposefully for the truck.

"THIS IS HOW I make my clothes, young man! If
I don't take this, I won't have a stitch to wear,
and I don't see how you can get any more 'per-

sonal' than that!" Mee-Maw railed at the foreman Murphy had sent to oversee the eviction.

"Ma'am…" The man shot a look of pure misery at Ryan, and then back at Mee-Maw.

But he didn't relinquish the hold he had on the battered old Singer. He cleared his throat. "I'm just doing my job. Murphy's list says nothing but clothing and personal items—"

"This sewing machine has been in my family for nigh over fifty years—I made my babies' clothes on it—"

Some of Mee-Maw's feistiness evaporated, and tears welled up in her eyes. She sank down on her bed. "I raised my babies here. And my grandbabies. Thought I'd see more of my great-grands running around barefoot under the pecan trees. I nursed my little ones right here in this bed. Sewed this quilt while I was expecting my youngest…"

The foreman shuffled his feet. "Aw, boy. This is the lowest… If I didn't have three kids to feed, I'd quit right this instant." He straightened up and met Ryan's eyes. "Go on. Put the thing on the truck. If Murphy finds out, he can just take it out of my pay."

Ryan didn't hesitate. He hefted up the machine and its cabinet and headed for the back door. If he could take anything from this place that would give Mee-Maw even part of her past, he would.

Murphy would have to come through him to get it back.

The sewing machine had been the last of the things he'd battled with the foreman over. He could empathize with the guy, understood that he didn't want to get on Murphy's bad side.

But this was Mee-Maw's stuff. Gramps was probably spinning in his grave right now at what was happening.

Jack, out of his cast, helped him load the sewing machine on the back of the truck—Jack's truck, not Gramps's.

A lump Ryan couldn't swallow formed in his throat at the thought of leaving Gramps's old pickup here. But, like Mee-Maw's beds and her rocker and the old kitchen table Ryan had crawled under as a baby, the truck was part of the "foreclosed estate." It would stay behind, no matter the pain leaving it cost.

He brushed his hands together and cast a worried glance at the lowering sun.

Jack seemed to read his thoughts. He said to Ryan, "It's getting late. I don't want to go head-to-head with Murphy. I'm surprised he's not already here. He said the close of business…and it's nearly six."

"Murphy wouldn't know a real business day if it bit him. The man starts at ten in the morning and calls it a day by three."

For all of Ryan's bravado, however, he, too, was concerned. Mainly he wanted to get this last load gone before Murphy had a chance to see it—and protest that it belonged to him.

"Let's go see what else there is," Jack suggested.

Ryan stopped at the door of Mee-Maw's bedroom to see her staring vacantly at her empty closet—a closet where just this morning her clothes had hung. She looked more than a little lost.

"Mee-Maw?" he prompted gently.

"Hmm?" she responded in an abstracted voice.

"What next?"

She didn't reply, didn't even act as though she heard.

Jack spoke up, a bit louder. "Mee-Maw, is there anything else? It's getting late—"

She stayed him with a hand, then let that palm trail over the top of her dresser, which was bare of the photographs that had weighed it down only last night.

"I know, I know. It's way past time. But how in tarnation is a woman s'posed to pack up a lifetime in a day? Just… Oh, Jack. Just give an old lady a chance to say goodbye to her home. Okay?"

Ryan pressed his lips together to hold back the scream of agony Mee-Maw's words caused him. This was his fault, all his fault. If he'd just—

What? Listened to his gut? His gut hadn't known what to do, either.

He looked over at Jack, who seemed as miserable as Ryan felt.

"You, um, go on. Get that load to your house. I'll stay here with Mee-Maw until…until she's ready to go, okay? I'll call you then to come pick us up."

Jack nodded. "Yeah. If you need me, if Murphy gives you any trouble, I'll be trying to figure out where to put all this stuff."

Ryan saw him looking at Mee-Maw, trying to figure out what words to say to comfort her…and like him, finding none. So instead, Jack about-faced out the door.

A moment later, Ryan saw Jack's pickup lumber down the drive past Mee-Maw's bedroom window.

The sound of the truck signaled something to Mee-Maw.

"One more walk-through then." She said it matter-of-factly and led Ryan on a tour of the house.

It looked gutted without her personal effects, but Mee-Maw didn't act as if she noticed the difference. Instead, she'd stop and touch this or that piece of furniture, patting it with a bittersweet smile on her lips. She halted at the door of the kitchen and beamed at the notches on the door frame.

"That's you, Ryan. See? You started out on the short side…" A gnarled finger trailed up the battered paint. "But look how you shot up…and just in one year." She closed her eyes and breathed out, long and low.

Ryan felt as if his heart had been ripped out of him by the time they stood on the back porch.

"Well, now. Just one more thing to do."

"What's that, Mee-Maw?"

Mee-Maw took his hand in hers and squeezed. "I want to say goodbye to Mac, Ryan. Who knows when Murphy'll let me back up here. So…can you drive me up there? I know Murphy said not to drive the truck off the property…but the family plot, well, that's not off the property, is it? Can you take me to say goodbye to Mac?"

Ryan closed his eyes and nodded. He'd take Mee-Maw anywhere.

THE OLD OAK TREE'S branches creaked in the light evening breeze as Ryan guided Mee-Maw over the rough path to Gramps's grave. Out before him, the sun hung low in the sky, painting the horizon vivid scarlet and orange. If the old wives' tales were true, then tomorrow should dawn clear and fair—perfect for plowing.

Plowing that Ryan wouldn't be doing.

For the first time, he thought about what the future would hold for him.

No cows to feed and tend to and persuade that the grass really was greener on the other side of the fence.

No hens to battle for eggs.

No butter beans to break his back over.

No cotton to plow and worry over.

Well, really, when he thought about it, the prospect sounded…like utter misery.

Mee-Maw's low-heeled shoes scraped along the gravel surrounding Gramps's plot. She knelt down, stiff and slow, and lay a palm on the smooth granite.

"Well, Mac. Never thought I'd see this day," she murmured.

Ryan would have stepped back, given her some privacy, but she reached up and twined her fingers around his.

"The boys think they can get the farm back, eventually. Don't know that I'll ever see it. I'm afraid, Mac…afraid that, away from this ground, I'll be as dead as a lamp unplugged. And about as useless."

Ryan wanted to run, get away from Mee-Maw's words, but losing the farm was his fault. Maybe, if the punishment fit the crime, this was the perfect, fitting punishment. He forced himself to listen.

"I know what you'd tell me. You'd tell me to fight. You'd tell me not to give up. So…I'm gonna do that. Best I can, anyway."

Mee-Maw fell silent. Ryan thought she was done, but she started again.

"I thought the day you died was the worst day of my life. Then I thought, no, the day we put you in the ground was the worst. And then, no, it had to be the day after the funeral… I miss you. Every day. I look for you. I miss you. I miss the way you left the razor on the sink—sixty years, and you never learned to put it away." Tears choked Mee-Maw's chuckle.

"I miss a lot of things," she whispered. "I miss the way you'd hold my hand when we said grace. I miss the way you never liked the weather. I miss your kisses. But I thought…living here that I'd always have a piece of you. Guess it wasn't meant to be. Guess you'll just have to wait for me to get to Heaven. Guess…guess I'll have to find some other place to be buried. You won't mind, will you, Mac? That I won't be here beside you? You'll understand, won't you?"

Now she hid her face in her hands and wept in earnest. "I wish I had flowers to put on your grave, but I don't. I sure am sorry, Mac. I sure wish I didn't have to say goodbye this way."

CHAPTER TWENTY-SEVEN

NEITHER RYAN NOR Mee-Maw said much on the ride back to the house. He pulled up in Gramps's usual spot and parked the truck. Ryan couldn't bring himself to look at Mee-Maw, so instead he just stared out the windshield.

Trying not to see what all they were losing.

Then Mee-Maw cleared her throat. She lifted a trembling hand to her hair, patting it.

"I sure thank you, Ryan."

He couldn't help himself. "What for? All I've done is lose this place for you. This is my fault."

"Pshaw. It's not and you know it. Well, not all yours, anyway. A good portion of the blame's mine. What could you have done anyway to stop Murphy?"

"I should have escorted Becca Reynolds to the county line and told her not to come back until she had a posse of federal investigators and a slew of warrants. I shouldn't have fooled myself into thinking I could win any standoff with Murphy. Jack warned me I was playing with fire. If I'd just not let Becca onto the property to begin with, this whole game of chicken with Murphy wouldn't have started. At least, Murphy wouldn't blame me for Becca's digging. That way, at least it wouldn't be my fault that Murphy got so riled up."

Mee-Maw made a disappointed clucking sound. "Wouldn't have solved anything, just put it off a bit. Becca was only doing her job. No point blaming her, either. You're not, are you?"

"She knew, Mee-Maw. She knew from the start who I was, what was going on…she baited me—"

"You don't know that, Ryan. Before you go jumping to any conclusions, you talk to her. Now, I'll tell you what you could have done. You could have gone to the insurance company the minute you knew something was up with that vine."

"Mee-Maw…" Ryan shook his head and closed his eyes, then opened them and looked straight at her. "I didn't feel like I could. Not with so many unanswered questions about J.T. and what with Murphy saying Gramps had something to do with bringing the vine here—"

"Should have asked me. I could have told you—didn't have to ask anybody, anyway. You should know better than to think Mac was mixed up with the likes of Murphy."

"It was that check. I—I'd think about that check you wrote…"

"See now, that was my fault. I should have told you about that, but I'd given J.T. my word, and I didn't know a thing about that old tax bill." Mee-Maw let out a long breath. "No point in it now. I have faith in Becca, even if you don't, and I think that girl will move heaven and earth to get Murphy behind bars. Maybe you can get the farm back after that. Until then, why, we'll just have to make do."

"I'm glad you've got faith in Becca. I wish I could."

Mee-Maw pinned him with a hard stare from her blue eyes. She shook a gnarled finger at him. "Now, you listen. We got in this mess because all of us were tippy-toeing around, too skeert to ask or say what was on our minds. You don't make that mistake with Becca. You care for her, right?"

Ryan's heart squeezed. He thought about the times he'd spent with Becca, the long e-mails he'd shared with Sunny. Were the two women so different? "I cared for who I thought she was."

"That's who she is, and you know it. Your heart won't steer you wrong, Ryan. You listen to it."

"Yeah, right. I listened to it to begin with and look where it got me," he started, but then he saw Mee-Maw about to blast him again. To appease her, he said, "All right, I'll talk to her. Later, okay? I just don't want to see her right now."

"Too late."

"What?"

"There she comes, if my eye ain't mistaken.

That her car? I believe it is. You go on and talk to her. I just need to rest a bit in the truck. Go on. I'll be okay."

Ryan peered around Mee-Maw to get a better look. Sure enough, the setting sun reflected off the light of Becca's car as it bounced up the driveway.

RYAN WAS WAITING for her when she got out of her car, Wilbur at his feet. Ryan stood there against his grandfather's truck, arms folded, mouth tight, eyes devoid of any trusting twinkle she might find.

Becca tucked her shaking hands in the back pockets of her jeans. "Hi."

Ryan didn't answer.

Okay, he was going for the stone-faced approach. Well, then. She swallowed hard. "I wanted to ask you…"

Why won't you listen to me? Why won't you answer my phone calls? Why won't you let me explain?

But Becca didn't ask any of those questions. Instead, she opted for the professional approach. "My dad has picked up J.T. at the airport, and they're on their way back here. J.T. wanted to see Charlotte—and Mee-Maw. He asked specifically to see Mee-Maw before he would talk to any federal authorities. So…Dad wants to know…where, um, you want them to go."

Ryan raised an eyebrow. "It could have been here if you'd gone along and bought us some more time."

Anger and hurt whirled inside of her, making her words hard to get out. "Look, I did the best I could—and you can blame me all you want to, but if you and Mee-Maw had just come clean earlier—"

"Well, we didn't, did we? And neither did you, *Sunny.*"

The taunt hit her hard—as he'd intended, she was sure. "I won't deny that I kept things from you, Ryan. But I didn't know anything about this case before I came down here. You can believe me or not. That's your choice. But what we had… what went on…it was real. To me, anyway. There was no lie."

For a moment, emotion shattered his poker face. She couldn't, in that split second, decide whether it was anger or pain or a mix of both, but then Ryan composed himself.

"When will your dad and J.T. get here?"

His cold indifference wounded her more than anything he could have raged at her. But if this was how he was going to play it… Becca glanced at her watch. "Probably another half hour or so. Where do you want to meet them?"

"We're taking Mee-Maw to Jack's. That's—" Ryan closed his eyes, compressed his lips.

She waited for him to say more. When he didn't, Becca asked, "Okay. Should I follow you?"

Ryan laughed, the chuckle hollow and sardonic. "You don't get it, do you? We lost everything, Becca. *Everything.* The house, the farm, the truck, the animals—well, except for Wilbur. He's considered a personal item, since he's the family pet. We're waiting on Jack to come back and get us."

His despair, fresh and raw, stabbed at her heart. "I'm sorry, Ryan. I am so, so sorry."

"Yeah, well, so am I. Sorry that I ever listened to you when you assured me that Murphy was just bluffing."

The passenger-side door of the truck swung open. "Ryan...help me out here. Getting so stiff—"

Becca realized for the first time that Mee-Maw had been waiting in the truck. She walked around to see the old woman trying to get her feet on the ground.

"Here," Becca said, "let me—"

But Ryan came between them. With accusing eyes, he said, "I think you've helped quite enough, thank you." He assisted Mee-Maw out of the truck.

"Thank you, honey," Mee-Maw said to Becca, as if Ryan hadn't spoken. "I was a-wonderin'...

since we can't take the truck, you reckon you could give us a lift into town? I'm mighty tired. I just want to lie down for a bit."

Becca exchanged a pointed look with Ryan. "Yes, ma'am. I'd be happy to."

"Did I hear you say J.T. was back?"

"Yes, ma'am."

"I sure have missed that boy."

"I'll call Dad and tell him to meet us at Jack's, then. Ryan, can you and Wilbur fit in the back-seat?"

He nodded without speaking. Becca knew from his stubborn expression that, if not for Mee-Maw, Ryan would have walked to California barefoot before he would have ever asked Becca for a ride.

Maybe it's for the best this thing between us is over. What was I thinking, anyway? That I'd get to play Green Acres with Ryan for the rest of my life?

Becca wound up sitting with Mee-Maw and Charlotte on Jack's front porch swing while they waited for J.T.'s arrival.

Charlotte couldn't sit still—or keep quiet. She peppered Becca with a thousand questions about what would happen next—would J.T. have to go back to jail? Or would he be in any sort of trouble?

All Becca could answer was an honest, "I don't know. We'll have to wait and see."

She knew her dad had been in contact with an assistant U.S. attorney that he knew. He'd fluttered a few hypotheticals the feds' way. Still, until the government heard J.T.'s story and decided whether or not he was a good enough witness, there were no guarantees.

The one bright spot was that Ag-Sure had already promised not to press charges of conspiracy to defraud against Ryan, Mee-Maw or J.T. if they agreed to testify in civil and criminal trials against Murphy. Becca knew that under federal and state statutes, Ryan and Mee-Maw were both subject to conspiracy charges. It didn't matter that neither had actually been active participants. Ryan and Mee-Maw had known about the scam and had aided and abetted Murphy with their silence.

As for J.T., he still had quite a bit of explaining to do. It was clear from what Becca's dad had told her of J.T.'s story, the hired hand was in up to his neck.

The rental car her dad had used to make the trip to Savannah turned into Jack's drive. Charlotte rocked the swing violently as she sprang up and hurled herself down the front steps.

"J.T.!"

The man of the hour stopped in the open car door to wrap his arms around Charlotte, holding her tight. Becca bit back tears of envy that flooded her at the sight.

Selfish. It was selfish to want that same thing from Ryan.

She glanced toward the door where Ryan stood. Their eyes met. His were cool and impassive.

The flicker of hope in her heart went out. She'd been stupid to think he'd ever be able to forgive her. She'd lied to him, kept pressing until Mee-Maw had lost her homeplace.

J.T. and Charlotte made their way to the porch where Mee-Maw sat. He knelt in front of her, his eyes full of concern.

Seeing that compassion, Becca couldn't believe she'd ever thought J.T. a common criminal in it for a quick buck.

"Mee-Maw? They told me…about the farm. I sure am sorry. I shouldn't have run, should I? I should have stuck it out. But I—I just couldn't face prison again."

Mee-Maw patted J.T.'s hand. "I shouldn't have let you run. I should have talked you out of it, should have told you we'd back you, no matter what. But I wasn't thinking too straight."

Now Ryan closed the gap and stood near J.T. He held out a hand. J.T. took it and gave it a brisk shake.

Anger rattled through Becca. How could Ryan accept J.T. back with a handshake, when J.T. had been the one to start the whole mess?

J.T. surveyed everyone assembled on the porch.

"I just want to say how sorry I am that I'm the cause of all this. If I'd known...I honestly thought me going away was the best thing for everybody."

Becca held her breath. Finally she'd hear the whole story, not someone else's version.

"Miss Becca..." J.T. nodded his head her way. "She and Ryan figured out that I was the one who brought those vines here. I didn't want to. But Murphy...well, he told me he'd jam me up with the local law. He said he'd make sure that I got found with drugs or a gun if I didn't get him the vines. I worried over it, and finally just figured, what could those vines hurt? The insurance company was rich enough—they'd sure not minded paying out all Murphy's claims before."

"Did Gramps know?" Ryan asked.

J.T. gave him a bewildered look. "That I was bringing those vines back? No. He didn't know until I came back with 'em. He saw 'em on the back of my truck, figured something was up..."

Now misery etched even more deeply into J.T.'s features. "I talked to Murphy, asked him how he figured the insurance company was gonna believe something wasn't up when he was the only one with those vines in his fields. Murphy just laughed. He said...he said I was gonna make sure that his wasn't the only land it was on. When I caught his drift, I said no. Mr. Mac had been real good to me. No way was I gonna let that vine

anywhere near Mr. Mac's cotton. I wouldn't let
Murphy have the vines after that."

Nobody made a sound as J.T. told how he'd gone
to Mac, told him everything. Mac and J.T. had met
with Murphy, the vines on the back of the truck—
that's when Murphy had shot that picture.

"Mr. Mac was sure giving him a telling-off, I'll
say that. I ain't never seen a man so angry. Told
him he was gonna go to Ag-Sure, tell them what
Murphy was up to—" J.T. broke off and stared
down at the beat-up brogans he wore. "He got
so worked up. And then standing there, Mac just
grabbed his chest. Murphy wouldn't help me—
wouldn't call an ambulance—just stood there. I
don't guess an ambulance could have helped, but
I'll never forget the way...that man died in my
arms. And it was 'cause of me. 'Cause I was too
scared to say no to Murphy in the first place."

Mee-Maw made a low hiss under her breath. "I
knew he was no good, I just didn't know he was
that low."

Becca wrapped her fingers around Mee-Maw's.
"You didn't know?"

She shook her head. "No. J.T. brought Mac
back up to the house. Said he was in trouble with
Murphy and that Mac had found out. J.T. said he
needed to leave right away, or else he'd wind up
back in prison, but I didn't know anything about
what Murphy was planning. I didn't ask J.T. what

the trouble was—didn't want to know, tell the truth. Later, of course, I figured it out. And I knew J.T. wouldn't have done it if not for Murphy puttin' a squeeze on him."

J.T. picked up the story again. "Murphy got the vines off the truck while I was trying to help Mr. Mac. He told me that if I wasn't willing to help him plant those vines, he'd fix it where I'd wind up in trouble with the law. He told me I had three days to make up my mind—made a big deal out of being generous about it. Generous!" J.T. spat the word.

"So you left…" Becca trailed off.

"Figured… I don't know what I figured. I just couldn't face planting those vines—not on Mr. Mac's land—or going to jail again. I knew I'd made a big mistake. I had no idea what Murphy would tell on me. That's why I laid low all this time. If I'd known…I guess I never dreamed that Murphy'd dare plant it on someone else's land without inside help, you know? But if I'd known what all had happened… Oh, Mee-Maw… Mee-Maw, I'm sure sorry."

In the ensuing silence, Becca's dad cleared his throat. "Mrs. MacIntosh, it's small comfort for you now, but Murphy will wind up in federal prison. Not only do we have J.T.'s testimony, but we have the corroborating testimony of the man who supplied the vines—he sold them to Murphy, not to J.T. I've tracked down the crooked insurance adjustor. A buddy of mine in the U.S. Attorney's office is driving up here tomorrow and we're going to present him a nice, tidy package— Murphy tied up with a bow. Becca's got some people from the state revenue department looking into the way your land was foreclosed. Eventually, eventually…you will get your land back."

Mee-Maw managed a tremulous smile, a dim version of what that smile usually was. "I am glad there are good people like you and Becca here."

"Well…" Now it was Becca's father who stared down at the rough floorboards of the porch. "When Ag-Sure first gave us this case, I sort of figured you'd all been tarred by the same brush. But…I should have trusted Becca's judgment. She thought your grandson wasn't involved from the start, and that should have been good enough for me. I just wish I'd come down here sooner to lend her a hand. After all, Murphy could have gotten my daughter killed."

Becca blinked in surprise. Her dad? Saying he'd been wrong?

Her gaze moved from her dad's bent head to Ryan's.

Ryan's expression didn't lighten. His arms folded across his chest, his jaw hard, he spoke up. "I take responsibility for that, sir. I was in over my head. I guess I was in over my head even before all this mess. I had no business thinking I could save this farm."

He met Mee-Maw's eyes. "Mee-Maw. You should know. I called my old boss. He said to give him a week or so to figure out where to put me back to work. Guess selling ag chemicals is what I'm supposed to do with my life. I'm sorry that while I was chasing my dream, I let you down— sorry I let Gramps down."

With that, he spun on his heel and let the screen door slam behind him as he went inside.

Becca's heart, which she thought was broken already, splintered as she saw defeat in the bow of his retreating back. Now she understood his earlier bitterness with her. Maybe she hadn't been the sole reason his dreams had gone up in smoke, but she'd definitely played a part in it.

CHAPTER TWENTY-EIGHT

THE SPRINGS IN Jack's sofa bed jabbed into Ryan's back like hot pokers.

Or maybe it's your guilty conscience.

Ryan sat up and rubbed his eyes. He'd had plenty to feel guilty about in the week since J.T. had come home.

For one thing, Mee-Maw had no roof to call her own.

And Becca.

Especially Becca.

A noise on the stairs made him look up. Jack stood at the foot of the stairs.

"Couldn't sleep, either?" he asked his cousin.

Jack shook his head. "Nope. I don't care that the cast is off—leg still hurts. Want to see what there is to eat?"

Ryan followed him into the kitchen. He nursed a glass of milk while Jack poked through the fridge, finally satisfying himself with a wedge of apple pie.

"One of the benefits of Mee-Maw living here is that she's a good cook." Jack forked up a bite of pie. It didn't look as if the pie went down that easy, though.

"She's pretty depressed, isn't she?"

Jack nodded. "Not surprising. But I see signs of life there, unlike you, buddy."

"Me?"

"I don't know who's the worst sad-sack—you or Wilbur. At least I know how to fix Wilbur—just take him out to the country and let him chase some rabbits. You? I don't have an earthly clue—except…"

At the sound of his name, the dog roused from his spot under the table and wagged his tail hopefully.

Ryan couldn't think of a reply. He stretched out an arm and dumped the last of the milk in Wilbur's dish. He watched in silence as the dog lapped it up.

"You heard from Becca?" Jack asked him.

Hearing her name from someone else's lips shook Ryan. He shoved back his chair and took his now-empty glass to the sink. "Nope. No reason to. Not with the feds taking over the investigation."

"The investigation isn't the only reason you'd hear from her."

"Figured you'd be glad I hadn't heard from her. You were right about her, I guess."

Jack raised his eyebrows. "Funny. I'd sorta come to the opposite conclusion."

Ryan finished rinsing his glass and set it carefully on the counter. "That's a change."

"Well…she's worked nonstop to get J.T. an immunity deal. And she can't help it if the state revenue guys can't presto-change-o fix what Murphy and Melton did, but she did kickstart an official investigation on the tax commissioner's office. That's something. Plus, Mee-Maw wasn't wrong about J.T."

"So by extension she's not wrong about Becca?"

"Sure you're not overreacting, buddy?"

"Me? Overreact? Oh, I don't know. The woman I thought I knew turned out to be *another* woman I thought I knew. Forgive me if it's taking me a few days to wrap my head around that little predicament."

"No need to get angry about it." Jack savored another bite of apple pie. "Me? I think Becca reminds you of losing the farm. You see her, you think about everything that's happened. It's all knotted up somehow."

"Aren't you the philosopher tonight."

"And aren't you the jerk."

"She's the one—"

"So she lied to you about the e-mail thing. Look at it this way, would you have ever gotten to know her if you'd known from the get-go she was an investigator for an insurance company?"

"I *did* get to know her."

"I'm talking about the e-mails. I mean, it's kind of like getting warm and fuzzy with a gal from the IRS. Even if you're not doing anything wrong, you still think, 'Hmm…'"

Ryan braced his elbows on the counter. "It's not just the e-mails. She wouldn't help. I just needed her to—I needed a little time. If she'd only sat on it—"

"Right. *We* sat on it and that turned out to be a flaming success, didn't it?"

"What's changed your mind about her?" Ryan narrowed his eyes. "You were so anti-Becca you didn't even want her at your kid's birthday supper."

Jack let a wry smile tug at the corners of his mouth. "Time. Distance. And seeing how sick she looked when you blew her off that last time."

Ryan closed his eyes. He didn't want to admit it, but the last glimpse he'd had of Becca, her face drawn and tired, haunted him.

"Oh, and one other thing changed my mind." Jack brought his plate to the sink counter and set it down with a clunk. "You."

"Me?"

"Yep. You've got it bad, cuz. Face it. You're done for."

BECCA STRAIGHTENED UP the pile of papers on her desk with a disconsolate indifference. The walls of their Atlanta office seemed to close in on her, and not even Gert could jolly her out of her sour mood. Becca hadn't even minded when Gert had asked for the rest of the day off.

Becca's opportunity to mope in private was lost when her dad came through the office door. "Hey. How's the fort?"

Becca shrugged. "Okay. No luck yet with the guys at the revenue department."

"It will take time."

"I don't want it to take time, Dad. She's eighty-four years old—"

"Sure this isn't about Ryan, instead?"

She didn't meet his eyes. "Why would that be the case?"

"Oh, I don't know. Crazy idea I had, that's all."

"I screwed up. He asked me…he asked me to hold off, and I didn't."

"Good for you. And understandable in his case." Her father seemed unperturbed. "Becca, in this business, you're going to see a lot of desperate people. And desperation makes people—"

"I know. Do desperate things."

"Okay, so you've heard this before and I can hit the high notes."

"I feel so guilty. I feel like… I'd never forgive myself if Mee-Maw didn't get her farm back."

"Correction—you think *Ryan* will never forgive *you* if Mee-Maw doesn't get her farm back."

"He won't. Maybe he shouldn't. You would have done things so differently, Dad. It wouldn't have—"

"Yeah, I would have. But in the end, you got the job done. You have to learn, Becca. You have to make mistakes and take the long way around." He fiddled with a paper clip. "Remember what I used to ask you? What is the problem? What do you know?"

Becca closed her eyes and forced her mind to quiet. The problem...

"Mee-Maw's farm. I need to get it back."

"And what do you know?"

She opened her eyes. "That...it was done unfairly. That Murphy bought it in a rigged auction. That Murphy..." She struggled for the answer he was awaiting, knowing from his expression that she hadn't got it yet. "What do I know about Murphy? He's...he'll be facing federal indictment, but the feds say that will take a while and they're keeping it mum... I know he's up to his neck in debt."

Now she closed her eyes again. "Wait. Wait..." Excitement pulsed through her, and she started scrabbling through the printouts on her desk. "His debt...there might be some way..."

Her father smiled. "'His own iniquities shall

take the wicked himself.' A banker or two might
be interested in knowing what's about to happen…
not, of course, that I would ever go against my
client Ag-Sure's best interests and tell another
party. But I might—" he winked "—let it slip."

Her joy flatlined. "It wouldn't do any good.
Ryan doesn't have the money."

"I know somebody who does."

"You do?" She frowned.

"Uh-huh. Someone who could call her lawyer
and get him to offer a rock-bottom settlement to
an aggrieved Atlanta bigwig—on a case I'm sure
said bigwig would like to go away—if, that is,
that someone didn't want to get back in the magazine business. Someone, who I hear, does some of
her best thinking in chicken coops, so she might
be interested in investing in a family farm." He
shrugged. "Up to her, I guess."

With that, he left Becca alone with a mind
swirling with possibilities…

And choices.

RYAN TOOK a folded up letter from his shirt pocket
and smoothed it out. He reread the bank's assur-
ances that they were extending a line of credit to
him and Jack for fifteen thousand dollars—they'd
borrowed the money against his paltry IRA and
Jack's home equity. Stupid really, but what choice

did they have when, once again, Mee-Maw's farm was up for bid?

Fifteen thousand was a fraction of what Mee-Maw's farm was worth, but you never knew. This was an auction, after all, and the banks didn't care how much something went for as long as they got their money out of the deal. He was just grateful that Murphy's creditors had decided to call in their loans before the feds had let slip their plans to indict Murphy. The feds had indicated to Ryan and Jack that, once the indictment was handed down, Murphy's assets would be frozen for the duration of the trial.

Now that Ryan knew herbicides would work on the dodder vine, he knew a lot more money in cotton waited for them in the farm's fields. Plus, Ag-Sure's grateful execs were even making noises that Mee-Maw might even get a partial insurance settlement, since J.T. had fingered Murphy. If Ryan could just put down fifteen grand in earnest money today…

More than one well-wisher came up to Ryan to assure him they didn't intend to bid against him. The whole community seemed to want Mee-Maw to have her farm back.

This time the auction was at the main offices of the Murphy farming operation. As the auctioneer geared up, Ryan felt himself sweating despite the cool September morning. This was it. This was his chance to redeem himself.

Mee-Maw's tract was the first one up—thankfully they hadn't subdivided it the way they had the rest of Murphy's acreage. The auctioneer started out the bid at ten grand and slowly started ratcheting up the price.

"I have nineteen. Do I hear twenty?" The auctioneer paused, and for a moment, Ryan's heart stopped. Had he gotten it for just that?

But then the auctioneer indicated a bidder in the back, and let loose again with his yodeled calls. Ryan raised his bidding stick. As soon as the auctioneer registered his bid, Ryan switched his gaze to the rear.

No. One of Murphy's son-in-laws apparently was determined to at least raise the price so that Murphy could get the most out of the land—or maybe they, too, had figured out how to leverage the money needed for the auction.

It meshed with the scuttlebutt around town. Murphy had been busy shooting down rumors of his imminent fall. He'd been mouthing off to anybody who'd listen that if the feds had anything on him, they'd have locked him up already.

Apparently he'd decided that since he hadn't been indicted yet, it wasn't going to happen at all. He obviously had no clue how slow and careful the feds could be.

Now, by the son-in-law's bid, it was equally obvious that Murphy didn't intend to give up Mee-Maw's farm easily.

"Twenty-twenty-twenty-five? Yes, I have twenty-five, do I hear twenty-six?"

The auctioneer acknowledged a bid from another section. Ryan didn't recognize this bidder. He had the look of a big city attorney, complete with the pinstriped suit.

Ryan's heart sank. No way he could win a three-way bidding war.

He stuck with it, though, until the bid topped out at the price he and Jack had agreed on. They exchanged looks of regret as Ryan dropped out of the bidding.

Mr. Pinstripes kept at it, hanging in as the farm price reached nearly fifty grand. Ryan gritted his teeth as he watched with impotent rage some land speculator show every intention of grabbing on to his grandmother's property…and for a song.

Murphy's son-in-law lost his nerve at forty-nine thousand. Ryan saw it in the man's sweat-beaded upper lip, the clenched fists. Now Ryan could see that Murphy was there, hanging in the very back, signaling with frustration for his son-in-law to keep up the bidding.

But the man shook his head and stalked off.

The auctioneer paused again, scanning the crowd. "Prime property, folks, cotton ready for the harvester... Surely it's worth fifty? Do I hear fifty? Going once? Going twice? Sold at forty-nine thousand to the man in the pinstripes."

Ryan barreled through the crowd. Who had just bought Mee-Maw's land—and what did the man intend to do with it?

The man took a few steps toward the office. Still more people came between Ryan and him. Ryan elbowed his way onward, not sure what he would even say to the man.

"Ryan! Ryan!"

The voice stopped him in his tracks. He turned, couldn't believe who it was.

Becca.

Ryan knew the man was going, knew the papers were about to be signed, but he couldn't move.

Not with Becca there.

She smiled at him. The smile was as radiant as any she'd ever graced him with. It bewildered and bedazzled him.

He connected the dots a halted breath later. He looked from her to where the man had stood just a few moments earlier.

"You? You had something to do with this?"

"Officially...no. But I'm now the proud owner of an old homeplace with lots and lots of cotton I have no clue how to harvest. I was thinking... maybe I needed to sell it back to its rightful owners?"

"How—"

She blew out a breath. "Remember the guy who was appealing the judgment I'd won in the countersuit? Well...let's just say he got a blue-light special on a settlement."

"You gave up your judgment? But that's crazy! Why would you—"

"I needed to make this right, Ryan."

He took in the earnest hope in her eyes—and something else. Peace.

The crowd's overlapping conversations filled the silence between them. Ryan pulled her over to the side, out of the throng of people.

"You didn't have to do this, Becca."

He kicked himself the moment the words were out of his mouth—what he'd meant to say hadn't come out right at all.

But it was too late. Already he saw Becca's eyes cool.

"Thanks. But I couldn't live with myself until I knew I'd done everything I could to get Mee-Maw's farm back. I'll have my lawyer draw up the papers, and you can set the repayment however you'd like. If I'd thought for a moment you would have gone along with my ideas, I would have just offered the money to you straight up." She shrugged. "But you never did answer my calls."

Before Ryan could reply, she smiled at him, this

time in a more impersonal way, and turned from him, walking toward the office.

"Wait! The reason...I was...Becca." For a panicked moment, Ryan thought she wasn't going to stop.

"Yes?"

"I couldn't figure out what to say. When a man screws up, it's hard for him to know...how to fix it."

"Fix what?"

"Us. You. Me. I'm not... I'm no good at this."

"Try?" A measure of pleading in Becca's voice let Ryan know he still had a chance with her.

She'd come closer to him, close enough for him to reach out and touch her, but he didn't dare. Not until he'd made things right.

"I kept thinking," Ryan said, "that the words would come. And all I could think to say was, 'I'm sorry. I love you. I'm sorry.'"

Now she closed the gap between them, wrapped her arms around him and stared up at his face. "Oh, Ryan." Her voice cracked. "Don't you know that's all I needed to hear?"

He kissed her then. He didn't care that half the town was probably thinking him a crazy man. He didn't give a crap about how people would talk.

All he cared about was what he held in his arms.

"Well, now."

Ryan and Becca broke apart to see Mee-Maw beaming at them. "Glad to see that's taken care of. Becca, I would have taken him up to Atlanta if you hadn't come back down—no point having somebody moping around all the time."

"Hey, Mee-Maw." Becca wiped tears from her eyes—and Ryan was amazed that he hadn't realized she was crying.

"Just talked to that shyster over yonder, and he said you was the one who just bought my farm."

"To sell back to you. I want you to have it, Mee-Maw."

"Yes, ma'am. But if you was aimin' to be a partner, that would be okay, too. I can always use an experienced hand with the chickens. 'Course, I'm hopin' Ryan'll change his mind about hauling off to go sell fertilizer."

Ryan met Becca's gaze again. He wiped another tear from her cheek. "I'm here to stay. And... Becca, if you're interested...the partnership comes with room and board—all of Mee-Maw's cooking you can eat."

Becca chuckled. "Now, that's an offer that's hard to refuse."

"Just one thing, though." Ryan held up a finger. "One tiny limitation. The contract's for life."

"Life, huh?" She smiled again.

"Comes with seven-days-a-week work schedule, low pay, skimpy benefits…but one gold ring and all the love I can give you."

Mee-Maw was not content to leave a tender moment alone. "And I'll throw in my best cast-iron frying pan. 'Cause you're gonna need it with this hardheaded numbskull."

Becca pressed her lips to Ryan's, then broke the kiss long enough to say, "Sold!"

* * * * *

HEARTWARMING INSPIRATIONAL ROMANCE

Contemporary,
inspirational romances
with Christian characters
facing the challenges
of life and love
in today's world.

**AVAILABLE IN REGULAR
AND LARGER-PRINT FORMATS.**

For exciting stories that reflect traditional values,
visit:
www.ReaderService.com

LIDIR11B

Love Inspired®

SUSPENSE
RIVETING INSPIRATIONAL ROMANCE

Watch for our series of edge-
of-your-seat suspense novels.
These contemporary tales
of intrigue and romance
feature Christian characters
facing challenges to their faith...
and their lives!

AVAILABLE IN REGULAR
& LARGER-PRINT FORMATS

For exciting stories that reflect traditional values,
visit:
www.ReaderService.com

LISUSDIR11B

Love Inspired.
HISTORICAL
INSPIRATIONAL HISTORICAL ROMANCE

Engaging stories of romance,
adventure and faith,
these novels are set in
various historical periods
from biblical times
to World War II.

NOW AVAILABLE!

For exciting stories that reflect traditional values,
visit:
www.ReaderService.com

LIHDIR11B